CW00433212

Nick Brooke was born and raised in various parts of Europe. He has spent the last twenty-something years wondering why he is here, what he should do with himself and, crucially, what nationality he is. After yet another brain-dead night on the graveyard shift making Minis, he decided to become a writer and New Head on the Block is the outcome.

He lives in Oxford, Dublin and Tipperary and has few vices that are printable though he supports passionately one of the teams in red and just as passionately, dislikes another.

NEW HEAD ON THE BLOCK

Nick Brooke

NEW HEAD ON THE BLOCK

AUSTIN MACAULEY

Copyright © Nick Brooke

The right of Nick Brooke to be identified as author of this work has been asserted by him in accordance with section 77 and 78 of the Copyright, Designs and Patents Act 1988.

All rights reserved. No part of this publication may be reproduced, stored in a retrieval system, or transmitted in any form or by any means, electronic, mechanical, photocopying, recording, or otherwise, without the prior permission of the publishers.

Any person who commits any unauthorized act in relation to this publication may be liable to criminal prosecution and civil claims for damages.

The author certifies that none of the characters depicted in this novel are based on any person, living or dead. Any of the events that transpire in the text are purely imaginary, and to the best of the author's knowledge have not happened to anyone in the real world. The author has not set out with the intention of offending anyone, but if he has, tough. No-one has a right not to be offended and everything is fair game. No animals were harmed in the writing of this book.

A CIP catalogue record for this title is available from the British Library.

ISBN 978 1 905609 40-6

www.austinmacauley.com

First Published (2008)
Austin & Macauley Publishers Ltd.
25 Canada Square
Canary Wharf
London
E14 5LB

Printed & Bound in Great Britain

DEDICATION

"When you treat someone with cancer, you don't just treat the patient, but the whole family too."

This was the motto of Jon Pritchard, whose life's work was to provide comfort and support to families going through the agony of dealing with a child's cancer – including my own.

I dedicate this book to his memory.

ACKNOWLEDGEMENTS

I would like to thank my family, for their patience, support and understanding.

Also, thanks to the publishers for the professional but personal way they have dealt with me and my work.

Finally I would like to thank all my friends for their persistence in badgering me about when they could read it.

.... well now you can!

CHAPTER ONE

Jack Nielson read through the fine print of the letter sitting on his table. *Blah, blah due to changing family circumstances, blah, blah right time in the current market, blah, blah enjoyed our time here etc.* He looked up out of the window in his front room to witness the letter's revelations being enacted not thirty yards from him. Mr and Mrs Doyle, a quiet and reserved couple in their seventies, had decided that there was no longer any need for a comfortable family home in the suburbs now that their kids had not only moved out, but also produced their own children and migrated to all corners of the globe. Apparently they had bought some disused farmhouse out in the sticks, away from the hustle and bustle of the suburbs and the hectic schedule of tending their garden and rounds of golf at the nearby course at least three times a week. They were both suffering from increasing ill-health, the decays of time beginning to take their toll, so for some reason they presumed a move to the country (and the ensuing extra half an hour on top of their journey time to the doctor's) would benefit them in the long run. Jack had trouble envisaging what a couple of retired seventy-something-year-olds viewed as being the long run, but then again being only twenty-five he was happy to assume it was just his own youthful ignorance.

In a way he was sad to see them leave. He wasn't exactly best friends with them, in fact he could only recall being in their house once. When he'd first moved in he'd been caught off-guard by Mrs Doyle calling round to welcome him to the Close. He'd politely feigned interest in all the small talk, though once he mentioned that he didn't, in fact, actually have a job, his stay was politely cut short by

Mrs Doyle's sudden need to "get on with things". He hadn't been invited back. He didn't mind, he was a largely a private person, who had little time for chatting about the weather or how so-and-so's kids were doing. Still, their leaving meant change, which to him was always a risky business. Jack liked the Doyles because he didn't have to see them, talk to them or integrate with them in any way. Having someone new move in was a gamble. It could be some axe-wielding serial killer. Worse, it could be a young couple with infants. Jack made a mental note to find the number of that salesman who had called the other day offering triple glazing for his windows.

The ensuing "party" he could see from his room was the final get-together of all the inhabitants of Appletree Close along with assorted friends and other guests. He had fully intended to go, but while picking his least scruffy shirt from on top of the laundry pile he had happened to notice the assembly on the Doyles' front lawn. It was now obvious that someone had forgotten to include the word "tea" on the invite letter next to "party". It wasn't that Jack didn't like the elderly, but having been raised by his grandparents until he was eighteen he did have a natural instinct to avoid them if possible, and the motley collection of bowls enthusiasts and pearl necklaces had made him think twice. Now he surveyed the scene from the comfort and relative safety of his front room. It all seemed so sedate, yet Jack smiled wryly as he witnessed the varying degrees of social etiquette performed to the letter by all. *Not for me, not today.*

CHAPTER TWO

A couple of weeks later Jack found himself enjoying his usual Saturday afternoon routine. Having already played his latest role in an affair he was having with the young wife of an old school friend, he was now sitting in the Rosebush, his local, watching the football scores come in on the TV. He was generally joined by one or two friends who didn't have work that day, and today it was the turn of Marky, a Manc and "dead proud of it." Marky was one of Jack's closer friends, in that he tolerated his quirks and never asked for money from him, something that those who knew him were generally inclined to do once in a while. Marky, save for pestering him when it was his round, didn't really care much for money, something Jack liked about him. Marky groaned again as the newsreel flashed up another goal against Man City.

"Fucking Jihai's well past it, get the lad Richards on there. Ah, I see your lot aren't doing so well either."

Jack looked up at the screen briefly to notice that Liverpool were one down and shook his head slowly before finishing his pint. "Another?"

"Sure."

Jack returned with two more lagers and saw Marky staring intently at the inside of a redtop. "Here, have you seen this?"

"What's that?" Jack asked indifferently.

"Some fucking knacker's won the lottery!"

"Some what?"

"Knacker. You know, chav, townie."

"Oh. So?"

"Well it says here that he was on probation for drink driving. Apparently he had a tag on his leg and all."

"Lucky boy. Honestly mate I don't know why you read that shite. Can't you just buy a normal paper and look at tits on the 'net like the rest of us?

Marky wasn't listening though. "Christ, it says he knocked down some old boy while three times over the limit a couple of years ago. And he only got 3 months. 3 months! Our Nellie got more than that for having a bit of weed!"

"Yeah well the law's an ass." Jack couldn't have been more disinterested. "Anyway, what you doing later?"

"Oh I gotta take me kid brother to the cinema. He wants to see some superhero bollocks and his ma's not feeling so good. You up for it?"

Jack politely declined. As far as he was concerned comic book heroes should stay in comic books, plus Marky's brother was a whiney little nuisance.

"Alright then, well I'll give you buzz if I'm going out later, but I doubt it. Laters."

Marky downed his pint and left to tackle his courageous quest of taking an eleven-year-old to the Saturday matinee. He'd left his paper. Jack looked at the picture on top of the article. A spotty, shrunken-eyed youth was giving the cameraman the bird outside his house. He was standing by a battered up Vauxhall Nova which had obviously been shamelessly attired with all forms of paraphernalia and random junk. His car looked less like a mode of transport and more like a mobile advert for every garage inside the M25. Jack's glance was drawn by the headline *Local yob nets £3 million lotto payday.* He laughed inwardly. The article went on to describe how the 'yob', a Mr Ashley Johnson or simply 'AJ', 20, was already a father of two, and declared that he had no intention of giving up his benefits.

"Dumb bastard," muttered Jack, who was not without tolerance, but simply knew that the press would give him enough rope to hang himself with, then eat him alive. As far as Jack was concerned this would turn out to be another 'build 'em up, knock 'em down' story, only without the build 'em up. The newsreel announced that Liverpool had now lost 2-0 and Jack finished his pint and set off home.

CHAPTER THREE

Appletree Close was the sort of place people went to get away from things. A secluded cul-de-sac about five miles from the M40. Backed into a golf course to the south, a woods and park area to the west, and other similar capillaries of suburbia to the north and east, it offered its inhabitants a haven of tranquillity away from whatever it was they disliked. Of course house prices in the area reflected this, but as the Major in Number 2 often reflected, "Got to keep out the riffraff."

In all there were six houses in the Close. The Doyles had owned the largest at Number 1, with the Major directly next to them. Number 3 was owned by Kathi, whom Jack referred to as "Career Bitch". Not to her directly though, as she was never around. She left for London every morning at 5am (including Saturdays) and rarely got in before 11 at night. Jack wondered what job could possibly be worth so much time devoted to it. Apparently she was something in the city, which to Jack meant she was screwing her way to the top of some bank or other financial institution. Almost every weekend (Sundays to her, Saturdays were part of the working week) she brought a different silver-haired tycoon back to the house, and every couple of months or so, she would be seen driving a brand new car, with a flashy new suit and all the bells and whistles.

If she ever needed advice on her new cars all she needed do was pop next door to Number 4. Ralph Blakeney owned a garage larger than Jack's entire house. It was home to a small but nonetheless impressive collection of sports cars. Every Sunday they came out one by one to be cleaned and then carefully manoeuvred back into place. Ralf was an artist apparently. Whatever he did, it certainly paid the bills and also caused him to speak in an irritatingly high-pitched squeak. He also spent most Sundays with a different silver-haired rich gent, probably for the same reasons as Kathi, Jack mused, just different motives.

Jack lived at Number 5, in his opinion the best placed house in the drive. He could see everything that went on from various positions in his front room, plus his meagre garden backed onto the golf course so he could smoke joints out the back without much bother from anyone. It was here that he did most of his thinking. Jack spent many hours just thinking. Not about anything in particular; life, the world, the increase in fuel tax, whatever just happened to be on his mind. His parents had been entrepreneurs, so his grandparents had said. Anyway they had died in a car crash when he was only two, and had managed to leave him a quite substantial trust fund. Substantial enough that he didn't have to work, much to his grandparents' irritation, and that he could afford a house in Appletree Close, or Luckyman's Close as he referred to it. Jack generally spent his time messing about on the internet (messing being the operative word, he once sent a year's subscription for Dildo World to his grandparents after one of their regular rants about his lack of employment). When he wasn't on the internet he could be found down the pub with any mates who happened to be off sick from work; generally this occurred whenever there was a decent football match on TV. Most of the time, however, he spent idling away in deep thought. He didn't hold any great ambitions, nor did he have any real hobbies, short of creating mischief towards those who annoyed him, or fluttering his money about recklessly (at least, it would have been reckless had there actually been a bottom to the pit that was his trust fund, but he could spend as much as he desired, within reason, and it was usually covered by the interest alone). Jack had had a decent education in a private school, he had done fairly well in his exams, especially economics, which he had studied quite hard just to understand how much money he could fritter each year without actually losing out. He just didn't have any real motivation to actually do anything; he didn't see the point. Most people went to work to earn money and pay the bills, well he had money, he reasoned, and therefore, sod work.

Finally next door to him in Number 6 were the Hamiltons, a family of five and two cats. They were everything Jack was not, nor ever wished to be. The father, Graham, worked a hard 9-to-5 job in town in some sweaty little office. The mother, Alice, was a librarian. The kids were 11, 9, and 7 respectively. Each one obviously planned, each one part of some grand scheme that Graham and Alice had drawn up shortly after realising they were meant to be together. The Hamiltons were also devout Christians, though there were doubts that the eldest child, Joshua (or Josh, as he insisted he was called) would last much longer in the religious community, he had the attention span of a partially demented gnat, and the energy of a Jack Russell on heat. They had the smallest house in the road, and yet a mortgage that would have crippled them if they'd even taken one day off sick. Out of sheer pity for their determination Jack had offered to pay off their mortgage completely; he had the money and they obviously needed it. They had said no outright. It seemed that they were so insistent doing it themselves that they couldn't take what they had referred to as the "easy way out". Whether it was out of human nature or just because he had gained all the interest he could from watching them struggle to keep afloat, Jack had quietly seen Graham Hamilton's boss in town and fixed it that Mr Hamilton would receive an extra few hundred quid on his salary each month, paid for by Jack, who had had to slip the boss a couple of grand as a sweetener as well. He was confident that they hadn't suspected a thing, and the sound of the youngest son Jacob ringing the bell on his brand new bike that weekend had confirmed to Jack that they weren't complaining.

The Hamiltons aside, this was Luckyman's Close. So called by Jack because you had to have had some titanic slice of luck to afford to live here. The Doyles had got in early when the place was built and the market was ripe. The Major had picked up a massive compensation payment from the Independent Police Complaints Commission in Suffolk after he had been falsely accused of paedophilia. He had had to move and even considered changing his name, but the Police had been so keen to hush him up that apparently they had even offered him their most lucrative set-up in the witness protection program, the type usually reserved for spies and defectors. Kathi had had a mortgage at one point or another, but it was obviously with the bank that she worked with, and a cosy evening with one of the directors had seen that disposed of. Ralph seemingly made a heck of a lot of money for dropping tin cans on the floor and calling it art, and Jack had his trust fund. One time Jack had joked to a couple of his mates that the only thing the Close was missing was a lottery winner. That was soon to change.

CHAPTER FOUR

Jack hated Sundays. In truth, he hated a lot of things. Not out of any sense of reason, just because they annoyed him. He hated snakes, even though he'd never even seen one in the flesh. He hated the Sun, but that was because he was a Liverpool fan. He hated politicians and tax inspectors, but he felt he shared that with too many people for that dislike to be classed as irrational. But he did hate Sundays. He wasn't sure whether it was because his grandparents had always dragged him off to church on this morning every week throughout childhood, or whether it was simply because he knew his parents had died on a Sunday, but certainly at regular intervals throughout his adult life he had considered taking enough sleeping pills on the Saturday night to last him through to Monday. He didn't in the end, because he hated feeling tired.

This Sunday was just the same as always. Jack woke with a splitting headache and a general feeling of suffering. He had gone out with Marky the night before after all, but only after they'd dumped the hyperactive child off at Marky's sister's. The sister had, at the time, been celebrating her two-year anniversary of her first date with her current beau. She had, after dressing rather rapidly and wiping trace amounts of white powder from her upper lip, been furious at Marky for interrupting, but had relented because she loved the nipper. That and Marky, who was particularly adept at them, gave her one of his heaviest guilt trips, before promptly going out on the piss.

The previous evening was not too blurry for Jack to remember; he always found it best not to dwell on trying to remember, it would come to him eventually. For now, he flipped up the screen of his laptop and played random on his media player. After several bars of speaker overload courtesy of Oasis, he fumbled around to find something less inclined to cause his head to burst. *Hotel California, that'll do.*

He had rigged his house so that music was able to play in every room, and Don Henley's fragile tones followed him downstairs as he went to put a brew on. He looked at the clock on the oven. 13:38. *Ah well*, he thought, *at least I can have a nap in a while and then this fucking useless day will be over.*

He poured his tea and scrabbled around to find his cigarettes from his jeans. After finally finding one, he felt around for a lighter. *Bugger, must've lost it last night.* He duly lit up from the hob on top of the oven and shuffled through to his sitting room, where the tune had now changed to Tequila Sunrise. He turned off the speakers in the sitting room, not having the energy to traipse upstairs to shut his computer off. After fumbling around for the TV remote in vain, he gave up and sat with his cup of tea contemplating what he would do in the evening. A dull melodic thud sounded in the distance. *Wap wap, wap.* Jack irascibly banged on the speaker control on the wall, no change. *Wap wap, wap.* He poked his head out into the hallway, still Tequila Sunrise. Jack went upstairs, puzzled. He finally shut down his computer, but the sound didn't leave, in fact, it seemed to be coming from outside. And it was getting louder. For a moment he was worried it might be the boiler. *Well what the fuck do I know about plumbing?* He composed himself with the thought that if that was it, then he could at least wait until there was water leaking all over the floor before he'd have to call someone.

Wap wap, wap. It was too regular; it sounded like that God-awful tune all his school friends had played when they'd got their first sub-woofer in their cars. Needless to say, Jack hated trance music. The louder it got, the more and more it reminded him of that. *It **is** that tune.* The windows began to shake, and he heard some piece of crockery downstairs jump onto the floor and smash. He looked out the window and saw a car pull into the drive. It had blacked-out windows and despite it being a bright sunny day a powerful blue light oozed out from under the chassis, which seemed to be mere millimetres from the ground. The wheels looked as if they were three sizes too large, and the car was plastered with adverts for various garages. Despite all the many thousands of pounds of upgrades, there was no mistaking it was a battered up N-reg Nova. Not just any Nova, the one from the paper. Jack went into the toilet to find Marky's redtop. (Being the Sun, the only suitable use Jack could find for it was as emergency toilet roll.) He shuffled through the pages until he found the picture. There it was in all its glory. He wandered back over to the window, which was doing well to not shatter under the vibrations. A white cap and blue shell-suit jacket poked out of the door. Then came the rest of the body, black tracksuit trousers with the customary triple white stripe down the side, and shoes so white they'd do a Daz advert proud. Ashley Johnson, aka AJ, had arrived at Appletree Close. He spat on the ground and kicked his car door shut, before sauntering over to the empty house on the left.

CHAPTER FIVE

Jack wasn't timid. He wasn't a man afraid to speak his mind or stand up to difficulty. However, he was also a man of logic. For the most part. He wasn't about to storm out and give the new arrival a piece of his mind just for having his music on. Albeit at a volume that, if you believe chaos theory, would have just started earthquakes large enough to end civilisation in Australasia.

Scrabbling round the assortment of scraps of paper littering his desk, he found the number of the triple-glazing salesman and went downstairs to call him. From the front room he looked out of the window while listening to Ticket to Ride playing down the receiver. *At least they've got some taste,* he mused, whistling along to the tune. A sleek-looking black vehicle pulled up behind the chavmobile. Jack assumed it was a Mercedes or Audi, but found himself with a wry smile when he realised it was a Skoda. *It doesn't matter what they look like, or who owns them; a Skoda will always be a Skoda.*

Jack watched a small flustered-looking man get out and brush himself down. He pulled a clipboard out of the car and held it against his chest like a shield before scurrying off towards the empty house that AJ had begun wandering around. A cheerful yet plastic voice cut into the music to tell Jack that they were thankful for his patience and his call was important to them.

Across from the side of his window, Jack saw the imperious figure of the Major marching decisively towards the two cars. He was wearing a very smart suit, but for all it looked like he might have been wearing full dress uniform with medals and insignia, such was the purpose of his stride. He was followed by Betsy, a small dog whose features were more rat-like than canine. *Must've forgot to shut the door*, Jack mumbled to himself, just as the tune on the receiver changed to Yellow Submarine. The shaggy rodent looked as if she was running to catch up, but, if anything, she was lagging further behind her ever-advancing master. As they approached the red death trap, Betsy stopped in her tracks and growled, staring rigidly at the boot door. The Major turned around, and seemed surprised not only by his dog's actions, but also by the mere fact that she had followed him this far without him noticing.

"Go back to the house, Betsy, there's a good girl." The dog continued to growl menacingly at the back of the Nova. "What is it, girl? Is this the car that made that raucous cacophony? Well aren't you a clever girl." The Major's tone seemed to soften slightly, but Betsy remained frozen.

The growl grew louder, and suddenly the Major realised that his dog was no longer accountable for the noise. He turned to face the back of the car and was greeted by a crashing deep bark. It didn't actually sound like barking, more artillery fire, and the Major's instincts hammered into him over years of army training took hold of and forced him to retreat. As he backed away, scooping Betsy up hurriedly as he passed her, he caught a glimpse through the darkened windows of the car of a very large, very animated outline of what appeared to be a Labrador. Appearances were deceptive though; no Labrador could make this noise. No aeroplane could make this noise, let alone any domestic land mammal.

The barking drew the attention its volume warranted. AJ came swaggering out of the house with the small sweaty man scuttling behind him.

"What the fuck do you think you're doing?! Get the fuck away from me car!"

The Major was already trying to compose himself after the dog's recitation of the battle of the Somme, and this latest outburst demanded a reaction.

"What the hell have you got in there?!"

"That's Vieira, me dog. And you've pissed him right off."

"I've done no such thing. That beast began barking for no reason. And another thing, how dare you come here with your car making a totally unacceptable amount of noise. I don't know what you call it, but it certainly wasn't music, it was an aberration!" The Major's face grew ever redder.

The small man began to interject. "Mr Johnson, perhaps we should view the rest of the property? I have a busy schedule today and…"

"You're not thinking of moving in here, are you?" The Major was now crimson.

"I'm thinking about it, yeah. What's it to you?"

"But that's ridiculous! You can't live here!"

"I can live wherever the fuck I like, old man, an if I wanna live here then I fucking will!" AJ turned to the estate agent, "I'll buy it."

The small man beamed. It was fair to say he disapproved of AJ and his manner (or lack of it) but a sale was a sale and he stood to make a large commission on this house.

The Major was lost for words, and turned and stormed back to his house.

Jack had been so engrossed in the proceedings happening outside his front window that he'd not noticed the Beatles had been replaced by a deceptively charming voice.

"Can I help you, Sir?"

"Yeah, I'm the occupier of Number 5 Appletree Close. I want you to replace all my windows with your triple glazing as soon as possible."

CHAPTER SIX

"And bless this food, and let us be thankful for that which you have given us, Oh Lord, Amen." Graham finally finished his five-minute grace.

"Amen," came the reply from three of the other four Hamiltons, Josh already having half a potato in his mouth by the time grace had ended. His father was about to chastise him, but thought that such matters were not appropriate for the dinner table.

"So, have you kids all finished your homework?" he finally asked, in between chomps of cabbage.

Jake and Mary nodded, Josh was suspiciously silent.

"What about you, Joshua?"

"Dad! I've told you before to call me Josh!"

"Well then, *Josh*, have you finished your homework?"

"Not yet."

His father rolled his eyes, this was becoming a regular cycle. Joshua would be sent to his room the same as the other children and while they would happily complete their homework and then their chores, Joshua would find new and ever more innovative ways of wriggling out of them.

"Joshua, how many times must we tell you that you must do your homework and your chores? You know we hate to have to nag you about this."

"Well then don't," came the youngster's rather caustic response.

"Right, that's it. Go to your room and finish your homework now. You can have the rest of your supper after you're done. I'll be up in ten minutes and if I find you're playing computer games there'll be big trouble."

Josh left the room as loudly as he could, with comments from his father on how kids nowadays were more trouble than they were worth following him out of the door. Mary, the middle child, found the whole scene immensely amusing, but kept her thoughts to herself following a sharp glance from her mother.

"I spoke with Jack today." Alice finally broke the silence.

"Oh yes, and what did he have to say?" Graham replied whilst helping himself to more potatoes, before offering them around sheepishly.

"He says that Number 1's been bought."

"Really? Well that wasn't long. I'm glad for the Doyles, they'll have been happy with a quick sale. Jacob use your fork properly, please."

"Well Jack didn't sound too enthused about the buyer."

"Jack isn't enthused by anything. That man is the laziest mammal I've ever met."

"Now Graham that's not very nice. I know you haven't exactly seen eye-to-eye with him after the time he offered us...help, but his heart's in the right place. Besides, it's not setting a very good example."

"No, I suppose you're right. Sorry. Anyway what did he say about the buyer?"

"Well the exact words he used are hardly er...appropriate, but he called him a 'chav'."

"A what?"

"'Chav'."

"Daddy what's a 'chav'?" Jake asked with the most innocent of expressions.

"I really don't know, Jacob. Probably one of Jack's, er, Mr Nielson's vulgar slang words." It was a rare admittance of perplexity from Graham Hamilton, who usually had to give an opinion on everything, whether he actually had one or not. "To be perfectly honest, honey, I'd prefer to reserve my judgement on people for when I first meet them, as opposed to being based on Jack's opinion."

Dinner continued with further questions to the children about school and then further discussion about the new arrival. It was decided near the end of the meal that when the new owner moved in the whole family would go over to greet him.

"It's only right that we welcome him properly to the neighbourhood. After all, the Doyles were the first ones to invite us over just the day after we moved in, so we shall invite him to dinner as soon as we can."

After dinner, Graham checked on Josh, who had reluctantly finished his homework. Graham took pity on him and let him off his chore for that night, which happened to be taking out the rubbish. After the children were all tucked into bed, Graham took the full black sack out of the bin and carried it outside into the garden. He had just deposited the sack when he saw a faint orange-red speck of light pierce the darkness over the fence. He wandered over to see Jack.

"I wish you wouldn't smoke that stuff. It sets a very bad example." Graham said softly after catching the pungent whiff of a joint.

"And good evening to you, Graham." Jack replied equally quietly, staring through the trees towards the golf course. One of the Hamiltons' cats rubbed up against his leg. He bent down to pet it. "Hello Jadis, you keeping my garden free of mice?" The cat purred as he tickled behind its ears.

"Jack I have a question, if you don't mind?"

"Shoot." Graham couldn't see it through the darkness, but Jack blew a smoke-ring over the cat's head. The purring got louder.

"What is a 'chav'?" Graham coughed deliberately as he caught another whiff of the almost-legal cigarette.

Jack laughed quietly. "I should have guessed you of all people wouldn't know."

"And what's that supposed to mean?" Graham suddenly became defensive.

"Nothing, don't worry. A chav is…" He got no further.

"You know your problem is you judge people too quickly." Graham interrupted before Jack could finish.

"Indeed. Well I guess I'm too young to change, and too old to educate." Jack flicked the butt out onto the golf course and turned to go in. "Just, hear me this once, Graham. This guy, AJ, the new owner of Number 1, well he's not really the sort of guy you're gonna meet at one of your church do's." Jack went in to watch South Park, leaving Graham even more determined to welcome this new arrival.

CHAPTER SEVEN

"No fucking way!" was Marky's reaction upon hearing the news. Jack took advantage of his lapse in concentration to score another goal against him on the Xbox. 7-0. Marky noticed the score. "You play this too much."

Jack nodded slowly. "So yeah, Mr ankle-strap's gonna be joining us in Luckyman's Close. Heard he finalised the deal yesterday."

"How the hell did you find that out?"

"When I heard he was in the running I asked about it in the estate agency. They said the deal had been closed. He'll be in in a week or two I suppose." Jack scored another goal.

Marky dropped his game controller on the floor. "Sod it, I can't come back from eight nil. So what you gonna do about it?"

"Play you again?"

"No, I mean what you gonna do about this kid moving in over the road from you?"

"What do you mean, do?" Jack sounded slightly concerned, he knew Marky's views on the matter before he heard them.

"Well you can't stand for that! The house prices will plummet! You gotta get rid of him."

"Oh yeah, sure. You got any spare revolvers or mustard gas I can use on him then? Seriously mate I don't really care to be honest. He can move in and bring half the estate with him for all I care, so long as he doesn't pester me. Can I get another?" Jack held up his empty beer can and Marky nodded. Jack went into Marky's kitchen to fetch two more cans.

"But that's just it, he'll pester you all day long. You were saying about his car stereo, yeah? Well that'll happen all night, seven nights a week. You gotta stop him, man." Marky opened his can and drained half of it in one go.

"Where's your missus?"

"Ah she's out with me ma. Some shopping bollocks or something. Don't dodge the question."

"Well look there's fuck all I could do even if I wanted to. I admit I did consider moving but to be honest I've only just got the place looking how I want it."

"There's no carpet on the top floor."

"Alright, I've nearly got it looking how I want it, and I really don't have the patience to move again."

"I would have thought anyone who has as little to do as *you* would've been some sort of patience deity." Marky used the remote to change the TV monitor over to Sky Sports News. "Hey Manure lost!"

"Nice one. Anyway I've decided that I'll at least give it a couple of weeks and see how stuff pans out. If he really is the Antichrist then I'll think about moving. But it's a hell of a lot of effort just cos I don't like someone."

"Nah mate it's not cos you won't like him, it's cos of what'll happen in the street. I saw this sorta thing happen up in Manchester. One moves in, they all move in, you can't get any peace for love nor money."

"Fucking hell Marky this isn't Burnage or the Bronx, he's only moving in cos he won the lottery, I doubt he's gonna be the sort of lad who buys up the entire Close just cos he wants his mates closer."

"Well at least yer can be thankful that the pigs will nab him for something or other sooner or later."

"How do you know that?"

"Did you not read that paper I left in the pub?" Jack shook his head.

"No, it was the Sun, I wouldn't read that shite to save lives."

Marky inhaled slowly. "His brother's doing time!" Jack's blank expression tested Marky's patience. "He's in Bullingdon Prison for GBH! Apparently he put a lad in hospital with a bottle. He got four years or something."

"When was that?"

"Couple of years ago I think."

"Well that's alright, he won't be out for a while yet."

"I'm telling you, man, you're making a mistake hanging round there."

"Well, maybe. But at least it'll make things a bit more interesting for the time being. Did you know my neighbours are gonna invite him over for dinner?"

"What, the bible bashers?"

"Yeah." Jack and Marky shared insidious looks.

"I'd give any money to be a fly on the wall when that happens," Marky stated before finishing his can.

"Me too, might even try to get involved." Jack contemplated ways he could invite himself into the prospective evening, but thought better of it. His imagination of what might happen would suffice for now.

"Another beer?"

"Sure why not, if what you say will happen really does happen looks like I'll be spending more time round here than usual." Jack muttered aimlessly.

Marky wasn't entirely sure that was a good thing.

CHAPTER EIGHT

Ralph stood back to admire his latest masterpiece. Glass of wine in his hand (well, it was already 10 am) he bathed in the delights of imaginary applause and cheers from invisible peers.

"Absolutely *divine!*" he congratulated himself.

Ralph had for years been trying to get his hands on the much-coveted Turner Prize, in the hope of snaring a big-money contract with one of the larger London-based dealers. (It was, unfortunately, through sheer pig-headedness that he refused to accept that the prize was suspiciously always awarded to a protégé of these dealers in the first place.)

"The Tate will become my stage, the world my congregation." Ralph felt giddy with the thoughts of all that would now come to pass. He drank some more wine, then realised that he had a slight headache. "Ah, the burdens of greatness." He went off towards the kitchen to find his pills, and promptly popped two Ibuprofen washed down with more wine and a pair of Valium for dessert. The sound of Puccini echoed down the hall and briefly set him off balance. It was the doorbell. Ralph literally danced down towards the magnificent operatic announcement. "The first of my proles hath come to seek an audience with mine greatest feat." He opened the door, whereupon his mood promptly fell from his face. "Oh, it's you, Major."

"Yes, ah, Blakeney, I wonder if I might be able to borrow a few minutes of your time?" Major Forsythe eyed the glass of wine with particular distaste.

Ralph recovered himself. "Of course, dear man. Now I've finished my magnum opus I can spare you all the time in the world. How can I help you?" Ralph found himself leaning ever closer to the wall, until he finally stumbled and spilt his wine over the pavement.

"Er, not right now, actually Blakeney. I was hoping to have everyone over to mine this evening. A rather grave situation has arisen and everyone in the Close must be consulted."

"Dear me, tell me, young poochie hasn't run off again?" Ralph did his best to sound concerned, but the Valium was kicking in and he rather oddly felt hungry for cheese strings.

"No, Betsy is fine. Actually it's about this new arrival. Well I'm not going in to great detail at the moment, just be over at seven sharp." The Major turned to walk away, confidant that his old army forcefulness would ensure that the fop would be there on time. He stopped at the end of the path. "I'm surprised you didn't hear anything yourself, after all, you work from home, you would have been here all day yesterday?"

"Hear what dear boy? I was in my creative trance. It's a state of focused mental control exercised by Tibetan Buddhists according to Time. I couldn't have heard a marching band once I was in the daze of inspiration."

The Major wandered off muttering about the state of youth these days.

Ralph went back indoors, and immediately sought to replenish the wine lost on the doorstep. His craving for cheese strings had grown, and also his mouth was feeling strangely dry. The sound of the doorbell had ignited his taste for music, and after discarding the glass and continuing his liquid intake straight from the bottle, he wandered back into his studio and fumbled about with the radio in a search for Classic FM. As the bravado of Mahler's ninth symphony finally trumpeted from the stereo, he swooned down into an easy chair and began playing with his hair. He was just drifting off into a mild coma when his unconsciousness was pierced by the phone.

"Hello? Marcus! Dear chap how are you?"

A similarly reedy voice replied from the receiver. "Simply wonderful, darling. I attended a superlative rendition of Madame Butterfly at the Oak last night. It really took my breath away. Anyway, enough of such small talk, how goes the tour de force? I believe you said you were close to achieving perfection the other night?"

Ralph's enthusiasm came bounding back. "Darling, you will not believe your eyes. I have created what the Guardian will surely call the rebirth of the Renaissance in our time." Ralph rediscovered the wine bottle in his hand and promptly drained half the remnants.

"That's marvellous. I'm truly jubilant for you. This is what you've worked so hard for. Eight years, Ralph, remember that. You've worked for this for eight years. Liverpool here we come!"

Ralph was caught in mid swig by the name. "Liverpool?!" he finally spluttered after coughing up mouthfuls of Bordeaux.

"Yes, dear boy, the Turner's at the Liverpool Tate this year. Surely you knew?"

"I'm not going to Liverpool! It's the most ghastly place!"

"Come come, darling, it's the European Capital of Culture. Or something like that. Anyway, your piece will triumph I'm sure. Well, I must get back, Shelley's going to take me to this wonderful new restaurant in Piccadilly tonight. Toodleloo."

Ralph felt distinctly ill as he replaced the receiver. *Liverpool!* He couldn't believe his dreams had been crushed so immeasurably by that one word. In less than a minute the rest of the wine disappeared and Ralph had passed out in disgust.

CHAPTER NINE

The Major had had to wait until the early evening to visit Kathi at Number 3. He had visited Jack early in the afternoon, conscious of the boy's predilection to sleep well past normal waking hours. On any normal occasion the Major would have called at 7.30 am sharp and hang the consequences if his visit met with disapproval. However, today was different, the Major felt that it was important to get on the right side of people to gain their support.

The effeminate nancy had agreed to come, as had Mrs Hamilton, who happened to be home that day by a stroke of luck. Apparently the family was having some new furniture delivered and she'd had to wait around for the truck to turn up. Where they'd got the money for all that was beyond the Major, but he was in no mood to speculate. While waiting for Kathi to return from work, he'd spent fruitless hours trying to contact the Doyles at their new address, but to no avail. Either they didn't have a phone or it wasn't installed yet. He was frankly incensed at their decision to accept the little hooligan's bid for the house, but while he was sure that they had an ample explanation, he wasn't able to contact them to hear it.

Finally Kathi's sleek Mercedes pulled into the Close at about a quarter past six, and the Major scurried out to meet her, formulating what he was going to say along the way. Everyone else in the Close was a subordinate to the Major, almost lesser beings, but Kathi was the sort of woman he knew not to trifle with. She had power, and she made sure everyone knew about it. The Major had come across similar personalities in the Army, and had, on more than one occasion, learnt the hard way not to cross them.

He was pleased to note that she was alone, he wasn't sure whether he wanted to interrupt if she had an important client over. Not out of any real sense of courtesy, more because he knew only too well that she'd be completely disinterested in him, the Close and life in general if she was talking shop.

Kathi was, in fact, not alone. She was still connected to an evening conference back in London via her mobile. With the latest Bluetooth handsfree kit strapped to her ear, she was, at the precise moment that the Major approached her, finalising the liquidation of some small company that had forgotten to pay its bills.

"Fuck 'em Fred. If they're dumb enough to miss a month's interest payment then they deserve to go bankrupt. No I don't wanna hear it, their sales are their own affair, they were aware of the consequences when they signed the contract, and now it's time to pull the plug. Ok, good. I'll see you at eight tomorrow to go over their assets for appraisal." She hung up without so much as a goodbye, and the Major tactfully made his approach.

"Excuse me, Miss West." He coughed quietly. She shot him an angry glance in reply, still obviously worked up about the temerity of a small shop daring to miss a payment.

"Don't call me that, Major," came the icy reply. "'Miss' is a feminine pronoun and therefore I find it sexist and offensive."

The Major found himself without a response. *What the hell am I supposed to call you, you heartless cretin?* "Ah, er, Kathi. I may call you that?" She nodded sharply. The Major couldn't see any difference between calling her by a feminine pronoun or calling her by a woman's name, but he wasn't about to split hairs. "Kathi, there is a meeting at my house this evening to discuss some matters that are going to affect us all in the Close. Everyone has agreed to come and I would appreciate it if you were there too."

"What's it in reference to?" Kathi asked disinterestedly while texting feverishly on her phone.

"Erm…certain events that have happened in the Close and that are about to happen. A new…person…has bought Number 1 and we all need to discuss it. Urgently."

"Oh Number 1 gone has it? I wonder how much they got for it. Well to be honest, Major, I really don't have the time for your little quirks, but I'll come over for five minutes only seeing as you're obviously anxious about something. I have a report to write tonight and I can't afford to be late with it."

The Major muttered something under his breath about how everything this woman talked about had something to do with affording or costing. "At seven then." Not that she heard him, she was texting once more. Obviously there just weren't enough hours in the working day to torture smaller businesses with.

CHAPTER TEN

Jack had a fairly shrewd idea what the forthcoming meeting would be about, but he was prepared to give the Major a chance to prove him wrong. Short of issuing uniforms and pitchforks, Jack was almost certain that the Major was about to attempt to rally some form of militia to combat the so-called 'imminent threat' to the civilisation that was Appletree Close. Those had been the actual words the old sod had used. *Once a soldier, always a soldier.* Nevertheless, Jack took it upon himself to clear his mind of as much prejudice to either side of the impending argument as he could while he trotted across the road to the dimly-lit front windows of Number 2.

His knocking on the door was greeted by a yapping reception from Betsy, and the usual doting comments from her owner as he fumbled around with the locks from the inside. The fact that it took the Major over twenty seconds to open all the locks said something about the guy's paranoia.

"Ah, Nielson. Good of you to come." The door was still held in by a slide-chain as the Major inspected the last street member to turn up. "You're a bit late, you know. I did say seven."

Jack was already growing irritable; he had only humoured the bumbling fool out of morbid curiosity. "And I did say that I had a lot to do today, and that I might be late." Jack reminded him.

"Yes, well. You're here now and that's the main thing. Come on in then." The door shut and re-opened minus the chain. Betsy snatched the opportunity for freedom in a flash. Shooting out of the gap in the doorway faster than a cat with its tail on fire, her flight for escape was ended as abruptly as it began, with her diving headlong into Jack's shins.

"Ow!" The shock more than anything causing Jack's outburst, "What the hell is your dog doing?!"

In one fluid movement the Major had swooped down and picked the now star-seeing animal up in his arms. "There, there, Poochie." He addressed her first, as always. Then Jack, "Don't mind her, she's a tad short-sighted in her old age."

Jack was still wincing from the sharp attack on one of the less fleshy areas of his legs, and had in mind a good few ideas on how to end the damn mutt's suffering. He hobbled after the Major into the hall and then the front room.

"Make yourself comfortable, I'll be in in a jiffy."

All but one of the seats was occupied. Kathi was sitting sharply upright in the chair by a desk. Mrs Hamilton sad timidly on the corner of a sofa, the rest of which was taken up by a very ill-looking Ralph, almost lying across the thing, a small shiny streak of drool gleaming from the corner of his mouth. The only available sitting place was an easy-chair that had obviously come as part of a set with the sofa. Jack approached it to take his place, but the Major's return to the room stopped him in his tracks.

"No! Not there, boy!" The Major marched past him still carrying Betsy, who now had a small bone in her mouth, and sat down in the only available seat with the mutt in his lap. Not wanting to disturb the semi-conscious Ralph, who looked like one movement would mean the re-appearance of his dinner all over the floor, Jack resigned himself to sitting on the floor, and squatted down near the door.

"Now then," the Major started. "First of all I'd like to thank you all for coming at such short notice." He eyed Ralph's mute form with distaste but continued. "As I explained to each of you, there is a situation that is about to affect us all that must be dealt with swiftly and decisively. This new vagrant who has bought Number 1. He's a totally unacceptable hooligan who has no sense of decency or manners whatsoever." He scanned the room for reactions, but he didn't have to look far to find a distinct lack of support seasoned with general disinterest and apathy. "Well, come on then. Someone start the ball rolling."

Kathi was the first to make herself heard, unsurprisingly. "Is that it? You dragged us all over here to moan about some kid you don't like? I've got a report due…" She was interrupted by her mobile. "Excuse me, I have to take this. She left the room barking down the phone at some poor colleague for no apparent reason. The Major was not amused.

"Mrs Hamilton, surely you're of the same opinion? This vagrant must be stopped."

Mrs Hamilton was, by nature, a rather quiet and reserved person - the archetypal housewife, who felt somewhat out of her depth without her husband. "Well, Major, it's not really my place to get involved. After all this young man hasn't actually done anything wrong."

Major Forsythe had begun to seethe loudly. "What about your children, Mrs Hamilton? Do you want them exposed to the sort of degraded tripe that comes out of the little bastard's mouth?" The Major caught his own act of hypocrisy and ignored it. Jack did not. About to interject, he was silenced abruptly by a fierce bark from Betsy, evidently attracted to his shins still, but now more so for their resemblance to the bone she had just stripped bare.

"Surely it's a case of embracing those who are less fortunate than ourselves?" Everyone turned to find out from where the mumbled comment had emerged, and the prostrate figure of Ralph stirred briefly as he tried to brush his hair out of his face, and missed.

"Less fortunate?! The sod could buy the whole Close on a whim!" the Major erupted.

"Oh well what's the problem then? Sell him your house and move somewhere else." Ralph was now attempting to sit up, a feat far easier said than done, considering his alcohol stream was lacking in blood.

"I will not be forced out by a child who wears his trousers inside his socks."

Jack felt he had heard enough, and braving retribution from the wind-up rodent, finally gave his thoughts. "For fuck's sake, why is everyone against this guy? You can't hate someone just cos of what he wears, or because he wasn't fed with a silver spoon from birth. I don't like the lad myself, but I'm not getting involved in some urban war to blackball him or whatever you had in mind, Major. Just ignore him if you don't like him, or take it up with him yourself if you can't do that. Anything's better than this underhand plotting. Jaysus, it's like the Ides of March here. If you don't mind, Major, and in fact even if you do, I'm off down the pub." Slamming the door behind him was less of a statement than an assurance that the bloody dog wouldn't follow him. He bumped into Kathi outside, who, seemingly for the first occasion in all the time he'd known her, was doing nothing. Just standing there, biting her thumbnail. "What's up with you?"

"Hmm? Oh nothing. Just...no, nothing. I've got to go. Well done by the way, I heard your little rant, glad not everyone's as mad as that geriatric. Anyway, bye."

He watched her walk out the door, without the usual swagger that had in the past both intimidated and excited him. It was the first time he had spoken to her without seeing the fire of power in her eyes. He had seen something else though. He couldn't place it, but it made his stomach feel slightly emptier than it had done five minutes earlier. Something was wrong, but he wouldn't pry. Especially not when the Rosebush was only doing 'pound a pint' for another hour.

CHAPTER ELEVEN

William Forsythe sat on his easy chair a depressed man. Depressed and outraged at the same time, two emotions dangerous enough on their own, but when combined are much more than just the sum of their parts. "I've been totally abandoned," he told Betsy, who was heartily tucking into another bone she had fished out while her master wasn't looking. The fact that he seemed not to care was to her a green light to help herself. At first his apathy towards her theft was reflected by her disinterest in whatever he was saying. Humans had far too many emotions, in Betsy's view, and they swung between them too quickly. As far as she was concerned he should be the happiest member of the pack; free access to the bin with the treats in it, able to leave the house whenever he felt like it. He had it easy.

Gradually though she sensed that her master deserved some attention, and she diligently left her bone and hopped up onto his lap to show him some affection. "Abandoned, left alone. No-one cared, Poochie." The Major's sullen mood was understandable, given how the campaign meeting he had carefully planned had ended up. First the snotty bitch had walked out without even feigning interest. Then the young layabout, with a parting statement that, in the Major's opinion, showed absolutely no respect for his elders and betters. The long-haired nancy-boy had barely been conscious, and when he finally did come round, he vomited in the toilet and staggered out without offering so much as an excuse, and he still found time to utterly condemn everything the Major said, and tell him that he was being a childish bigot. Finally Mrs Hamilton had made her excuses politely, but remained firmly on the wrong side. She'd even gone so far as to imply that she was having the new arrival around for dinner as soon as possible. The Major found it hard to resent her for this, assuming, quite rightly as it happened, that she was merely putting across her husband's views without actually having any of her own.

To be fair to the crowd, each of their reasons for failure to support what he had thought to be a noble quest were all valid, and the Major knew this. As is so often the case in warfare, timing is of the essence, he had pointed out, and failure to act while they had the chance would mean that soon it would be too late. By referring to his campaign as a 'pre-emptive strike', he had earned himself an acid comment from the fop that even compared his suggestion to some of the most questionable military actions in history. Had the Major been an outsider on the conversation, completely lacking in military jargon and an ignorance for tactical appraisals, while also having missed out on the first Gulf War and having been retired for the second, he would have probably agreed, but unfortunately such were the only terms he thought in.

From the Major's dejection, the spark of his lifelong training suddenly ignited. His whole life he had been brought up through the Army ranks never to give up, no matter how great the adversity, and now the long painful hours on the mock field of battle overpowered his depression and jolted his consciousness. He recalled the story of Colonel Herbert Jones, who, faced with fierce odds, charged to his death during the Falklands War. The Bulldog spirit.

"No!" Came the rebellious outburst. "No I will not give in!" The Major leapt up, spilling Betsy onto the floor, an act she forgave almost instantly as she landed next to the unfinished bone that had been momentarily forgotten. "Damn it I will see this through! I won't have my life ruined by a wastrel, and I won't stop for those fools." A mess of ideas, few of them pleasant, began to piece themselves together in his mind, forming the embryo of a plan. The Major stood bolt upright, as if at attention to some higher invisible force.

"From time to time in the history of this island race, it has come upon a few to defend that which we all hold dear, even if some of us do not realise it." Betsy realised that something momentous was happening, and duly sat up attentively wagging her tail in encouragement. "The Armada, Trafalgar, the Battle of Britain. Sometimes it takes the actions of a few to restore order, and so it shall be with me. I will show the way, then they will follow." He remained at attention for several minutes, forming his tactics in his mind. Betsy had grown impatient, and trundled off with her bone to see if the back door was open. The Major didn't notice her leave, he was not to be distracted from this, his darkest yet finest hour.

He finally decided that his plan was viable and, even better than that, it was subtle. He couldn't involve the police; after the way they treated him he wouldn't trust them to catch a cold, let alone so obvious a rascal as this. Picking up the phone, he punched in a number, only to hang up shortly after realising that he'd dialled so quickly he'd missed out several digits. This time he was just as voracious, but also more careful. After a few short tones from the receiver, the call was answered.

"James my boy, I need a favour." The Major started without waiting for pleasantries. His son didn't mind, he was used to the manner.

"Yes, Dad. What can I do for you?" The Major dictated his request to his eldest and only, who frantically tried to write everything down. He goggled at the other end, more than a little disconcerted at his father's requirements. When the Major had indicated that that was all, he hung up, having told James to be round first thing tomorrow, ignorant of any plans that may have already been made.

Feeling that his ingenuity deserved some reward, Major Forsythe fetched a bottle of the finest Glenfiddich from the drinks cabinet. At 40 years (when he bought it) and of an exceptional quality it was a drink he delighted in only for the most special of occasions, such as the Queen's Jubilee or the re-election of the Tory party. However, tonight, he felt, surpassed all the above in terms of significance. To him, it was the beginning of the fight back. Against adversity of the coarsest nature, he celebrated the birth of his plans. An hour and a half later he was snoring loudly with an empty glass in one hand, and empty bottle in the other, and a contented pooch in his lap.

CHAPTER TWELVE

"Ah I'm fucking stuck. I've got 9, but can't figure out me last one." Marky flung his pen down on the table in disgust. "It's between that bird who played Kaylee in Firefly and Carrie Fisher."

Jack took the piece of paper out of Marky's hand and examined it closely. For them, choosing their entries to the annual hundred sexiest women awards was an important time of the year. "Ten years of loyalty and only now are you finally over your Princess Leia obsession."

"Come on mate, that was part of our childhood."

"Bollocks. We're too young to make that claim, and even if it was the case I don't much think these awards should be based on anything connected to the word 'childhood'. It sounds more than a bit wrong."

Marky sighed in resignation. "Well, either way I gotta get this done before I go home. The missus don't like me doing this anymore."

"I'm not surprised," Jack concluded. "You've picked, well, eleven brunettes and your bird's a blonde."

"Well, not really."

"So I've heard," Jack mumbled slyly. Marky either didn't hear the slur or ignored it. "But you know what I mean." Jack was on his fifth pint in an hour, all bought at the same time, obviously, to take advantage of the pound a pint offer. "This stuff isn't half watered down."

"That's why it's pound a pint like. There's only about a quid's worth of beer in that glass." Marky drained his in appreciation of what little water seemed to be in his. He wasn't about to tell Jack that his definitely wasn't watered down for fear of an attempted exchange. "Anyway, how did that meeting you had go?" Jack appeared not to hear. "Well?"

"It was a load of bollocks. Major Disaster tried to organise a lynch mob," he admitted after a brief pause.

Marky chuckled, he could picture the scene, and in fact his vision of it was not entirely different from the actual event. "So what happened?"

"Well what do you think? He got shot down. By everyone."

Marky sighed. "You're all a load of fucking weirdoes you rich 'uns. It's only when people have money that they somehow seem to care about those without it." A blank look from Jack brought a sheepish return from Marky. Though he made a point of very rarely actually asking Jack for money, it was fair to say that Jack happily paid for them both to do things that Marky would never usually be able to afford. "Sorry, mate."

"Ah forget it." Jack relented. "I just get a bit wound up about everyone getting on this lad's back when apart from having a loud stereo he's not actually done anything wrong."

Marky was about to interject but thought the better of it. In any case, he'd solved his problem regarding his list. "Sorry, Jessica." He addressed the slip of paper, "But I can't choose between these two." He scratched a name off and replaced it with his new choice. "Done." He was pleased with himself, it had taken him over an hour. Jack looked over the final copy and shook his head wistfully.

"Talking of fit brunettes, have you told your ball and chain about Prague?"

Marky's contented grin washed off his face in a tide of bloodless colour. The incident in question regarded a weekend he and Jack had spent a few months previously in Europe's new capital of liberalism and student loan expenditure. They had been sampling the local delights and, due to high alcohol intake, had spurned their hotel rooms for much less comfortable but much more enjoyable rooms in the red light district with a pair of leather-clad female locals. "Why've you brought that up?" he asked quietly.

"No, I didn't mean a guilt trip or anything like that, sorry. I meant, I wanted your views on infidelity." Jack's expression was as innocent as a puppy's, something he had perfected in school as a way to get out of trouble. However this time it was genuine.

"Whose infidelity?" Marky was wondering where Jack was going with this, the topic made him edgy.

"Mine."

The relief that should have been due to Marky was barged out of the line to his thought process by perplexity. "You don't have a bird though."

"Yeah, Anna."

"You mean that bird you're doing who just happens to be married to your old school mate? I hardly think that if you shag someone else she'll be able to have words about it."

"I suppose." Jack agreed. He hadn't actually asked the question to find out Marky's views on infidelity. He didn't really care about them. This was a conversation he was taking elsewhere. Marky unwittingly obliged.

"Why, who's the target?"

Jack mumbled while halfway through a swig of his beered-down water. "Kathi."

"Career Bitch?!" This had been the response Jack had been expecting, which comforted him somewhat, as it meant he wouldn't have to beat around matters to get an opinion from the Manc. "Well fair play to you. She's hot alright, but she's the most stuck-up tart I've ever met."

"Yeah, I know. Well, I thought I knew, but just earlier as I left Major Disaster's pad I bumped into her and she looked...well..."

"Well what?"

"I dunno, fragile."

"Fragile?! She's not a fucking vase!"

"No, you know what I mean. Delicate, insecure, that sort of thing."

"Oh." Marky took a sip as he contemplated this most seemingly unfitting of descriptions of a woman who had once threatened to repossess his house after he had wolf-whistled her. "So?"

"Well, I dunno. I looked at her differently, she didn't seem to be this power-mad lunatic. She looked, well, different." The normally perfectly eloquent Jack found his tongue tied for some reason he couldn't explain.

"You're going soft. Get yourself back home and watch some porn, that'll sort you out proper."

Jack rolled his eyes not inconspicuously. He knew he'd been a fool to try and explain this to a guy whose idea of sensitivity was giving his significant other flowers freshly nicked from a graveyard on his way home from a night on the piss.

CHAPTER THIRTEEN

AJ had grown increasingly frustrated at the amount of patience involved in moving house. At the painful behest of his solicitor, he hadn't been able to take the month long holiday to Ayia Napa he'd hoped for, due to the apparent need to stay to make sure everything was finalised. To AJ, the fuss seemed needless. Pick a house, give the owners money, move in. All this fucking about with lawyers and estate agents was beginning to grate on him. Now, however, he had received the long overdue phone call from Mr Terrace, the estate agent with a more than apt name, to tell him that he could move in on Monday.

"Fucking sorted," he said, replacing his brand new mobile in his jacket pocket. His mum looked up from the TV.

"What's that then, love?"

"The house, Ma. We can move in on Monday. 'Bout fucking time too." AJ had retrieved his phone once more and began texting the news to all and sundry. "Hey, Wayne!" he yelled through the flat without looking up from his phone. "Get off the fucking computer and start packing."

A spotty kid with a crew cut and an ear piercing thundered across the floor making more noise than you'd think an eleven year old could. "What's that then bruv? You got the house then?" he chirped in a voice that rasped rather than sang.

His elder brother eyed him darkly. "You been smoking weed again haven't you?"

"Yeah, but just a little bit. S'alright bruv I had the window open."

"I fucking told you enough times not to smoke weed. That's how Kev got in jail. Anyway, go pack your stuff, we're moving on Monday." The kid tore off back up the stairs, making even more noise than before. AJ watched him go. "He's gonna end up like that old dear from across the road with the voice-box if he don't give that shit up," he told his mother who had gone back to the TV.

"Ah don't worry about it, love. He'll grow out of it."

"Ma, you don't grow out of weed. He's too young to be smoking that shit." The mobile buzzed a bassline meant to sound like a recent hiphop hit, but in fact was nowhere near it. "Yeah? Jonesy! Yeah I know it's fucking sick ain't it!" He breezed out of the room into the kitchen to make himself a brew.

Several hours later, and several dozen phone calls and texts, AJ had decided to take a spin down to his new house to survey the scene before he picked up his kids from their mother. He'd been recommended the place by his elder brother Kev, who'd burgled one of the houses a few years earlier and found the owners to be 'minted' in his words. It was certainly a far throw from the Greenmeadow Estate where he currently lived in his absent father's flat. The burnt-out wrecks of many joyrides were replaced by well-trimmed hedgerows and signs that weren't covered in graffiti and pirate radio station flyers. The urban jungle of high-rise flats and concrete Abaddon seemed another country compared to the small white fencing designed more for show than keeping out armed junkies on the prowl for their next score.

No, this was certainly a different world to the one he'd been brought up in. This was a world that hadn't heard of Jobseeker's Allowance or if it had, chose to feign incomprehension. A world where the sight of a policeman didn't send gangs of youths scurrying round dark alleys throwing small pieces of cellophane down drains as they ran. AJ had dreamed as a child of one day leaving the

54

Greenmeadow Estate, if only for the total abject boredom of the place. To him, suburbia was a haven of innocence, almost sheltered from the real world by the incumbents' ability to afford ignorance.

He pulled his car into Appletree Close and parked by the junction. Not out of respect or consideration regarding his music volume, it was off anyway, but because he wanted to see the Close in its entirety. He rolled up a cigarette and pulled his hood over his cap before leaving the car and wandering down the quiet road. It was mid-afternoon and most people would be at work. In actual fact, hardly anyone in the Close was out. Only the Hamiltons' house was empty, the parents being at their jobs and the children at school. AJ shuffled slowly through the invisible line between his house, Number 1, on the left, and the Hamiltons, Number 6, on the right. He saw a small roundabout that he hadn't noticed before, sat in the middle of the drive with the other four houses facing into it like scouts round a campfire. The circle was obviously more there for show than anything else, with several quite impressive trees in the centre, and even a park bench nestled in their shade. He wandered over and sat down, and he found it was many times more comfortable than any public seating that could be found on his side of town. Looking around, AJ regretted his rather boisterous first introduction to the Close. Not for the sake of the Major, as far as AJ was concerned that old fool was just being bloody-minded. No, for the peace that seemed to be the life-blood of the place.

AJ finished his rollie and flicked it away into the grass. He thought briefly about picking it up, but in the end decided he couldn't be bothered scrabbling around on the ground looking for a dog-end. Especially with his brand new trainers on. He got up and wandered back to his car, thinking all along about his new life here and how different it would be.

CHAPTER FOURTEEN

The Major looked proudly at his new weapon. An impressive array of loudspeakers of all shapes and sizes had been set up perfectly to roar out of the sitting-room and into the garden via the French windows. His son, James, amidst regular confessions of bewilderment, had warned him not to push the volume up beyond a set level. The Major had other ideas. Years of training in the field with mortars and artillery firing all around him had reduced his ears to all but total inefficiency, and now that would work in his favour. Unlike his target, he could simply remove his hearing aids and wear his army-surplus mufflers.

"They'll produce anything up to a hundred twenty decibels," James had informed him. "But that's louder than a plane taking off, so you'll deafen yourself and anyone in a half a mile radius if you push them that far." The Major had simply patted him on the back and told him to expect a cheque in a week, provided he was happy with how they performed. James didn't see the point of arguing, he had never won an argument with his father in his whole life, even when he was unquestionably right. He had paid for the equipment himself the next day.

Anxious to test out his brilliant plan before the big day, the Major had waited until the Close was empty, as far as he could tell. The Hamiltons were out doing their usual weekday routines, Ralph had been driven off early in the morning by a man with green hair and a suspiciously gaudy jacket and Kathi's car wasn't in her drive. Just the layabout Jack would be in, and the Major no longer cared what happened to him.

Ironically, that very morning Jack had been overseeing the installation of his new triple glazing windows. "Sure, it'll make your house almost completely soundproof," the technician had told him several times, "and you'll not be having any more cold mornings in winter, I'll tell you that much." Jack had run out of tea that morning following the installation, and had gone off down to the corner shop to pick up more.

The Major looked through his collection of dusty LPs. He needed something boisterous, something patriotic, something to remind the young vagrant just what country he was in and what the pecking order in these parts was. *Why not.* he thought, as his eyes settled on a copy of Last Night of the Proms. Elgar's most famous work, Land of Hope and Glory no less, was more than adequate, at least for a test run anyway.

He pulled the vinyl out of its sleeve and blew away the dust gathered from years of lingering. The Union Flag stood proudly in the centre of the disk. He flipped open the lid of his elderly record player and laid the precious recording in place. His first mistake was not to notice that the player was set to forty-five RPM instead of the regular thirty-three. Upon dropping the needle into place halfway into the record, he was blown backwards by a howling scream of a chorus. As he staggered backwards, the screech of what was originally a soprano, but now more resembled a Formula One racing car, grew louder and louder. The Major just about realised that it was building to the climax of Land of Hope and Glory, and leapt back to prevent the final high note from shattering his nerves, eardrums, the windows, and his dreams of this madness actually working. He got there just in time.

As he tore the needle off the top of the record, creating what can only be described as a sound effect from a Carry-On film, Betsy shot into the room howling in tune with the now finished anthem. The Major sat down in his easy chair for a moment to recover. His ears hadn't wrung this much since an idiot TA had accidentally let off a flashbang inside a lecture hall during a safety briefing.

Any remotely normal sentient being would have probably called it a day following this first setback, but after half an hour's quiet contemplation over a strong cup of tea, the Major determined that he'd organised this plan and paid for all this equipment, (at least he intended to). No, he would press on, and more importantly, press on the button that made the damn thing play at the right speed. Anyway, he hadn't even tried the speakers out to their full extent yet.

After carefully removing his hearing aids, which he was now sure didn't work anyway, and putting his mufflers in place over his ears, he approached the sound system with a degree more caution this time. After spending a good five minutes searching the entire plastic casing, he found what he was certain was the button that set the errant machinery playing at the right speed. After moving it to the correct position, he then replaced the needle at the beginning, and listened happily as the gentlemanly opening to the famous march filled the room.

Louder, he thought, and pushed the dial around a quarter turn. No real change. In fact, no change at all. He pushed the dial all the way around, just as his son had explicitly told him not to. No change whatsoever. He then looked at the new equipment. It all seemed to be working fine. What was it James had said? "Turn on the amplifier to use the new speakers." *Ah yes*, thought the Major as he located the 'on' switch for the amplifier. The new speakers lived up to their promise. Just as the power flowed into them, the crash of drums flowed out, shattering the antique desk they were perched on. The Major was, for a second time, knocked backwards by a sudden noise, only this time it was not the shock but the diaphragm of the sub-woofer blowing out so quickly it flew into his chest and rebounded off in search of new targets. It found them in the form of a collection of priceless ornamental crockery above the fireplace on the other side of the room. Major Forsythe landed with a heavy bump, not that it could be heard for the cacophonous death of the new speaker system.

The Major's accident was nothing compared to poor Betsy's. As the shattered desk collapsed the speakers landed on the floor and began a mini-tremor throughout the room. Convinced that some inconceivably large predator was in the area, Betsy was in no mood to hang around. She darted for what looked like salvation and the woods outside the garden. The Major had, however, recently cleaned the french windows, not that that was to deter the committed animal. She crashed through two layers of apparently invisible reinforced glass as though they weren't there, and shot up the nearest tree, where she found herself sitting next to one of the Hamiltons' cats, who had had the same idea.

CHAPTER FIFTEEN

Despite being around a half mile away at the time, Jack had heard the bedlam. Actually that wasn't much of an achievement, half of the M40 heard the bedlam. More curious than concerned, Jack had jogged towards the sound, only to discover that it was coming from the Close, so jogging became sprinting. By the time he turned the corner into Appletree Close he stopped abruptly to cover his ears and backed off down the way he came. Whatever was making this much noise definitely wasn't worth approaching. He ran a mental checklist of who would be in. Ralph was away, the God Squad were all out, Kathi was at work, that only left...*Oh fuck what's the old fool gone and done now?* After deciding that he couldn't afford to wait, not knowing whether the Major's life was in danger or, more likely, someone else's was because of him, Jack raced down the road with his hands over his ears. It was futile, he had a headache within three seconds and felt sure he could feel blood inside his ears, not that he dared take his hands away.

Displaying remarkable quick-wittedness and dexterity for a man whose idea of exercise was playing air-guitar, he kicked the Major's door in and raced into the front room. He found the Major lying on the floor in a strange contorted position, and noticed the glass on the back door had been smashed. That was about as much information as he was able to take in, as he literally couldn't hear himself think, or move, or yell, as he found himself shouting at the Major to see if he was awake.

Jack wrenched all the plugs out of their sockets by the speakers, and a blissful peace descended on the room. The pounding beat of the final part of the march was still throbbing inside his head, but at least he could take his hands away from his ears now. He looked down at the body lying at his feet. Major William Forsythe was certainly alive, of that much he was sure. He had begun writhing around and foaming at the mouth, and his mouth was moving as if he was trying to say something. Jack couldn't tell whether he actually was speaking or not as his hearing was still several degrees worse than deaf.

"Are you alright?" he asked and immediately regretted it. It was the most pointless question in the history of language. He fumbled about in his pocket looking for his mobile, only to discover that he had left it at home. Cursing, he tried to speak to the Major again. "Where's your phone?" The lack of response led to him asking it again, but slower and louder, as though the Major were some tongue-tied foreigner.

The Major shook his head violently. Jack was unsure whether he was trying to say that he had no phone, or that he didn't want him to call anyone, or whether he was just having a seizure. Jack went to leave the room in order to find a phone. "No!" came the yell after him.

Partly happy that he now knew he wasn't deaf, and partly bemused by the outburst, Jack knelt down by the old man. "I think you should go to hospital." he said slowly while surveying the room carefully. "What happened here anyway?"

The Major indicated that Jack should help him up into his easy chair, a process made harder by the fact that the bottom half of the pensioner's body seemed unwilling to comply. After a few minutes of struggling, and the rather unpleasant experience of receiving a consignment of roaming saliva in his ear from his charge, Jack had successfully placed the Major in his easy chair and handed him a cigarette for good measure.

"Don't usually smoke, but thanks, I feel as if I could use one right now," wheezed the Major. "Must say it's very good of you to help me out." He looked down at the damage for the first time. "Well I'm glad I won't have to pay for all that. James can take it all away as far as I'm concerned."

Jack wasn't listening. He'd been taking a closer look at the broken glass at the back. There were faint drops of blood and white hair. He looked down the trail to see it lead towards the closest tree to the fence. Usually a proud tree of that size would have squadrons of birds perched at the top chatting aimlessly to each other, but none today.

"So are you going to tell me what happened or should I let my imagination have a pop at guessing?" Jack asked, his attention now drawn to the remnants of the antique crockery collection lying around the fireplace.

"Oh nothing, just a little experiment I was carrying out. All fine now."

Jack wanted to believe him, in fact he wanted nothing more than to get out of this bombsite and neck a packet of painkillers for his head, but the residual foam around the Major's mouth and his nervous twitch left doubt hanging in the air. "Are you sure you don't need to see a doctor or something?"

"Yes, yes," came the irritable reply. "Honestly I'm fine. Now thank you for your help but I've got a lot to be getting on with." He gestured towards the door, and Jack reluctantly took the hint.

Outside the house, his ears now finally starting to settle back down, Jack made plans to stay round at Marky's for a few days. Sure, his missus wouldn't be best pleased, and of course Jack would miss the fun at the Hamiltons' 'dinner', but something was happening and intuition taught Jack that he'd do well to stay away.

Inside the wrecked front room the Major was seething. Deep down he was actually pleased that his plan had shown such promise, but he realised now that it was just as effective 'friendly fire' as it was to others. He decided to shelve the idea. Not that this was the end. No, this was what test runs were for. As he settled down with a cup of tea he began to think of a different way to win his war.

CHAPTER SIXTEEN

AJ realised his first mistake fairly early on. Instead of hiring a professional removal company, he had decided to get a mate to 'sort it' for fifty quid. The battered and rusty white van had barely been able to take the weight of all the furniture, and while taking a corner at well over fifty in order to avoid a red light, the sofa in the back threw itself across the cabin, crushing several lamps and one large plant pot that had tried to escape by rolling away. The noise hadn't deterred the driver though, and while holding the steering wheel in-between his knees as he tried to simultaneously light a joint and make a phone-call, the van had careered through a bicycle rack and clipped the wing-mirror off an unsuspecting taxi, which thankfully happened to be empty at the time.

It was only after one of the back doors had flung open and pieces of a table began falling out causing following traffic to swerve violently that AJ, following behind in the Nova, had forced the driver to stop. After a brief but loud altercation by the side of the road, while young Wayne ran back down the road dodging cars trying to dodge him whilst picking up the pieces of the broken table, the van doors were slammed shut and held together by TV cable, and the procession continued. After a further fifteen minutes of traffic violations, they miraculously arrived in the Close, relatively unscathed.

Following a brief survey of the damage, the driver of the vehicle which unknown to him now had its number plate racing across the airwaves of the Thames Valley Police, agreed to cut his fee to twenty quid and a pint. They unloaded the undamaged furniture onto the spacious front lawn, then argued further when it was discovered that AJ had left the keys to the house back at the flat on the estate.

Forty-five minutes later AJ had returned with the keys to discover that the driver and the white van had both vanished following a tip-off from a friend with a police scanner. He finally opened the door to his new pad, and walked in to survey what he hoped was the start of a new life.

"Right we'd better get this stuff in, I gotta pick the young 'uns up in a couple of hours. Charlene said they could stay here for the night," he said to Wayne, who was already kicking a football around in the road. They began lifting in some of the smaller items, and after about a half hour all that was left was one partially broken sofa-bed and a few other large items of furniture which Wayne couldn't lift. "I'll see if anyone's around to give us a hand." AJ told his brother, who took that as a sign that he could go and watch TV.

AJ looked around, and decided to try the house directly opposite his, which happened to be the Hamiltons. After ringing the bell a few times, and banging the door so hard anyone inside could be forgiven that there was a debt collector outside, he decided that no-one was home. He moved along to try the next house: Number 5.

Jack had had a pretty good day so far. He'd managed to avoid the dread of Sunday by playing a mammoth computer gaming session on the Saturday night. Having just got into internet games, he'd been rather proud at the way he'd lasted until 11am the next day, at which point he'd realised what day it was and promptly went to bed. Having only dared to rise after the clock had turned midnight, he'd then been back on the online game for a few more hours, then back to bed. It wasn't the most productive day and he'd be the first to admit it, but anything to get out of the horrors that Sunday usually presented.

At that moment, Jack was in the process of deleting the game which had taken up nearly twenty hours of his time out of the last forty-eight, and when the doorbell rang he thought it was the game complaining about being removed. When the banging on the door started, Jack became somewhat more concerned. He ran a quick mental checklist to see if he could think of any bills that he'd ignored recently. None sprang to mind. He trotted down the stairs still racking his brains as to whom he owed money, as it was the only explanation for such ferocious knocking.

He opened the front door to find no-one there. The banging had stopped a few seconds earlier, so Jack looked around the road to see if there was anyone about. He saw the infamous Nova parked across the road, and some large items of furniture lying around the front lawn of Number 1. *Please don't tell me it's that bumbling old fool trying to rope me into another stupid scheme,* was the first thought on Jack's mind, but as the Major's house was quiet and still, and there was no other movement in the Close, he assumed it had been a door-to-door salesman. *Must've got a sale next door.* he thought. Next door was Ralph's house, and the artist was always too gullible to say 'no' to salesmen, in fact as far as Jack could remember Ralph had changed his electricity supplier four times in the last six months, simply due to being visited by different companies.

He closed the door again and turned around back into his hallway to find himself staring straight into the eyes of AJ. After he'd recovered from the initial shock that had nearly seen him hit the roof, he finally addressed his intruder.

"What are you doing in here?! How did you get in here?! What are you doing here?!" he blurted out.

"You've asked that twice." AJ replied calmly, as though it were an everyday situation.

"Well what *are* you doing here?!" Jack finally asked, silently cursing himself for having said it a third time.

"Your back door was open. I heard music and you didn't answer your doorbell. I dunno, you could've been being attacked or something." AJ looked around the hallway at the stacks of opened envelopes and junk mail lying around on the floor.

"You mean attacked by someone who comes in the unlocked back door without me knowing?"

"Yeah like that."

Jack rolled his eyes, but AJ didn't seem to gather the irony.

"Well thank you for your concern. Now what do you want?" Jack half-heartedly started picking up some of the junk mail that was lying around, as if by some warped instinct to clean for visitors.

"Oh right, yeah, well me and me bruv are moving stuff in over the road and we need a bit of help. It'll only take a couple of minutes."

Jack's eyes were caught by a scratchcard that had fallen out of one of the envelopes, and he nodded slowly not really listening. "Yeah, ok. Sorry, what?"

"Come on, then." AJ shuffled past him and opened the front door. "It'll be well easy."

Jack followed him out, and they were both greeted by the sight of young Wayne running out into the road to greet them.

"The fucking leccy's not working Bruv. I can't get the TV to work either," the youngster bawled.

"Ah for fuck's sake." While AJ jogged over to the house with his brother to find out what was wrong, Jack looked over towards the house next door, to see the dark figure of the Major looking out of the front window with an unpleasant smirk on his face.

CHAPTER SEVENTEEN

"And that should fix it." Jack took a step back to admire his handiwork. All he had done was to flip the mains switch back on, but knowing approximately as much about electricity as a five-year-old, was determined to bask in his little triumph. AJ tried a light switch and the small toilet was bathed in yellow light. "Why do they put the switches in the toilet anyway?" Jack mused.

"Sweet, nice one mate." AJ turned the light back off and went off to tell Wayne that he could now watch TV.

After seeing the Major's gloating satisfaction the rebellious nature in Jack had urged him to help AJ. The old fool just wouldn't take the hint that his plans were futile and stupid. *How did he get in here anyway?* He wondered. Maybe the Army trained people to break into houses. Jack didn't immediately see how being able to burgle people's homes helped with the defence of the realm, but he didn't really care. Fact was, the Major had now upped his resistance, and it was worrying.

"You want a cuppa something?" AJ called from another room, presumably the kitchen.

"Sure, cheers. Tea, please." Jack shut the cover of the fuse box and went out into the hall. It was already a mess of junk. Half-inflated inflatable chairs, a collection of lava lamps, a dartboard. *Why would anyone buy this stuff?* Jack's attention was drawn towards a stack of Xbox games that stood as high as him, yet he could see no Xbox. He reached up and picked the top one off of the pile. It was the new Fifa, the one that hadn't even come out yet.

"Hey, how did you get ahold of this?" Jack asked while walking into the kitchen. "It's not even been released yet!"

"Ah me mate's bruv works down the docks in Southampton. He picked up a few of them games for cheap. I got another if you wanna buy it?"

Jack thought for a few seconds about the law and the ways he would be breaking it. Possession of stolen property, failure to report a crime, aiding and abetting. *Sod it, it's the new Fifa.* "How much?"

"Ah seeing as you fixed the leccy and helped with the sofa you can have it." AJ handed him a cup of milky tea with the bag still in the cup. Jack ignored it.

"Cheers, man." Jack looked at his new toy and couldn't wait to see Marky's face when he thrashed him with all the new moves in the game. "So is it just you and your brother, then?" Jack knew that AJ had children from the newspaper report, but was somewhat stuck for conversation.

"Nah, me mum's coming round tomorrow. She's cleaning up the flat for the council. And I got me two kids as well. They're coming over tonight." AJ put his tea on the table and began rolling a cigarette. He offered one to Jack, who declined, saying that he preferred his own brand. "Suit yourself. So yeah they're great kids. Thierry's already fucking sweet at footy, and Hayley's well clever. She don't get it from her mum that's for sure."

"Thierry?" Jack stifled a small laugh. "You wouldn't be a Gooner then?"

"Fucking right I am. Arsenal 'til I die. Why what are you?"

"Liverpool." Jack almost whispered while drinking his tea, which he now found out was actually a cup of milk and sugar with a teabag in it.

"Sorry to hear that." AJ replied with a cheeky grin. "Ah they're not all bad. Good manager, and Stevie G's the fucking dog's. And at least you're not fucking Chelski. Fucking hate those wankers."

Jack nodded in agreement. The unwritten law of supporters of English football that everyone should hate Chelsea seemed to know no boundaries.

"So where'd you live before then?" Jack made a mental note to improve on his conversation skills, as he found himself trying his own patience with his inane questions.

"Down the ghetto. Fucking nightmare over there. Greenmeadow Estate, why'd they give such a shithole a name like that? All the worst estates have nice-sounding names."

"The ghetto?" Jack emitted an involuntary laugh. "This is South England not South Central, we don't have ghettos."

Jack was surprised by how aggravated AJ seemed by the comment. "It fucking *is* the ghetto man! You haven't lived there. Last month a guy got stabbed fifty times while sitting in his car!"

Jack had heard about that on the local news, but as was normal had ignored it as being someplace else and nothing to do with him. Suddenly he thought about all those times crimes had been reported on the local news and he'd ignored them. There were a lot. The Greenmeadow Estate seemed to be mentioned regularly. Jack suddenly realised how naïve he had been. "Sorry, mate. I guess I didn't know."

AJ relented, it seemed he just wanted to forget about that place and move on. "Ah, it's alright. Don't have to worry about that shithole any more now." He chucked the rest of his tea down the sink and went to the fridge. "Shit, no beer. You got any?"

Jack shook his head. He didn't know why. He did have beer, but for some reason his instant reaction had been to deny it, almost as though his subconscious didn't want AJ in his house. Again. "Oh yeah, sorry I forgot, I got some the other day." He inwardly cringed at his lying and poor acting, but AJ didn't seem to notice.

"Sweet, let's go then." AJ pulled his jacket up from a chair and lit his cigarette at the same time. Jack followed him out and peered though into the living room as he passed. Wayne was unpacking an Xbox from a cardboard package and furiously trying to connect it up. His speed was surprising. AJ seemed to read the thoughts from Jack's face.

"Yeah well it has been almost two hours since he last played it. Quick we'd better shift before he figures out I've left the controllers at the flat." They made a hasty exit just as Wayne discovered.

CHAPTER EIGHTEEN

That evening, in the Hamilton household, Josh was once again presenting his more rebellious side to his parents. After a brief but conclusive argument about whether he could go and see the new Harry Potter film at the cinema with his friends, he had stormed up to his room in a tantrum. According to his father, Harry Potter was evil and to be avoided by all respectable God-fearing people.

"I do think we should at least encourage him to read the books." Alice had meekly suggested following the sound of angry footsteps rumbling up the stairs.

"Absolutely not. I don't want his head filled with ideas of occults and pagan witchcraft. If he wants to read he's got a perfectly good Bible upstairs."

Alice sighed. She had not been quite so fundamentalist as her husband in previous years. Indeed, she had only been at the parish barbecue to help her mother out when she first met her future partner. Sure it was well enough living a good honest life and attending church every now and then, she could handle that much. But now and then had become twice and then thrice weekly, and a good honest life now more resembled the brand of penance and devoutness normally associated with Asian monks who lived in wooden huts halfway up Mount Everest. It wouldn't have been so trying if there was some form of ending to aim for, but these days it seemed to be a case of 'enjoy the way it is while it lasts, because there's worse to come'. The incident over the car had been a particular warning. Graham had discovered a fanatical belief that in the interests of saving the ozone layer, they would sell the car and travel everywhere by foot or bicycle. After her insistence that she was not about to walk five miles with the children to their school every day, and then a further eight miles in to work, and then again in the evening, Graham had reluctantly relented and settled instead on trading their car in for a hybrid. Come to think of it, that argument had been the last one she could remember winning. And that was well over a year and a half ago.

"Are we ready?" Graham more demanded than asked as he opened the front door.

"Yes. Are you sure the kids will be alright?" Alice never liked leaving her children alone, even if it was just for a few moments. She was one of those bundle-of-nerves people when it came to her children, who believed that as they had a gas cooker in the house, there was therefore the obvious liability that one of the kids would find a reason to stick their heads inside.

Graham didn't bother to answer, merely ushering his wife out of the front door. They crossed over the road towards the newly-occupied residence. The sound of rummaging could be heard as they approached the front door, and almost the second Graham rang the doorbell a spotty child of around eleven poked his head out inquisitively.

"What do you want?" Wayne challenged them impatiently. His search for an Xbox controller had proved fruitless, and now he was scrabbling around for money to buy a new one.

"Erm, is your father home?" Graham didn't understand how he could feel intimidated by the child, who was half his height and probably less than a quarter of his weight.

"Nah me father's never home. He fucked off on us. Why, you Social?"

"What? No. Well, er…" Graham shuffled uneasily, suddenly he had forgotten why he was standing there. Finally his professed sense of moral superiority decided to intervene on his behalf.

"You know I really don't believe that a child of your age should be using language like that." He tried to look down his nose at the youth, something that he always believed made him look authoritative, but in this particular recipient's case it made him appear autocratic.

"I'll bear that in mind." Wayne began shuffling behind the door, he'd now gone nearly three hours without his computer gaming fix, and it was starting to annoy him. "So what d'ya fucking want?"

Graham abandoned his attempt at moral superiority. "Is your mother home?" He decided to get this interrogation over as quickly as possible.

"Nah she's back at the flat. She don't live here yet."

"Then who owns this house?"

"Me bruv. He's out at the moment. I'll give him a message if you want." Wayne had now also decided to end the conversation as quickly as possible, having remembered that his brother always kept a stash of money hidden in his room somewhere.

"Fine, just tell him that we'd like to welcome him to the Close and we wish to invite him to dinner with us sometime soon." He checked his watch deliberately, ready to give the age-old excuse that he had to be getting somewhere.

"Oh 'dinner'?" He over-emphasised the word in a poor imitation of a posh accent. "Nice one, we ain't got a thing in the fridge and Ma's not up to cooking at the moment. I'll tell him when he gets back." He shut the door and thundered up the stairs in search of lost treasure to pay for a new controller.

Alice, who had remained quiet throughout, more due to the fact that her mind was on her own children's safety than current developments, turned to walk home. Graham remained stationary, trying to work out what had just happened.

"You know, I think we're a little harsh on Joshua sometimes. I mean, he's nearly a teenager and he's bound to go through a slightly rebellious phase." He turned to follow his wife home.

"What do you mean?" Alice slowed slightly to let him catch up.

"Well, I mean boys will be boys and all that. Let's just thank the Lord that if the worst young Joshua gets is a reluctance to do his homework then I believe we've been blessed." As he finished the sentence he cast a glare back at the front door of Number 1.

They arrived back at their house to be greeted by the sight of Joshua's legs hanging out of the oven, after he had apparently lost one of his Action-Man figures at the back. After a sharp berating to his son for being so stupid, and mild chest pains for his wife, Graham poured himself a stiff drink, breaking a vow of abstinence that had lasted all of three weeks.

CHAPTER NINETEEN

"Alright, take care mate," Jack mumbled out of ceremony as he closed his door. He was still perplexed by his own discomfort. He and AJ had spent the last two hours chattering on about football, music, women and their shared distaste for the working life, and had, to a neutral observer, appeared as though they had been friends for years. Yet as Jack watched AJ stagger slightly across the road as the fifth can of Carlsberg began to take effect, he could not help but feel that it somehow felt wrong. Maybe it was his upbringing, his grandparents having been somewhat closeted in their opinions towards people from differing classes. Or perhaps it was his friends, notably Marky, to whom the tags 'chav' and 'townie' meant instant shunning. A slight pain in his bladder made Jack realise that his fifth can was also kicking in in a different way and he trundled off to consider these strange thoughts in his favourite thinking place.

AJ had also received a similar call of nature, but was having rather less success answering, having stopped in the middle of the road to roll a cigarette. Ignoring his body's plea in order to finish, he was just about to lick the paper when a sharp blast from a car horn made him jolt, spilling his almost-complete rollie over the tarmac. As the wind whipped the wreckage away from his half-hearted attempt to recover it, he cursed and turned to view his aural assailant. A bright yellow BMW stood some six feet away, with Ralph fidgeting impatiently behind the wheel. AJ was, to Ralph's limited driving skills, an impassable obstruction in the middle of the road, and this was the last thing Ralph felt he needed, as having just returned from Liverpool he was anxious to get to his drinks cabinet.

He stuck his head out the window and the wind caught his hair and blew it straight into his mouth just as he was about to launch a tirade. "Get out of the way, you wretched urchin!" he finally yelled after removing his mop. He silently wondered what this creature was doing outside of the horrible place he had just left; his self-absorption leading him to briefly believe that it had followed him down from the north. He banged the car horn once more to underline how much more important his getting home was than whatever AJ was doing.

AJ was fuming. Having watched the last few strands of tobacco creep down a nearby drain, he shot Ralph a look so dark it made what little blood that was in the fop's face run away to hide.

"What the fuck do you think you're doing you fucking faggot? You made me fucking lose my fucking baccy all over the fucking road!" AJ began marching up to the car door to deliver his next bombardment directly into Ralph's ear. He needn't have bothered.

Spurred into action by two whole days of nauseating whiney Scouse accents, and this bigoted attack on his sexuality, Ralph had had enough and leapt out of the car to give this underling a piece of his mind. "How dare you speak to me like that?! I've a good mind to call the police and tell them exactly what you just said. You know your sort are exactly what's wrong with this world, you and your filthy narrow minds…"

He got no further. AJ had raised his arm to strike, but had pulled out at the last second. He didn't want to end up spending the next two years with his brother in HMP Bullingdon. In any case, the gesture had had the desired effect. Ralph had been instantly silenced and was now cowering behind the car door in apparent prayer.

Jack had heard the fracas, and after having been initially miffed that his throne-time was being interrupted, had then rushed outside when he realised who was involved. He had had a vague idea of what would happen when AJ would eventually encounter Ralph, and had hoped to, if not avoid it, at least delay it until he was away from the area so as not to be put to the inquisition by the police following any incidents. Now it seemed that was unavoidable, so he raced out to try to detour the situation away from as many serious crimes as was possible. He arrived on-scene just as AJ pulled his punch.

Ralph initially viewed Jack's entrance as one of a saviour. "Ah, you, whatsyourname, Jack!" he wheezed between pants of shock. "Go and call the police. I'm being attacked!"

Jack stood still and arched an eyebrow in the fashion of a Roger Moore imitation. Far from attacking the cowering wreck, AJ had begun rolling another cigarette quietly and wasn't even paying attention to proceedings anymore.

"Well don't just stand there, go and get help!"

Jack would have found the situation a lot funnier had he not known that Ralph was being serious, not only in believing that he was being attacked, but that Jack was actually going to call the police at his command.

"Piss off, for fuck's sake. You're not being attacked, you're barely being bothered." Jack turned to AJ who had finished his roll-up and was cradling it in a bizarre Gollum imitation. "You'd better hop it," he whispered away from Ralph's earshot. "I know he's an idiot but he will do it. I'll try and shut him up."

AJ nodded, he appeared now completely disinterested in current events. As he slunk away having lit his cigarette Jack suddenly realised that despite having felt just a few moments previously distinctly ambivalent about AJ, now he was covering for him. Fair enough it was more a call to uphold common sense than aiding and abetting, yet it still felt the other way around. Jack made a mental note to quiz a friend he had who was training to be a shrink about this when he next saw him. A whimper from behind the car door brought his attention back to present matters.

"What's the matter with you?" he demanded of the artist. "Anyone would think you're allergic to not getting your own way or something like that."

"The Major was right. *He* must be removed." An icy glare followed the statement in the direction of Number 1.

"Go home. Drink some wine. Wake up tomorrow with a hangover and you won't remember a thing," Jack ordered. In his 'fragile' state Ralph felt compelled to oblige.

CHAPTER TWENTY

"It's not my fault!" Marky protested to Jack. His face was the colour of the Liverpool strip Jack was currently sporting.

"How, exactly, is it not your fault?" Jack asked as straight-faced as he could muster, which was very little.

"I have two lazy eyes. I can't control where they look. They always seem to point towards large-breasted women." Marky had a few moments earlier received a sharp slap from the barmaid in the Rosebush. Supposedly his unique syndrome had displayed its symptoms while he was trying to order a pair of pints.

Jack hid his amusement behind his drink. He'd needed a good laugh. Especially after having been told by Frank, his friend studying psychology, to bugger off and stop wasting his time when he had asked for a 'session on the couch'. Looking back on it, Jack could see Frank's point of view, and using those exact words to a man with very little sense of humour at the best of times hadn't helped matters.

"Do you ever get the feeling that we drink too much?" Jack asked more by way of conversation than actual interest. He'd been the subject of another rant from his grandparents on the telephone the previous evening, and even though most of the beer from his time with AJ had worn off by then, he slightly slurred a couple of words when he could get them in edgeways, and his sharp-eared grandmother had instantly picked up on them. The resulting condemnation had ended in him hanging up out of boredom, but the suggestion that he drank too much had lingered.

"How do you mean? Generally?" Marky asked between precious sips, suspicious that their evening in the pub may be ended by this train of thought.

"Yeah, I suppose."

"Look, put it this way. Did you have a drink yesterday?" Jack nodded slightly sheepishly. "Kay...what about the day before?"

"No, yesterday was the first time since we were here last week."

"Right. And have you thought about drinking at any point in time at all in between those days?"

"Well, no. Why should I?" Jack was initially puzzled by the question, but his answer's significance struck him as he said it.

"There you go. If you were an alky you'd have been banging down the door of an offy after just two days. Problem solved."

Jack felt a little more relieved than he thought necessary. He'd let his bloody grandparents wind him up over nothing. He began plotting his next retaliation prank. Obviously the subscription to 'Dildo World' hadn't been enough of a message.

"Oh by the way, the drink I had yesterday..."

"Christ will you shut up about that? You're not an alky, there's monks in Andorra who are more alcoholic than you."

"No, I know. Well actually I don't, but anyway, I mean, yesterday."

"Yesterday what?"

"It was with your favourite townie. He's not all that bad, you know. Bit weird, supports the Gooners but then again no-one's perfect."

"You went out with that twat?!" Marky nearly stood to deliver the line, but sat down abruptly when he realised that he'd already been part of one embarrassing scene in the pub tonight, and that was enough.

"Nah, I had him over. He'd just moved in and I fixed his electric for him. It'd gone on the blink somehow."

"Let me get this right…You fix his leccy for him then have him over to *your* house to drink *your* beer?"

Jack, who had never had much time for the tit for tat etiquette of favours, ignored the question, despite the fact that for seemingly the first time in his life, Marky had pronounced 'your' properly, rather than the Mancunian slur which was usually used in its place. "He's alright. Nearly dropped Ralph in the middle of the road but he didn't in the end."

"Who's Ralph?"

"You know, the guy who lives next door. With the long hair and luminous sports cars."

"Oh him. Not surprised by that in the slightest."

"Yeah, well, anyway he gets my vote for that. It was about time someone brought that gormless knob down to earth."

Marky was goggling. "He gets you to fix his leccy, drinks your beer in your house and nearly lays out your neighbour and you're fucking best mates with him?"

"I didn't say that."

"Nah, well you needn't have bothered."

Jack eyed his friend darkly. He was getting tired of arguing this lad's case with everyone, including himself, but he wasn't about to get in a fight with his best friend over it. After a silent acknowledgement that it would no longer be mentioned, the two of them drank up and decided to head out clubbing. It seemed, Marky reasoned as they walked out to the taxi rank, that the best way to ignore things you didn't wish to ponder on was to get so absolutely shit-faced that the next day you're more worried that half your mortgage has been spent on champagne than anything else.

Jack nodded agreement out of appeasement. Inwardly he found himself chewing over the irony of this statement by a man who had not ten minutes earlier described the pair of them as the exact opposite. *The nineties 'lad culture' dies hard*, he mused, and, as if on cue, a blast of Oasis from a nearby car stereo set them in the mood for the rest of the night.

CHAPTER TWENTY-ONE

That evening was also a one for revelation back at the Close too. Ralph had come to the decision that he had been wrong. A considerable moment, and not one that made him any happier. He had always believed that those with less money than him should be helped, that those who were not given the best start in life should be afforded even more chances then their peers. Actually, 'believed' would be the wrong way of putting it; he more agreed with other people when they expressed such views in the interests of being accepted. Artists take their breaks wherever they may fall, and if a small amount of cajoling is involved, who should care?

Now, he realised, things were different. It was all very well supporting the 'valiant and brave' Tamil Tigers of Sri Lanka when speaking to the latest recipient of the Duff Cooper Prize at a book launch in Claridge's, but to be honest with himself, Ralph didn't give a toss about the Tamils any more than they cared about him. In fact, come to think of it, he didn't even know where Sri Lanka was. *Somewhere they play cricket, probably Africa or the Caribbean.*

These realisations of fallibility on their own would not so much have bothered him had he not been ripped quite so forcefully from his blissful ignorance. Instead, he had now been thrust into the face of an alternate life without so much as a hint of preparation, and he was pissed off.

He ran over what he was going to say in his head. Last shreds of hubris led him to believe that the Major would welcome his change of position. That hope was soon diminished. He rang the bell tentatively, part of him hoping the Major wasn't in, though this logic confused him, as if the Major was away he would be unable to join his cause. The sound of muffled footsteps from inside told him that there was no backing out now. The door itself seemed to be broken, Ralph couldn't distinguish why, but there were large cracks in the wood running down the framework near the locks.

"Hold on, I'm just coming," came a grumbling response from inside. Ralph heard what he could have sworn was a deadbolt being removed from behind the door. As it opened up, Ralph shuddered slightly, a last thought of escape flashed through his mind, and was gone as soon as it arrived.

"Blakeney, what do you want?" The Major appeared thinner than when they had last met, with his receding hairline even further back, were it possible after only a few days.

"Ah, er, could I come in?" Ralph had completely forgotten his pre-prepared speech.

"No."

"I see, er, well, I was wondering if I might, er, that is to say, whether you'd be so good as to let me, er, help you?"

"Help me? Help me do what?" The Major had begun tapping his foot ostentatiously.

"Ah, well, you see, this new…person. I wanted to, well, see if I could join you in getting rid of him."

"You? You want to join me? After what you did when I first asked? I hardly think so. Good day." The door began to close and Ralph saw his last chance disappearing.

"No, please! I really want to help."

The Major hesitated. "Why? What happened to you to have such a drastic change of heart?"

"Erm, well, that bastard living next door to you attacked me in my car!"

The Major squinted, as if checking for any signs of bullshit. All seemed clear. "Why didn't you call the police?" he asked sardonically.

Ralph saw straight through the question. It was a well-known fact that the ex-army man had very little time for the police, following his wrongful arrest and subsequent legal battles to clear his name on supposedly falsified paedophilia charges. He spoke about it little, but several irresponsible websites on the subject could be found by 'Googling' his name.

"I didn't think they'd listen. You know what they're like when it comes to his sort." Ralph thought he was lying as he spoke, but then realised that there was probably more truth in that statement than fiction.

"You're lying, Blakeney."

"No...but..."

"Well I suppose if you're concerned about it enough to come to me and lie to get my help then at least you must be genuine." The Major opened his door fully and gestured for the artist to come in.

"Thanks. I, er, was wondering, how do you lock this thing when you go out?" Ralph asked as he eyed the old-fashioned deadbolt.

"I don't go out. I have a son to do that for me. I'm not leaving my house for a second while it's on the front line."

As if on cue, James Forsythe, erstwhile of the Stadhampton Army cadets, now manager of a small electronics shop, wearily came downstairs to see what was going on. The Major didn't seem to notice him, and didn't bother to introduce anyone.

"The front...I see. Tell me is that how this happened?" Ralph indicated the broken front door.

"Good Lord, no. No that was...collateral damage. Friendly fire and all that. Still that's what test runs are for, eh?" The Major patted his son on the back as if to emphasise the point.

"The vet called. Betsy will be kept in overnight and we can pick her up in the morning." There was no emotion in

James' voice, just the dull monotone more generally found in call centres and rail station announcements.

"Good, good. You can take care of that. So, Blakeney," the Major led him into the partially cleaned front room and offered him a drink. Ralph barely let him finish the offer as he accepted.

"How exactly do you plan to help me?"

Ralph was about to speak, having ripped the glass of scotch from its donor's grasp, before he checked himself, and eyed James ostentatiously. The Major took the hint.

"James, my boy, I wonder if you'd be good enough to run down to the shop for me and pick up a bottle of soda, it looks like Blakeney here will be needing it."

Ralph watched James leave without a word of protest. The man seemed to have no character of any form, just a mere robot. Ralph paid it little attention though, after all, he'd had enough of sympathy for others for one day.

"So, what are you prepared to do?" Ralph found his glass refilled as the question was presented to him.

"Anything." He immediately regretted saying it.

"Splendid. Now, here's the plan."

CHAPTER TWENTY-TWO

Jack awoke during what he presumed to be the next morning to unfamiliar surroundings. He wasn't in his house. Of that much he was certain. He was also pretty sure he wasn't in Marky's house either, having passed out in every room of that building enough times to recognise it by sight. He was on a sofa, a leather one, so it seemed, except there was a sheet in between him and the cow-hide. There was also a duvet on top of him, and a pillow with a case on it under his head, which was in agony. *What the fuck happened?!*

He tried to sit up, and regretted it instantly, the sudden increase in two feet worth of altitude gave him enough of a headrush to make him feel queasy. He lay back down and stared at the ceiling. It was not a ceiling he had seen before. It appeared yellow, though that might be down to his vision.

A long familiarity with this type of situation had installed in him a contingency plan to act upon. Instead of the somewhat futile task of trying to remember everything that happened the night before, he instead concentrated on establishing a few small certainties.

Fact – I went out last night with Marky and obviously drank my weight's worth. Immediately the first thought was that he'd picked up a girl. *No, I wouldn't be on the sofa.* Plus he knew from painful experience that he never picked up girls when he passed a certain level of drunkenness, and the black hole that was his current short-term memory implied that last night he reached and breached that level with gusto. *Did we meet anyone unexpected?* The idea was that somehow he was staying with a friend whom he'd met the night before, but he dismissed that thought immediately. None of his friends that he could think of would put down a sheet and duvet for him, he'd have more luck finding en-suite bathrooms in a rail station, which, by the way, he had once tried to do.

Did Marky hook up with a girl and drag me along? Jack thought he was scraping the barrel a bit with that suggestion. Marky had left that part of his personality behind after that night in Prague. He abandoned his attempts to figure out why he was here, and concentrated on trying to work out exactly where 'here' was.

For the first time he blearily gazed around the room. It was very chic. Sparsely decorated, the owner was either heavily into feng-shui, or some form of minimalism. A couple of strange paintings hung on the walls, Jack couldn't figure out what they were supposed to be. A sharp black coffee table sat a few feet away from him, with a glass of water and an unopened Alka-Seltzer on it. Jack felt around for his mobile to find out the time, only to realise that he wasn't wearing his jeans. In fact, he wasn't wearing anything save for his boxers. *Odder and odder.* What was stranger, was that gazing around the room he couldn't seem to see his clothes anywhere. Usually they were to be found in a heap on the floor at times like these, if removed at all, but today they'd vanished.

There was a creaking sound from outside. Someone was coming down the stairs. Jack thought quickly of a list of the most versatile excuses he could think of and prepared to deliver them, but the sight that greeted him coming in through the doorway left him silenced.

"Oh, you're awake. You feeling alright?" Kathi asked sleepily. She was still in her dressing gown and slippers, with no make-up and her hair in a morning mess. It was a sight Jack had never seen before, and he was incapable of replying. Kathi took his muteness as a symptom of a hangover. "Take that Alka-Seltzer and drink the water, you'll feel better. I'm making tea, you want one?"

Jack nodded slowly. He was about to ask some of the more obvious questions aroused by this scenario, but by the time he'd arranged the words in the right order, she'd wandered through the room into the kitchen and he could hear the sound of a kettle boiling. He dropped the tablet into the water and watched it fizz around the glass. When the liquid had finally settled, he downed it in one go, but was still unable to avoid the salty taste. As he replaced the empty glass back on the table, Kathi re-entered carrying two large mugs of tea. She handed him one and sat down on the table expectantly.

He took a long sip, not actually drinking, merely figuring that whatever embarrassment and indignity that was coming his way would at least hold off while he had a drink. Kathi obligingly waited for him to finish.

"So...er...how did I get here?" It wasn't the most tactful way he could have put it, but there was no avoiding the subject, so best just to get it over with.

"Well, after I got in last night, at about two-ish, I saw you lying on your porch in the rain grinning like a demented idiot. I asked you what you were doing and you gave me some silly answer about how you'd lost your keys on the golf course and you were thinking about going to get them. You were obviously in no fit state to find them and I couldn't find any way into your house, so rather than let you catch your death of cold I had no choice really. You should be more careful, you're not eighteen anymore."

That last part bit Jack. It brought back the memory of how he'd been feeling in the first place when he and Marky first went out last night. "I'm truly grateful. Really I am." He smiled weakly, feeling more than a little ashamed that this was how he should first get to properly meet one of his neighbours.

She nodded appreciatively. "It's OK. I'm sorry you lost your keys. Come on, drink up and get up and we'll go and find them." She rose before he could interject. It was one thing helping out an acquaintance like she had last night, even if she had gone above and beyond the call of duty, but now she was offering to go and help him find his keys. Jack's mind was drawn back to the meeting in the Major's house. Kathi had, he could remember distinctly, been her usual authoritative and organised self, and when he had met her in the hallway one phone call later she'd seemed distant and fragile. As though she'd had some major shock.

He hadn't given it much thought at the time, but the more he considered it now, the more the idea grew on him that that phone call had changed her. He was intrigued, and wanted to know more. He tried to sit up again, but the Alka-Seltzer hadn't kicked in properly yet, and he was brought back down on his back by dizziness. Whatever else he would find out today, it could wait until he'd shed his hangover.

CHAPTER TWENTY-THREE

"This is it," Jack tried to proclaim dramatically, failing in the process. In reality the Rosebush looked no more than what it was, a typical suburban pub that was run down and destined for demolition as soon as its owners admitted defeat and gave up the futile struggle to keep clients. In one of his more ambitious schemes Jack had toyed with the idea of buying the place himself. He soon realised that it was a lot of money to spend just to keep your favourite watering hole up and running, and the whim passed as soon as it had come.

AJ grunted in acknowledgement. He'd been thrown out of the place five years previously for drinking his own cheap cider out of a flask in the corner, and subsequently barred when it was discovered that he was only fifteen at the time. He didn't bear the place any resentment over it, fact was he'd been barred from half the pubs in the area at some point or other, it was just a part of his teenage-hood.

Wayne had been happily trundling along behind. Having never been to this area before, his sense of mischief was already eyeing up possible practical joke candidates. He noticed that almost every door on this street was directly opposite another one, and had large solid doorknobs on them. He made a mental note to return when he had some spare time with a length of rope and a partner in crime.

"You sure they'll be alright with him, yeah?" AJ nodded towards his younger brother who was sauntering up towards them.

"Shouldn't be a problem. There's always some couple in here with a noisy child running around the place, they should be fine with Wayne." Jack inwardly hoped otherwise, however. During the journey he'd become increasingly tired of Wayne's manner. While walking past a shopping outlet on the way, both he and AJ had had to physically restrain the youngster from getting in a fight with a street busker, who had not taken kindly to seeing his day's earnings being pilfered in front of him as he tried to play some Beatles covers. "So what you having anyway?"

"Vodka Martini. Shaken, not stirred." Wayne interrupted in his poor posh accent imitation before AJ could answer. It earned him a cuff from his brother.

"Don't fuck about, Wazza. I'll have a pint of wifebeater cheers, and get him one of those Jay Two-Oh thingies would you?"

Jack nodded and led the way in. He walked over to the bar while AJ indicated that he was going to the pool table, which was free. "Two Stellas and a Jay Two-Oh, please." He looked over to the pool table, where Wayne had begun mimicking a sword fight with one of the smaller cues. "And could you put the Jay Two-Oh in a plastic cup, please?"

"Call it." AJ called as Jack returned with the drinks.

"What? Oh, heads." He placed the drinks on the table, watching for Wayne's reaction to his drink not being served in a glass bottle. Thankfully none came.

AJ bounced the coin off the table and caught it, revealing tails. "You break."

"I hear you're going over to the Hamiltons' for dinner." Jack half mumbled as he chalked a cue and lined up a break.

"Yeah, tonight. How'd you hear that?" AJ sat back rolling a cigarette as Jack took his time over the shot.

"Ah you know, it's a small Close, everyone knows stuff like that. How well do you know them then?" Jack skewed his shot horribly and barely hit the formation of balls. He mumbled a few choice swear words and set about re-setting the table.

"I haven't met them yet, only heard what Wazza told me and then they called last night to ask. Seem like a nice family to me. Some sort of weird religious type ain't they?"

"Some sort, yeah." Jack chuckled as he shot his break again, this time spraying the balls all over the table, potting two of each colour.

"Why, what do you think they want?"

"Fuck knows. Probably want to convert you." Jack lined up a shot and missed.

"Convert me?! Fuck that. You serious?"

"Dunno. They tried to convert me when I first met them. That wasn't a pleasant experience. I suppose they're just the sort of people who like spreading the Word."

"Well they can spread it somewhere else as far as I'm concerned. If that's the case you gotta come with me."

Jack mulled over the idea briefly. It was true he felt he'd have a great laugh watching whatever drama there was to be had at the dinner unfold, but was almost afraid of an anti-climax if he turned up and it wasn't as entertaining as he hoped.

"Ah I can't I'm afraid. I gotta sort out my finances tonight." he lied.

Jack hadn't been paying attention to the game, but AJ slotted the black and won. He was about to put more coins in and set up a new round, when a burly looking man with a half dozen sovereign rings and a crew cut strode up and slapped down one pound fifty on the edge of the table, to indicate that he had reserved the next game, before pacing off again with barely a look of acknowledgement.

"Sorry mate I can't really be bothered to play another." Jack mumbled. As he replaced his cue in the rack on the wall, he spied Marky and his girlfriend in the corner having a rather deep discussion. "Hey come and meet Marky," he said, "He's a bit northern but a good laugh."

AJ nodded and whistled to his younger sibling to follow. Wayne, who the whole time had been playing a game on his phone, hopped up with his drink and trotted along after them, picking up the burly man's pound fifty as he passed the table.

CHAPTER TWENTY-FOUR

"AJ, Marky. Marky, AJ." Jack introduced them to each other. "And this is Wayne," he said indicating the youngster, "and here's Rachel."

The quartet of new acquaintances shook hands informally, and Marky shot Jack a sharp look of scorn, before recovering his manners.

"How's it going man, you alright?" Marky slurred disinterestedly in the direction of AJ, without really looking at him.

"Yeah, safe cheers. You?" AJ responded in fashion.

"Aye, not bad."

An awkward silence settled down. Jack pretended to count his change for another pint, Wayne was back on his phone, AJ was smiling at Rachel, who was blushing, and Marky was staring at Jack again. Mercifully, Wayne's lack of social situational awareness broke the atmosphere.

"Hey, Bruv. Get us another." He waved his empty glass under AJ's nose.

AJ fished a twenty-pound note from his wallet and handed it to his brother. "Get it yourself, and get a round in while you're at it."

"They ain't never gonna serve me."

"Sure they will, just tell them it's for us."

Wayne impatiently took everyone's order, forgetting everything instantly as he joined the queue that had formed at the bar following the five o'clock rush.

Jack and AJ sat down. Marky had now noticed that AJ was eyeing up his significant other and tried to intervene.

"So, AJ, how's the moving going? I hear you've taken the yard across the road from this tit." Jack 'this tit' made no comment, well aware that Marky would have words with him later about bringing the new guy to their pub.

"Yeah, it's all sweet, cheers. The furniture and stuff is all in now, just gotta fucking sort it all out now. You should come round and see it when it's all done. Gonna be fucking sick."

"Sure, will do." Marky lied. He'd been having a fairly serious conversation with Rachel about their relationship and 'where it was going' before being interrupted. In truth, Marky had wanted to have the conversation in the Rosebush on the off-chance that Jack might turn up and save him from any potential uneasy situations the discussion might lead to. However, now he was coming round to the idea that suffering his girlfriend's continual nagging for more commitment on his part was definitely more enjoyable than sitting around with AJ. None of his prejudices had been disproved by the meeting so far, and he was getting increasingly pissed off at the way the townie was looking at his girl.

"So, Jack, how's things going with that Kathi bird you were after?"

Jack went red. He hadn't thought about Kathi since that morning he'd woken up at her house. In a way he felt guilty for not having done so, as though even though nothing happened he should still have felt some form of mental loyalty to her.

"Er...nothing much going on," he mumbled while hiding behind his pint.

"Ah come on. You seemed to think she was well into you the other day. Now what with her and that Anna lass on the go you must be the luckiest bugger going. Two women and all that, fair play to you, son." Marky grinned sickly, knowing full well the discomfort the question would put his longest friend in.

"I don't think that's funny, Mark." Rachel scolded him. "How'd you like it if I went off with another guy twice a week?"

"Be fucking glad of the peace to be honest," came the unwise retort.

"I suppose you think that's funny, do you?!" Rachel yelled in response. "I wanted to speak to you about serious matters in our life and even whether we should have kids or not and all you do is act the fucking large one..."

Jack wandered away from the table. He'd no interest in listening to more bickering from Marky and Rachel, as she would surely find a way to blame him for things that Marky had done wrong. The argument was drowned out, however, by an even louder confrontation at the bar. The burley man had obviously discovered that his pool money was missing, and had found Wayne using it in the cigarette machine.

"Gimme back my money, you little twat!" He tried to grab Wayne by his shirt collar, but the boy slipped his grasp and slapped his arm out of the way.

"Get the fuck off me! Bruv!" he called out to his brother who was up in a flash.

Jack walked outside, he wasn't going to get involved. He'd seen enough pub brawls to know how this one was going to end. He sparked up a cigarette he'd rolled earlier and waited patiently by the door. Sure enough, as soon as he'd put his lighter back in his pocket, AJ and Wayne came clattering out of the door, escorted out by the landlord.

"You done?" Jack asked once they'd finished hurling abuse back into the pub.

"Fucking prick. No-one talks to my family like that." AJ gestured at the door. "So, what now?"

Jack sighed. He spotted some kids in the park across the road kicking a ball about. "Shall we?"

"Uh?" AJ didn't follow.

Jack pointed to the kids. "I fancy a kick-about. Let's go join in."

It turned out that Wayne knew the kids, and they were only too happy (and too scared to refuse) to let them join in.

Back in the pub, things had gone back to normal instantly. No-one had batted an eyelid at the scuffle, apart from Rachel.

"You really want one of those?" Marky asked, referring to Wayne.

"No, I see your point. You were right, it is too soon." Rachel sat with her empty glass wondering what she would do if she were to have a son like that.

Marky silently thanked the first God he could think of for the postponement of 'the talk', before making a note to have a 'talk' of his own with Jack.

CHAPTER TWENTY-FIVE

"But I wanna wear me fucking cap!" Wayne was adamant. He already felt like an idiot for wearing a shirt when he wasn't going to school, and now he thought his brother was taking the piss.

"Look it's just tonight, alright? And stop swearing too. These people don't like that sorta thing." AJ chucked Wayne's cap onto the sofa and took another look at his younger brother. It wasn't the smartest sight in the world. His shirt was hanging out, his trainers were scuffed and muddy from the kick-about earlier, and his trousers were frayed at the bottom. "Can't you wear your school trousers? Just for tonight, yeah?"

"Can I fuck. I'm not wearing them when it's not a school day. Why are you so keen to impress these people anyway? What's they ever done for us?"

"They're our neighbours. I got asked over for dinner and I don't trust you on your own here. Now come on, we're gonna be late." AJ didn't really want to take his brother, and the Hamiltons hadn't really said anything about him when they called, but he just knew that leaving him alone in the house with all the beer in the fridge and no dinner save for thirty packets of crisps would result in the new world vomiting record waiting for him when he got back. "Come on, for fuck's sake we're gonna be late."

"I thought you said no swearing."

"Shut the fuck up and get ready." He hurried his brother out the door, patting his dog on the head as he left. "You guard boy, and I'll try and get you a bone for when I get back." Vieira recognised the 'b' word, and sat attentively. It was a vast beast, capable of eating lesser canines on a mere whim, and it had been brought up to understand that being told to 'guard' meant that it was to bite the leg of the first person it saw, unless said person was AJ or a member of his family bearing a pacifying gift.

AJ and Wayne hurried across the road. The street lamps were already on as the light was fading away, and the first specks of rain were making themselves felt.

"Aw I wanna go back for me cap, this rain's messing up me fucking hair."

"No amount of wind or rain could make your hair any fucking messier." AJ hushed his brother just as he was about to be reminded of his no-swearing policy. They walked up to the Hamiltons' front door and Wayne banged on the door loud enough to wake the dead. "Oi! Keep it down you knobhead, they're not deaf."

"How do you know?" Wayne replied innocently.

The door was opened by a young lad of around eleven. Wayne burst out laughing as soon as he saw that the kid was wearing a bright yellow tie. AJ cuffed him round the ear while himself trying to keep a straight face.

"Yes?" The boy asked timidly.

"Hey mate, we're here for your food." Wayne blurted out before AJ could stop him, and got another clip round the back of the head for it.

"Er, could you get one of your parents for us? Cheers, lad." AJ asked as politely as he could.

Josh ran off to fetch his parents, and to hide. As far as he was concerned his family were about to be robbed and he had no intention of letting them get hold of his computer.

A few seconds later Graham Hamilton came to the door. His pleasant greeting smile was fractured somewhat when he saw their clothes, and also that they hadn't brought any wine, but he regained his composure instantly, drawing his breath as if in preparation to begin an arduous task.

"Welcome, welcome, come in, come in before it really starts raining. You must be Ashley." He thrust out his hand so firmly it nearly caught AJ in a sensitive area.

"Er, yeah, how you doing mate? I'm Ashley, but everyone calls me AJ." He shook Graham's hand quickly, the grip was unnervingly sturdy. "This is my little bruv, Wayne." He pushed his brother forward slightly by the elbow. Wayne stuck out his hand in the same manner, this time actually hitting Graham in the groin, causing the older man to double back quickly.

"Ah, yes. We've met actually," he said quickly, trying to remain placid. He eyed the youngster carefully. "How are you then?"

"I'm hungry." Wayne replied unaffectedly.

"Yes, yes, of course, of course." Graham replied, still weakly beaming. "First though, a drink. To welcome you to the area. Come through, come through." He led them through the hallway towards the living room, where a decanter of what looked like whiskey was waiting elegantly on a neatly laid out table.

"Does he have to say everything twice?" Wayne whispered to his brother.

"Shh…" AJ hissed hastily.

"I'm sorry?" Graham asked half-heartedly as he poured some of the whiskey into a glass.

"Oh, nothing. Wayne was just admiring your…er…windows." AJ gambled.

"Ah, yes. Triple glazing. Had them installed last month. Really good value too." He held out the glass, AJ almost snatched it away before Wayne could get a hand on it.

"Must be a fucker to break into." Wayne muttered under his breath. AJ elbowed him in the ribs before Graham could hear.

"Apparently Mr Nielson next door is having it done too." Graham mentioned indirectly in a faint hope that AJ might have them fitted as well to boost area house prices.

"Ah you know Jack then?" AJ asked enthusiastically as the conversation moved away from topics he didn't give a toss about.

"Er, yes. He's our neighbour, we've known him for a few years now." Graham mumbled quickly. "But anyway. A toast. A toast to welcome you to the Close and to say that if there's anything you need you only have to ask."

AJ raised his glass slightly before throwing the scotch down his throat. Wayne raised an empty hand in a gesture, and almost immediately a glass of orange juice was placed in it by Mrs Hamilton, who had entered the room silently.

"Ah, my wife. Ash...AJ I mean, allow me to introduce my wife, Alice. Alice, this is AJ."

"Pleased to meet you."

"Hello again missus." the younger Johnson squeaked irritably, he was already bored, and knew when he was being ignored.

"Oh yes, you remember Wayne, AJ's younger brother?" Graham murmured impassively.

Wayne shook the lady's hand carefully. In his experience, women who had kids the same age as him usually stored sweets somewhere in the house, and it paid to be nice to them.

"You must meet the kids." Alice leaned out of the door to call them. "Joshua! Mary! Jacob! Come down here, please!"

CHAPTER TWENTY-SIX

Remember, all we want is a bank statement. Don't waste time looking for anything else. Just something with his name on it and an account number.

The Major's instructions had been as clear as he could make them, but Ralph was barely twenty minutes into his mission and already he was wondering what he was meant to be doing. He'd been sitting in the hedgerow in between Number 1 and Number 2 for a while now, and was extremely bored. He'd watched AJ leave the house with his brother, and remembered how turned on he'd been after the initial shock of his first confrontation with AJ had subsided. It was a long time since Ralph had had a 'bit of rough', and he'd been musing as to whether he was doing the right thing. However, now that he'd passed the point of no return, and as he watched the two boys go into the Hamiltons' at Number 6, he crept through the weak bush and into the back garden of AJ's house.

The Major had given him a skeleton key but had told him to try the door first. "You never know how stupid people can be until you see it for yourself," he'd said. Or something like that. Frankly, Ralph was fed up of being ordered around by the geriatric already, and had decided that he'd get this job out of the way and then pull out. He reached into his pocket and fished out his bottle of Valium. He popped two to steady his nerves, replaced the bottle, and crept over to the back door. *The old fool was right, it is open.* He gently pushed the door open and hopped inside, closing it quietly when he was in.

Vieira had heard the door open. In fact, he'd known that there was someone lurking outside for a while now, but had been patient. In his ample experience of unknown humans entering his domain without his or his master's permission, he knew that it was always best to be patient, and savour each occasion. He was up on AJ's bed when Ralph had entered, and as he listened to the human (who sounded like a male but smelt like a female) he lay frozen in place, the thinnest drip of saliva running off his gums in anticipation.

Ralph's entrance had gone well, he thought, but now came the part he wanted to get over with as soon as possible. He found himself in the kitchen, fumbling around for a light switch, before remembering the torch in his pocket. He fished the large object out and was in the middle of a fairly lewd thought when he heard a creak upstairs. He stood perfectly still. Nothing. *Must be my imagination. These pills **do** work quickly.*

He shone the torch around the room. As far as kitchens went it was fairly sparse. A fridge, a microwave, an oven and a freezer were all there, but no food was in sight. He thought about looking around for some out of sheer curiosity, but another creak from upstairs made him flinch and he set about his task even more quickly.

A brief frisk of the top layer of rubbish in the bin was fruitless, and Ralph was resigned to searching further through the house. Through the hallway he found the living room, and saw some papers lying on the coffee table in the middle. *Bingo.* He shone the torch over them to find that they were exactly what he was looking for.

He grabbed as many as he could in one hand, not caring which was which or whether their owner would miss them. By now he just wanted to get out of the house as fast as he could. He had heard another creak, this one sounding closer than before, but after waving the torch in the general direction of the stairs he'd seen nothing. He stuffed the papers into his back pocket and gave a short contented sigh. As he spun around to leave the room he was greeted by a sight that drained the blood from his face. A huge black shadow stood in the doorway. He wasn't sure if it was a horse or some other large farm animal, but any thoughts of petting it and handing over sugar cubes were dismissed instantly as the creature began to growl heavily.

Vieira had his kill now. There was no other way out of this room of the house other than through the clear walls humans liked on the edge of the lair. And having been through one of those clear walls himself, he knew that this prey wouldn't be dumb enough to try it. It hurt.

"S...s...stay boy..." Ralph whimpered. "Good boy. S...stay there." He began to edge towards the door sideways on, but the beast would not budge. It nearly filled the whole lower half of the doorframe, and there was no way Ralph could see to get around.

What is it on about? Vieira thought in the basest of cognition. *It wants to escape!* Vieira had no time for that. He'd been patient enough and now he was reaching the climax of his hunt there was nothing that could stop him now. As the human edged closer, the full force of his muscular body leapt towards the man, pinning him beneath him in one swift move. *That was almost boring.* Vieira wasn't done with just that, he sank he sizeable teeth into a leg and to his utter joy he felt the familiar texture of bone. He clamped his teeth down harder to reach the tender interior and ignored the screams coming from the other end of the body.

Ralph hadn't known pain like this since he'd accidentally caught his arm in a revolving door, and even that had felt like a massage compared to this. He tried to beat the demon dog with the torch, but the animal didn't even flinch. He tried to wriggle out of its clutches, but its grip was like a vice, and not only could he not move, but trying caused even more agony. With the final thought that this was to be his end, Ralph fumbled around in his pocket for his pills, hoping against hope that they'd work doubly quickly this time.

Something was rattling in the human's clothing. In Vieira's experience this usually meant a treat of some sort. He'd discovered that this man's blood tasted funny, and decided that he'd let him go if there was a decent treat on offer. He released the tattered limb and sniffed around the arm, which was frantically trying to pull something out of the clothing. *Let me do it, useless-limbed creature.* He barged the hand out of the way with his head and bit down into the clothing. There was something solid in there. He wrenched his head away, leaving large gashes in the flesh of the same limb he'd been chewing a minute ago. In one gulp he swallowed everything in his mouth, bottle, pills and trousers. *Not the nicest treat ever.* But he'd had a bit of fun and some exercise. *Time for you to go.* He looked at the human as if to emphasise his point. There was no reaction. He barked to make his point clearer.

Ralph barely felt the pain of the new wounds in his leg, having witnessed the monster devour half of his trousers, pills and all in one mouthful, he was too afraid to move. Then the barking started. Actually, less barking, more the roar of thunder. Not waiting for a second telling, Ralph leapt up as fast as he could and raced out of the house at full pelt. His leg was gushing blood from so many different areas he was terrified he'd run out before he got out of the garden. Actually right now, it didn't matter how much blood he lost, or even how many limbs he lost, nothing was keeping him in the vicinity of that house. With his one good leg he hurled himself over the hedge to the Major's garden, and let out one last cry of agony.

CHAPTER TWENTY-SEVEN

"For what we are about to receive, Oh Lord, may we be truly thankful." Graham kept his usually extensive evening grace to a short sentence on this occasion, mindful of the company.

AJ looked at his plate curiously. Roast beef, potatoes, three different vegetables. Well, four if you count the potatoes. In his lifetime AJ usually only ate a meal of this proportion once a year, at Christmas. Three hundred and sixty four days a year it was microwave curries and frozen pizza. He began prodding at the meat, unsure whether there was some ritual involved in eating this sort of meal, like you had to have one mouthful of meat to two vegetable. Or you could only eat potatoes if you had beef on the fork with them. He scanned the others for some form of clue, they all seemed to just be tucking in. Especially Wayne, who had begun shovelling the food back as though it was his last.

"Use your fork properly, please." Graham had said, looking at Wayne, before remembering that he was a guest. "Er…Joshua."

"I am, Dad." Josh replied, spraying some gravy from his mouth as he spoke.

"And don't speak with your mouth full."

"But you do it all the time! For…"

"So tell me, AJ, how has the moving in been going?" Alice interrupted before Josh could continue his protests.

"Yeah all sweet, cheers. Had a bit of trouble with the removal van, he got flashed on the fuzz radio and had to shift before we could get all the stuff in the house, but Jack next door gave us an 'and so it was all safe."

"I see." Alice clearly didn't. "So what do you think of the Close, then? How long has it been now you've been here?"

"Couple of weeks, yeah. It's all cool, cheers. Had a bit of an issue with the er...guy across the road trying to run me over, but other than that all good." AJ was beginning to wonder if he'd be allowed a moment's peace to actually eat his food at all, seeing as apparently you weren't allowed to speak with food in your mouth. He looked across at his little brother's nearly empty plate with envy.

"Someone tried to run you over? What on earth happened?" Graham asked, genuinely shocked, but just for the slightest of seconds feeling aggrieved that whoever it was hadn't made a better job of it.

"Ah it was that fu...er I mean that guy with the long hair. He wasn't looking where he was going."

"My goodness," Alice started, but finished abruptly when she realised that there wasn't anything else to say.

Wayne had meanwhile jolted as he felt something rub up against his shin under the table. He looked down to see a small tabby cat sitting in between his feet looking back at him patiently. He picked a strand of fat off the meat on his plate and dangled it down in front of the cat's nose. A paw travelling quicker than the eye could see with claws at the ready snatched it away from him. He yelped in pain at the shock of it.

"That little fucker! That little fucking knobhead cat just scratched me for no fucking reason!" As everyone was in the process of gasping at the outburst, Wayne kicked the cat sharply in vengeance. It howled as it sped across the floor and into a cabinet on the other side of the room, where the glass decanter had been moved to before the meal. The decanter rocked slightly before tumbling in almost slow motion and landing on the dazed cat's head, shattering instantly, and sending the now semiconscious moggie careering out into the hallway and up the stairs.

"Young man, I don't know where you think you are but around here we do not use language like that!" Graham stood up sharply, actually subconsciously enjoying the chance to dress-down the unruly youth. "And look at what you've done to the decanter, just look at it! And the cat! What in heaven's name did the cat do to deserve that?!"

The three Hamilton children sat silently, each of them knowing that one false movement would mean they'd be sent from the room if there was going to be a row, and if there was going to be a row they certainly didn't want to miss it. AJ tried to intervene.

"Now wait a minute, he didn't mean to hurt the cat, and I'll replace your broken drinks thingy. He's sorry, alright? It was an accident." He placed a hand on his brother's shoulder protectively. Wayne was fuming, but AJ didn't want him letting rip into their hosts.

"He's right, sit down Graham." Alice pleaded. Inwardly she was probably the most incensed of anyone at the table, as Jadis was her cat, but she wanted to avoid a scene in front of the children.

Graham reluctantly retook his seat, and an uncomfortable silence descended around the room, broken only by the sound of Wayne chomping loudly on a potato. On the surface, he seemed to have calmed down instantly, but AJ knew that his little brother always ate noisily when he was annoyed about something. The sound seemed to grate Graham, who poked at his plate disinterestedly. What had he been thinking? Had Jack been right about warning him? Only now did his determination to prove Jack wrong show itself as sheer pig-headedness.

AJ sat quietly. He'd decided that it had been a mistake coming here after all. These weren't his people. Why was he apologising for his brother to them? He missed hanging out with his real friends back on the estate. They weren't the most honest people in the world, or the most decent, but then again he couldn't help the fact that he was one of them.

Even Jack bore all the traits of a former posh boy, no matter how much he tried to hide it. The grass wasn't greener on this side of the road, it was just a different colour altogether.

"When's the kids coming over, Bruv?" Wayne asked while chewing as loudly as possible in an attempt to provoke Graham. The eldest Hamilton wasn't paying attention.

"Tomorrow. Charlene's dropping them off before she goes off on holiday." AJ pulled out his phone and ran through the text messages to check whether that was right.

"You have children?!" Graham asked incredulously. It was only his last shreds of cordiality as a host that stopped him from adding 'they let you lot breed?!'

"Yeah, two kids." he beamed, ignorant of the malicious undertone of the question, just pleased to be talking about something he loved. "Thierry and Hayley. Best things that's ever happened to me."

Mary, ignoring her mother's orders before dinner to not speak unless spoken to, couldn't help her curiosity. "Where's your wife, then?"

"My what?" AJ almost laughed, before he saw the innocence on the young girl's face. "I don't have a wife."

"But you must have a wife? How can you have babies without a wife?" Butter wouldn't melt in her mouth.

"That's enough, Mary." Alice tried to hush the child up, but now Josh was keen to join in.

"But Mum, you always said that you had to be married to have children. Did that mean your wife died, Mr Johnson?"

"No, what? No! I never had a wife! Me babies' mum's called Charlene. She lives on the estate." AJ was getting frustrated now. Wayne wasn't listening to the conversation, he'd spied the last pair of roast potatoes and had swiped them while no one had been looking.

"But then how did you have children?" The youngest child, Jacob, chirped in. "Mummy says…"

"I don't give a shit what Mummy fucking says, alright?!" AJ blew his top. "I don't have a fucking wife! I don't have a fucking career! I don't have a fucking perfect family like all you knobheads in this shithole!" He hurled his glass across the room against the wall and dragged his half-protesting brother out of the room and out of the house.

CHAPTER TWENTY-EIGHT

"For heaven's sake shut up!" The Major was having enough trouble concentrating on the task at hand without being distracted by Ralph's screaming.

"Take me to the hospital! I don't want to die here!" Ralph took another hefty swig from the near-empty bottle of brandy the Major had given him as a painkiller.

The Major looked at him darkly. More than once tonight since the weak-willed fairy had crashed through his bushes yelling blue murder the Major had considered knocking him over the head to keep him quiet. Frankly, quite how nobody had heard the cacophony and come over to investigate seemed bizarre. Yet as well as relief for not being disturbed, the Major also felt a pang of sadness, that maybe the community in the Close wasn't quite so conscious about each other as he'd imagined.

His mind returned to the job he faced. The bite wounds were deep, but the bleeding had subsided somewhat, so it seemed that no major arteries had been damaged. "You'll live, and I'll guess you'll be a damn sight more careful in future as a result."

"How do you know?" Ralph asked in between burps. The brandy had gone now, and with it his mind. "I want a second opinion! I want to go to London!"

"What on earth for?"

"They're the best. Specialists. They'll stop me from dying!"

The Major rolled his eyes as he wandered off to his medicine cabinet to find further painkillers for his wounded trooper.

"Where are you going?! Don't leave me here to die!" Ralph's squeaky voice had become so high-pitched that Betsy, who was still feeling somewhat fragile from her run in with a glass door, howled in harmony. With her lampshade neck brace dragging along the floor, she trundled over to the limp body and began licking the wounds that her larger peer had inflicted. At first it made the pain come flooding back to Ralph, and his new wave of cries were barely audible to humans, then, however, whatever magical juices there are in dog saliva began to numb the pain and eventually Ralph started to giggle at it. The sudden change in sensation, coupled with a bottle of France's finest working its way through a depleted blood system, caused Ralph to vomit so quickly he didn't even have time to turn onto his side. Unfortunately for her, Betsy caught the main volume as she raised her head to see what was happening.

The sight that greeted the Major as he returned was foul. His cashmere rug had taken on a new colour in addition to the deep red from the leg, and Betsy seemed half her normal size now that her normally fluffy coat was sopping wet with reconstituted brandy. Without saying a word he splashed through the mess and thrust a pair of small white pills into Ralph's mouth. The victim swallowed them obligingly without liquid, and began hiccupping loudly.

"These are analgesics. They will relieve you of the pain but they'll make you feel drowsy." he muttered as he replaced the cap on the bottle. He picked up the sheets of crumpled paper Ralph had managed to 'recover' from his mission and began flicking through them, pleasantly surprised that they were actually quite useful. The hiccuping from his patient grew louder and began to irritate him, so he popped another pair of pills into Ralph and returned to looking at his prize.

"Yes, this is excellent. We'll get him with this for certain." he said to himself. Ralph muttered something incoherent in reply.

"How maneeey roads must a maaan walk dowwwn." Ralph began singing inanely. The Major looked at him suspiciously. He'd seen strapping six foot six privates in the Army floored by taking two of these things in a matter of minutes, Ralph obviously had some form of resistance built up due to years of taking similar drugs.

"It was evil! A demon! It wanted to drain my blood and my fucking soul!" Ralph's eyes had glazed over, he turned his head and saw a five foot tall dog's shadow against the wall. "It's back! Get a gun! Get a fucking priest! Don't let it near me!" He cowered.

The Major looked over to where he was pointing. Betsy was standing on the arm of a chair with a light beneath her, casting a shadow over a whole wall. "It's nothing," he said, but as he looked back at Ralph, he saw that the artist had slipped out of consciousness. "Finally, some peace."

Peeling the bandage away carefully, the Major examined the wounds. He'd live, that much he already knew, but they'd never fully disappear no matter how well they healed, and he'd probably have a limp for years as a result. He replaced the bandage and patted the sleeping Ralph on the head.

"You did well, lad. Your sacrifice will not be in vain." He smirked as he read through the papers. Bank statements, phone bill, credit card statement. The Major had once had his identity mistaken by the police with unthinkable consequences. This time there was no need for the police, not that he trusted them after that anyway. He could achieve his goals on his own.

He didn't want to harm the yob. Well he did, but he accepted that there was a limit as to how far he could go. Much as the Major would have loved to see the youth taken down a peg or two with some physical pain, he knew that he'd probably run crying to the police or those damn Social Services buggers, who seemed to enjoy persecuting victims more than culprits. No, simply getting him out of where he didn't belong was the only target, and if a little humiliation was served up along the way then so much the better.

Ralph had begun snoring now, which was also beginning to annoy him, and Betsy was still whining about being covered in a brandy and bile cocktail, so the Major placed the papers in a drawer in his desk and locked it carefully. *Don't want any old sort to find these.*

He breezed off into the kitchen in a fine mood, with Betsy sloshing behind her tail both wagging and spraying. Turning on the taps in the sink to give his precious pooch a good bath and a treat, a thought occurred to him. *They'll find the blood! They'll know something's missing. Damn and blast it, why the hell did that idiot poof have to get himself in a fight with their beast?*

He marched out of the back door to look at the house. It was dark, no lights, no car outside, no sign of life whatsoever. His mind made up, he went upstairs to fetch some equipment. There was nothing for it, he'd have to clean the mess up himself.

Once the gear was laid out on the table, he took a piece of bacon from the fridge and wrapped it round a handful of the pills he had given to Ralph. Shooting back a quick dram of malt, he went off to do his duty.

CHAPTER TWENTY-NINE

AJ hadn't even gone back into his house that evening. So pissed off had he been at the infuriating interrogation he'd virtually thrown Wayne in the back of his car and driven off, only to stop five yards down the road when his younger brother reminded him that the dog hadn't been fed. He opened the front door of his house and yelled for Vieira to come out.

After a brief pause, the monstrous animal hurtled out of the building as though its tail were on fire, crashing through the opened car door and flattening Wayne, who gave it a piece of his mind in return.

"What the fuck's got into you, you fucking knobber?!" He was about to slap it to calm it down, when he noticed the blood around its mouth, and in its eyes. "Bruv, I think the dog's wasted a rat. He's got blood all round his mouth and that."

AJ wasn't listening, he didn't care. He slammed the car door shut after he got in and thumped the accelerator down.

"Can't we have some beats?" Wayne quizzed from the back, keeping both eyes firmly fixed on Vieira, who seemed to be growling out the window.

"No." AJ mumbled.

"Where we going anyway?"

"Home."

"But that's our home back there." Wayne seemed puzzled.

"No it fucking isn't. Not with all these fucking wankers it isn't. We're going home to Mum's."

"Put the kettle on, love." Flo, AJ's mum, was one of these people who believed that the first thing to do when facing a crisis was to brew up. "Now, what exactly's the matter?"

"I've fucking had it, Mum. All these knobbers with their posh accents and fucking perfect lives. They keep fucking having a go at us for no fucking reason." AJ scalded his hand as he poured the hot water into the mugs a little too energetically. "FUCK'S SAKE!!!" He threw the mug he'd been holding into the sink, his second crockery missile of the night.

"Now, calm down," his mother said in the tone of patient understanding only mothers can manage. "What makes you think that these people's lives are so perfect?"

AJ slumped down on a chair holding his hand, which was throbbing. "They just are." He pinched one of his mother's cigarettes from the packet lying on the table.

"You told me you'd quit." Flo said matter-of-factly as she held out a lit lighter for him.

"Well, I haven't, and I feel like I fucking need one right now." He coughed slightly.

"So these people," she continued. "Have they got bigger houses than you?"

"No, it's not like that..."

"Do they have jobs?"

"Well, yeah but that's not the point..." he tried to protest.

"Are they all happily married with children and cats and stuff like that?"

"Yeah. That's it you know, they're all so fucking stuck up about it too."

"So what do you care?" She eyed him closely. "Ashley, love, if there's one thing I've tried to tell you over the years, it's that there's nothing wrong or right about where people come from, they just come from wherever. If they talk differently it don't make them better or worse, just different." She got up and poured the tea properly, handing her son a mug carefully.

"You now have everything you've ever dreamed of, your own house, no more worrying about Jobseeker's, enough money to keep you for the rest of your life." She grabbed his arm and dragged his vision into hers. "You remember when you got sent down?" He nodded slowly, still edgy at the mention of it. "You remember what I said then? I said that luck evens itself out, and now your luck has changed. Don't let it all go to waste because of a bunch of bastards who look down on you because of where you're from." She sat back and lit another cigarette to replace the one that had burned out while she'd been talking, content that her little speech had made the point.

"But I can't fucking deal with all the hassle and shit they keep giving me."

"Well if you can't stop them, and you can't ignore them, then give them shit back. What's the point in trying to get on with someone who doesn't want to know? You get out there and punch your weight, son."

AJ smiled, a sincere smile. To an outsider looking in it would appear that the Johnson boys were textbook fatherless children, but in reality their mother had always handled the job fine on her own.

"Mum, you fancy looking after the kids for me tomorrow night?"

"Sure, you know it's not like I have my own life to lead and my own things to do."

"Please, Mum?"

"Are you going back to the Close?"

"Yeah. Tomorrow. I got an idea."

"OK then, I'll look after them, but don't do anything stupid though."

"Oh I won't." AJ's smiled turned into a nasty smirk, and he left the room with his mobile.

"Yeah, Danno? Get the crew, fucking massive rave at mine tomorrow night. Yeah, get your mate from London to bring his speakers down." He closed the top of his phone, and then had a second idea.

"Wazza?!" he yelled through the hallway. "Get your mates from school on the phone. Free party at ours tomorrow!"

"You know that's not quite what I meant, love." Flo called from the kitchen without looking up from a magazine she'd started reading.

"I know, mum. At least that means you won't be to blame."

CHAPTER THIRTY

"Why haven't you called me? It's been a month already!" came the sobs from the phone. Jack sighed. He knew as soon as he'd seen Anna's name on the screen that this would be a trying call. Now he was on the receiving end of a distraught woman who really had no right to complain. *When's that ever stopped them though?* he mused wistfully.

"Look I'm sorry Anna, I've just had a lot on my mind recently."

"Don't you want me anymore?" she blubbered. "Don't you miss me at all?"

Why the fuck do women have to put us through this? Jack slumped down in his chair and held the phone away from his ear while the moaning continued. He'd always thought that affairs were temporary arrangements. At least that's how it appears in the movies. One way or another you either get found out and it ends, usually messily, or the unfaithful party realises the error of their ways and calls it off. Ten months this had been going on, and the relentless barrage of text messages from the former object of his affections, ranging from the distraught to the down right disturbed, had driven him further and further away from wanting to start up again. Finally his tether snapped as the bawling from the phone grew louder.

"Look, Anna, you're a married woman. You should be planning kids with your husband or worrying about how much debt your fucking mortgage has put you in. It's time to grow up and feel ashamed for what you've done, cos I know for damn sure that I do. Now if you don't sort yourself out and go back to Charlie, then I'm gonna tell him what we've done. And yes, I know he'll kick the shit out of me, but any beating is better than listening to you fucking whining all day." He closed the flip-top lid of the phone and put it back into his pocket. *I'll never hear the end of this now.*

Surprisingly, the phone didn't start ringing again, making Jack wonder if he actually had done the right thing. Come to think of it, he still wasn't sure why he'd done it at all. He wasn't really the type who enjoyed committed long-term relationships, which was why when the affair had started he'd been more than happy to ignore the risks and consequences. He didn't even like Charlie, not that that justified it now. But what would he do now? He'd live, surely? Of course he'd miss the bi-weekly appointments, but putting it bluntly when you've got as much money as he did lying around you're never going to 'starve'.

As he calmed down his thoughts turned to Kathi. That night he'd spent at her house had been one of the most unusual experiences of his recent life. Well, what he could remember of it that is. The next day she'd helped him find his keys on the golf course and had joined him back at his house after for coffee. Jack had wondered at the time why she didn't have work to go to, but hadn't mentioned it. He hadn't seen her since. A couple of times he'd gone round to her house, but she was either out or didn't answer her door for some reason, while her car hadn't left her driveway.

I don't get it. We didn't have sex, we didn't do anything like that. Why would she avoid me then? The complexities of female thought processes occupied him for a while before he drifted off to sleep.

"Oi!" AJ kicked him on the leg. Jack awoke bleary and irritable. He'd been having a most enjoyable dream, needless to say, that involved Kathi.

"Don't you ever knock?" he asked wearily.

"I did. I nearly broke your fucking door down I knocked so hard."

"I might have been out."

"The only time you're ever out is to go to that pub of yours." AJ lit up a cigarette and offered Jack one. He took it with his eyes still half closed, put it in his mouth and lit it, only to realise that he'd got it the wrong way around. After a short fit of coughing, he accepted another and sparked it properly this time.

"Well I might have been there," he finally reasoned.

"Yeah well I was gonna go there, but I thought I'd better check here first, you know, see if you were being attacked again." He smiled wryly.

"Fucking comedian. So what do you want?"

"Having a piss-up at mine tonight. You should come, gonna be banging."

Jack looked exasperated. He could guess that with the sort of piss-up AJ would throw he wouldn't have to leave his house to be involved. "I've got a headache."

"Don't lie. Take some fucking aspirin. Anyway, come over whenever, some lads have turned up already and now I gotta go out and get more beer. Come to the shop with us."

Jack didn't argue, he could see it was getting him nowhere. *Maybe getting hammered will take my mind off Anna and Kathi and all that shit,* the ageing nineties soul inside him concluded. *Hell, maybe there'll be some fit birds there and I'll get lucky with one of them instead.*

"Oh, get your northern mate to come along, and bring his missus." AJ said as he jogged down the stairs with Jack following slowly. "And don't bring any drugs." Jack stopped. Had he heard that right? *Don't bring any?*

"Why not?" He was puzzled.

"Cos if the pigs find them you're fucked." AJ obligingly held Jack's front door open for him while he waited for him to catch up.

"I know that, but what are you saying? You saying that you expect the cops to come?" Jack flicked his cigarette butt out of the front door and looked nonplussed at AJ.

"Nah, but you gotta be safe. Now come on then silly bollocks, fucking shop'll be shut by the time you get out of this house."

Jack shrugged his shoulders and followed him out.

CHAPTER THIRTY-ONE

Jack looked over the various bottles on display. Whiskey, Gin, Schnapps, whatever that was, it was all here. "What are you lot getting?" he asked AJ and his collection of mates. They were a weird bunch, to him. One of them, while speaking in the car, had said 'fuck' or a version of it no less than forty six times in two minutes. Jack had been counting, as he'd been unable to concentrate on what was actually being said.

"Just some beer for us and some Alco pops for me brother and his mates. Why, what you want?"

Jack didn't answer; he wasn't really in the mood for anything on display here. That felt strange to him, almost as though he'd grown twenty years older in the car drive over. He'd certainly felt it. The lads in the car with him had been no more than a couple of years younger, yet he'd felt like it was a generation gap. He wandered off towards the crisps aisle, thinking that while he was here he might as well get some stuff for himself. That thought made him feel even older.

He stopped dead as he passed the fruit and vegetable rows. There, standing not ten feet from him, was Kathi, holding a bag of oranges, looking just as vacant and dazed as she had at the Major's. He didn't know what to do. Should he go up to her and try to talk? Should he ignore her completely? He still hadn't decided whether she'd been avoiding him or whether he'd just missed her whenever he'd called round, but his hesitation worked against him. She looked up and saw him, and he pretended to be looking at the nearest thing on the shelf, which happened to be an empty box.

"Hiya," she said after coming up to him. Jack tried to scan the voice mentally, there was no malice he could detect, nor any sign of tension.

"Er...hey. How's things?" He shuffled about on his feet, refusing to meet her gaze.

"Oh, all's good thanks. You? I haven't seen you for a while, where've you been hiding then?" She smiled playfully as she spoke. Jack felt as though she was almost teasing him.

"I've er...been busy," he lied. "Listen, I never really got a chance to thank you properly for taking me in like you did. At least, thank you while fully sober." He looked up sheepishly. Why had he been so afraid of her? There was not the slightest hint of ill will in her eyes, though they did seem sad, for some reason.

"Don't worry about it." she said, half laughing. He hoped it was with and not at him. An awkward silence surrounded them. It even seemed as though the rest of the store had gone quiet too, and Jack was beginning to sweat. Though he still wasn't sure why, and definitely wasn't sure as to whether it was a good idea or not, he bit the bullet.

"So...what are you...you know, up to...er...tonight?" His tongue felt as though it was three times heavier than normal. He'd never had much trouble with chatting up women in the past. *Why the fuck is this so difficult? Why am I even asking her out though?*

Her smile grew wider, but not before her eyes bristled slightly. "I don't have any plans." She paused, before realising that she was going to have to drag this out of him. "What did you have in mind?"

"Well, er...AJ...have you met him? Well anyway he's having a party sort of thing at his house, and I'm supposed to be going." Jack wasn't sure how that was supposed to sound, but the slight return of the downcast expression on Kathi's face made him add a footnote. "We can go somewhere else though, if you want that is. Or, you know, whatever." The last part was meant to sound laid back and cool. It did not.

The warmth of her captivating smile returned. "I'd love to go with you." She looked at her watch, the universal signal that a conversation is either over, or should be. "I have to go. Come round to mine before it starts, OK?" She pecked him lightly on the cheek and glided past him through to the next aisle.

Jack couldn't move. He kept replaying the scene over in his head, wondering how a situation that had, from his end, sounded so wrong, yet turned out so well. The outside world squawked its way back into his consciousness in the form of his mobile ringing. *This better not be Anna.* He fumbled irritably around in his pocket and looked at the screen on the lid. Marky.

"Alright, mate. How's it going?" he answered distantly.

"Fucking nightmare, man. Missus has pissed off on me. Gone to her parents' for the weekend." Marky sounded like he'd been drinking.

"What?! Why's she done that then?" Jack tried to sound concerned, but really couldn't have cared less right then, which made him feel somewhat ashamed.

"Ah it's all a load of shite. Me dad got me tickets to go see City next month in the Derby match. Fucking tickets to see City take on the scum! In the cup! At home! And she's said I can't go, cos it's our anniversary."

For the first time in his living memory Jack saw the argument from both sides. Marky and Rachel were always rowing, but they were just one of those couples who seemingly liked to argue. In this case, though, neither side was going to back down, and it was plain to see why. Rachel had quite obviously been meaning to move their relationship forwards lately. The word 'kids' had apparently been mentioned a few times, and the usual hints about marriage had also been dropped. She worked the hardest on the relationship and when Jack was in some of his more fair-minded moods he'd often wondered why.

Marky, on the other hand, lived and breathed Manchester City. He loved Rachel, that was for certain, even if he did have a funny way of showing it on occasion. However, there were few things that would stop him watching City play, and nothing would stop him if it was against United. If his family were all tragically killed in a freak weather incident, he'd miss their funeral if it coincided with a Manchester Derby, and there was no way an anniversary was going to get in his way.

"I know how you feel, mate." Jack finally answered sympathetically. "Women need to learn that nothing in existence should come between an Englishman and his football team." He wasn't sure if he meant it, though he knew that Marky would probably quote him in his next argument with his estranged girlfriend. "Look man, there's a piss-up in the Close tonight. Open invite as far as I can tell. Come along and we'll sort it out then."

Marky agreed to come after Jack had reminded him not to drive if he'd been drinking. It wasn't actually out of any sense of safety that he'd warned him, more out of worry that if AJ expected the Bill to turn up, then they'd pick up Marky as soon as look at him.

CHAPTER THIRTY-TWO

Jack's jaw hit the pavement as Kathi opened the door. She looked stunning. Had he had any less self-control he would have been drooling.

"You look...incredible." he said once he'd finally found his tongue. She was wearing a short black dress that matched her raven hair perfectly, and he had no idea what she'd done to her eyes, but they shimmered deep blue as they penetrated his gaze. He shivered slightly, which made her giggle. He followed her inside and saw two wine glasses waiting patiently on the coffee table in her sitting room. For a moment Jack was worried. He'd made what he considered an effort for this party, namely, shaving and changing his T-shirt. She, on the other hand, looked as though she was off to the Proms. She was certainly far too overdressed for a house party, even one in this end of suburbia.

"You know, if you wanna go out someplace else..." he began before she hushed him with a finger on his mouth.

"I know I'm overdressed. I don't mind." she whispered, before handing him a glass of red wine. He hadn't even seen her pour it. He held it cautiously for a moment, waiting for an invitation. None came. She took a slow swig from her glass with her eyes never leaving his. Certain that the ground beneath him wasn't going to swallow him whole and save him from this most pleasurable of uncomfortable situations, he drained most of his glass in one go, and coughed slightly as some of the wine went down the wrong way. Placing his hand over his mouth, he was almost grateful for the break in tension, and when he looked up, he saw that Kathi had finished her drink and was putting on a silk scarf. Ironically, covering more up seemed to make her appear even more infatuating, and Jack was beginning to wonder whether she had some form of agenda tonight, or whether he was, for one night only, the luckiest man alive.

"Come on, then," she cooed. "We mustn't upset our hosts." Taking his hand, she led him out of the house and across the drive to AJ's.

AJ answered the door with a series of sarcastic comments about how Jack didn't need to knock, until he saw Kathi with him, and Jack found himself relieved that he wasn't the only man incapable of controlling his expression, speech, manner and general appearance upon seeing Kathi. Amazingly the usually silver-tongued AJ was left speechless as the two of them walked in.

As they entered the main room, silence fell. A ring of around twelve lads hushed immediately as Kathi linked her arm through his, and it all became clear to him. He felt like a God. This woman, this ridiculously attractive lady had stunned all these men with her beauty, and she had made a gesture to show that she was his. Had he not been quite so awe-struck he would have been wearing the most inane grin imaginable.

The introductions were made, and beer handed out to the newcomers. Kathi politely declined, but then relented when offered a glass of wine. The murmurs of conversation grew back into the room and, unsurprisingly, most of the questions were directed at Kathi. Each of the lads in the circle had a turn at smooth-talking her, and to each one she smiled or laughed slightly, but never showed any signs of interest. Eventually they grew bored and went back to their original topics; football, friends and films. Jack took a moment to quiz a lad of about nineteen who happened to be sitting next to him, why AJ had put out a no drugs rule.

"It's the raids, you know right? Fucking pigs'll be round tonight sometime and none of us wanna get busted."

AJ had gone out to answer the door, and by now newcomers were arriving by the dozen. The room had started to fill up and others were going off to different parts of the house in groups. The attention to Kathi had subsided now, as a fair few of the latest partygoers were women in the somewhat more obtainable bracket, and now the lads had more realistic targets for their affections.

Jack took the opportunity to ponder exactly what had happened to the woman on his arm when the conversation moved away from things that he was interested in. Before that meeting at the Major's, she had been a domineering career bitch whom he had heard liquidate companies and livelihoods over the phone. She'd had rich old men over to stay at regular intervals, and on occasion, had spoken to both him and Marky so brusquely he'd wondered if there was actually any functioning oestrogen glands in her entire body. But something had happened that night, something during that phone-call she'd taken, had changed her immeasurably. Whereas before he'd always assumed that she'd looked at him with nothing but contempt, now there was, well, almost worship. Could it just be an act? Was it all part of some grand scheme? He decided that whatever it was, he might as well enjoy it while it lasted.

CHAPTER THIRTY-THREE

Marky hadn't been able to wait for the party to tank up. He was so miffed at his girlfriend's behaviour that almost the same minute that she'd slammed the front door on her way out, he'd broken out his most expensive brandy and had begun swigging straight from the bottle. That had been at around four in the afternoon. Jack had said turn up to this thing at eightish, and in that time Marky had finished his bottle of brandy, been to the store to buy more, finished that, and was now lying semi-conscious on his sofa.

A swarm of thoughts were whizzing noisily around his mind. Rachel knew how much he loved City, she knew how important this game was to him. It was quite easily the biggest game the Blues had had in recent history since the promotion run in last time they went up. How could she not understand? It wasn't as though this was unexpected. After all, he was a man who'd cancelled their second date when they were first going out in order to see City reserves play Leeds in a friendly! She'd still wanted to date him after that, how could she now possibly justify this betrayal?

He glanced at his watch, an action that took a considerable amount of effort considering that his left arm was at the time underneath his stomach in a vain attempt to soothe the feeling of impending illness inside him. Seven-thirty. *Shit, I'd best be getting to this do.* His mind was ready and willing, his body, however, was not. As he swung a leg off the sofa down onto the ground, his stomach protested in the only way it knew how, by wrenching itself together and forcing its unwelcome cargo back the way it had come. *Wank French piss.* Marky grumbled as he crawled off towards the kitchen to fetch a mop.

His eventual return brought home the full extent of the damage. Dry cleaning couldn't sort this mess out, and when the smell hit home, a further reversal of gear by his digestive tract merely exacerbated matters. *Christ's sake, will this never end?* He dabbed at the mess half-heartedly but it was clear he was getting nowhere. *Bollocks to you then* he thought, flinging the mop down into the swamp, and pulling out his mobile to call a taxi. Privately thankful that Jack had insisted that he should call a cab, as he would have surely forgotten in this state, he slurred out the instructions to the voice at the other end.

The voice, unfortunately, belonged to a Polish man who was new to the country, and whose English, while technically sound, was not accustomed to Mancunian dialect at the best of times, and certainly not able to deal with this particular slurred northern accent minus consonants. As he tried to explain for the seventh time, a shrill beeping interrupted to inform him that his credit had run out. Cursing pay-as-you-go phones and life in general, Marky decided to walk to the nearest taxi rank, a good mile and a half, hopeful that by the time he got there, the fresh air would have sobered him up, and that there would be an English cabby available.

About halfway down the main road from his house, the warm familiar sight of the Rosebush almost swam into view. The fresh air had done little to sharpen his senses, but the sudden purging of excess liquid from his stomach had made him thirsty, so he decided to stop off for a refuelling at the watering hole. Even though it was late on a Saturday evening, the pub was virtually lifeless, just a few elder statesmen with their standard-issue farmers caps and pipes reading the Racing Post. Marky steadied himself, aware that the staff in this pub weren't afraid to throw you out on a whim, especially if they thought you'd had too many. He slowly walked over to the bar, where the barmaid who had given him a rosy cheek in retribution for his supposed 'two lazy eyes' had seen him come in and was watching him disdainfully.

"I'll have a pint of lager please, lass," he tried to say as clearly as possible.

"You will not, and don't call me 'lass'." was the reply.

"What?! Ah come on Maggie I've had a rough day."

"I know, I can smell it from here. And don't call me 'Maggie' either. It's Angie but 'miss' to you."

Marky indiscreetly smelt his T-shirt. Even to someone who'd been drinking heavily, it reeked of both regular brandy and the regurgitated variety.

"No, no, you see, this isn't my top. I borrowed it off a mate." But Angie wasn't a half-wit, and she wasn't fooled.

"Come now young man, you've had a lot to drink and I think you should go to bed," came the polite warning.

"Is that an offer?" Marky retorted cheekily. The desired effect was not achieved. After calling for the landlord to help her out, Angie oversaw Marky's ejection from the Rosebush and left him with the statement that if he ever came back she would file a sexual harassment suit against him.

After sitting in the park opposite the pub for what seemed like an eternity, wondering just how his life could get any worse, a cab crawled by on the road. After flagging it down and virtually giving the Asian driver instructions letter by letter, Marky found himself on his way to Appletree Close.

Twenty minutes later, he woke up from a brief nap in the taxi to find himself in Verity Road, the most expensive street in the area, and the complete opposite side of town to where he wanted to go. A brief but loud confrontation with the driver ensued, whereby Marky had to agree to pay an extra ten pounds just to be taken to where he had originally wanted to go.

By the time they finally found it, Marky felt his second wind rising. *About bloody time too,* he thought as he gave the cabby what he thought was fifteen pounds but was actually thirty. The music had started by then, and only now did he realise whose piss-up it was. Jack hadn't mentioned who'd been throwing it, and now that he was here with no way of getting home until the morning, Marky's second wind turned into a renewed feeling of anger. He didn't want to spend the next six hours sitting in a room full of fucking townies and pikeys, and he certainly didn't want to try and sort out his problems with his missus with Jack in front of them.

His mood blackening by the second, he turned towards Jack's house and banged on the door. No reply. Jack never locked his back door, he remembered, so after negotiating his way around the dustbins and other obstacles that weren't actually in his way, he made it into Jack's house, and, after calling out once for him, promptly fell asleep on the sofa.

CHAPTER THIRTY-FOUR

Things weren't quite so muted across the road. Having spent the best part of an hour trying to find enough plugs for all the equipment in the speaker system, now AJ was trying to get the damn thing to work. Danno and his mate from London had hauled the lot down in a rented (stolen) van, but as soon as they'd arrived they'd celebrated completing the hour and a half journey by cracking open a few beers. Now Danno was sitting in a corner staring at a lampshade, while his cockney friend was trying to teach one of the girls rhyming slang.

"Nah nah nah, 'battle cruiser' is a pub, cos 'cruiser' rhymes with 'boozer' got it?" He held back a look of exasperation, certain that he was impressing the girl.

"Oh yeah, I got it now. That's fucking clever an' all," she agreed in between guzzling her Breezer.

AJ wandered in looking for him. "Oi!" He found him. "You gonna give us a hand fixing these fucking speakers or what?"

"I told you, man. Just plug them into the amp and you're sorted." He ignored the frustrated plea from his host to come and help, certain that he was as good as on a promise now, and he wasn't about to leave a nice-looking girl like this half drunk here on her own to get picked up by someone else.

AJ went back to the job at hand. Stumbling over an ever-increasing pile of mostly empty beer cans on his way through the hall, he found Jack sitting on the stairs rolling a cigarette.

"Alright?"

"Hey." He finished his rollie and offered it to AJ, who took it.

"Cheers. Where's your bird?"

"Ah, piss. I think." He began rolling another. "Dunno she's been gone a while, probably fucked off home."

"And you don't care?"

"Not really," he lied.

AJ stared at him as though he was some form of mutant zombie. Or gay. "Well, whatever you say, mate. Oh, you know anything about rigging sound systems?"

"A bit, I suppose."

"Well then you know more than me. Come on, I need you to fix this for me."

Jack followed him through to the sitting room, where he noticed a large pale stain on the carpet by the doorway. "What happened here then? You spill some wine or something?"

"Oh, I dunno. I never seen that before. Wazza must've spilt something, though he doesn't normally bother cleaning up. Anyway, here's them speakers. Apparently you gotta plug them into the amp or something."

Jack looked over the four colossal units. They were at least his height and width, jet black and menacing. He had flashbacks of the ringing in his ears following the Major's bungled flirtation with similar equipment, and these were twice the size of his.

"Jesus, man. You starting up your own nightclub?" He fished around the back and found a spaghetti mess of tangled wires, each as thick as his thumb. He picked out two that happened to be unattached and looked around for right sized holes to put them in.

Upstairs, Wayne and his friends from his school class were ploughing through their allocation of Breezers. AJ had been very specific when telling his brother the plan for the night. On no account was any one of the kids to get hammered and hurl everywhere, and every bottle had to be hidden under a bed when not in use. Wayne had spent much of the so-called party wondering why he'd bothered inviting the eight other youngsters around, as they clearly weren't happy at not being allowed to get pissed, kept pestering him for cigarettes even though they didn't smoke, and continuously wanted to play on his Xbox while he was using it.

"So you let them come over, let them drink, but then tell them that you *don't* want them getting hammered?!" Jack asked in bemusement when AJ told him where his brother was. "In the name of buggery, why?"

"It's all a surprise." He winked. "But no one's gonna find out why unless we get this fucking speaker set working."

"All right, calm down." Jack had found a home for one of the loose wires, and after fruitlessly searching for the others, gave up and jammed it into the back of the amp randomly. The speakers let out a wail of pain not dissimilar to a foghorn and were then silent.

"Sweet." AJ plugged his CD player into the amp and instantly the loudest, fastest, roughest drum'n bass mix ever conceived shook the house to its very foundations. "There we go. Shouldn't be more than half an hour or so." AJ yelled before finishing his can and throwing it across the room casually. "Better check there's no drugs or anything lying around. Gimme a hand would you?"

Jack couldn't think of any excuses quickly enough to refuse, and soon found himself asking random people for their drugs, an act that lowered his popularity level considerably. AJ had to rescue him from one guy, who was obviously pretty heavily into steroids, who'd taken offence to being asked to hand them over.

"Nah you fucking idiot, you wanna get shot or your neck broken or something? You only gotta clear up any you see lying around, any stuff that people's got on them is their problem."

"Alright, but for fuck's sake why?" Jack's patience was wearing thin. He was now beginning to wonder if Kathi had gone home, and if he'd blown his chance with her.

"Well…" AJ began, before his mobile interrupted him. "Hang on." He answered the phone. "Yeah? You just heard it now? Fucking hell that was quick! Alright, sweet, mate, so how long you reckon? Nice one. Laters." He put his phone away and faced Jack again with a sly grin. "You wanted to know why? Well, come outside and find out, they'll be here in a moment."

He led Jack out into the hall, turning the music down to almost a whisper as he went out.

CHAPTER THIRTY-FIVE

"So what are we waiting for again?" Jack crossed his arms impatiently. It was around eight in the evening, and still fairly light, yet there was a sharp chill in the air.

"That." AJ indicated the flashing blue lights entering the Close slowly. There was no siren, and no noise coming from the houses, so the strobe effect of the lightbars cast something of an eerie effect over the otherwise docile houses. The police car pulled up in front of AJ's house silently, and two dark blue uniforms surveyed the scene before getting out.

"'Scuse me, sir," the taller one said as they approached AJ. "Are you the tenant of this house?"

"Yes, officer, yes I am." AJ spoke in as polite and elegant a tone as he could muster. It sounded horribly out of place. "Is there something wrong?"

"Er...yes, I'm afraid we've received a number of complaints about excessive noise coming from the building. Would you mind letting us take a look around to make sure everything is OK?"

"Absolutely." AJ over-pronounced. "I can't possibly imagine why someone would think that we're disturbing anyone, but you're welcome to look around to satisfy your curiosity." He led them in.

"Satisfy their curiosity? Where did you learn to talk like that?" Jack whispered as he followed him in.

"Shut it." AJ hissed through a plastic grin, before turning to the policemen in the hallway. "As you can see I do have a few friends and acquaintances visiting for a little celebration, but it's all very well ordered and there's no question of unruly or loutish behaviour."

The policemen nodded sceptically. Jack stared at him as though he'd turned green. "If you'd like to look around please feel free, and don't hesitate to ask if something seems out of place."

Jack watched the cops shuffle away uneasily. "Seriously," he said when they'd gone, "where'd you learn to speak like that? You got some sort of warped split personality?"

"Ah, you spend enough time listening to lawyers fucking going on and on you learn to copy the way they talk. There's fuck all else to do in court anyway."

Jack was lost for words, and while he stood there trying to think of something else to say, one of the constables called them from the sitting room.

"Ah, sir? Would you mind telling me what these are for?" He indicated the four gargantuan speakers, that were now softly playing chill-out tunes.

AJ heroically resisted the temptation to point out that they were for playing music. "Yes, they belong to my good friend Danno here." He said, grabbing a half-pissed Danno from his place in the toilet queue. "Danno here is DJ-ing at one of the clubs in town tonight and I said he could keep his equipment here until he needs it."

Danno stood edgily, whether it was due to the presence of the police, whom he was no friend of, or the fact that he desperately needed to piss didn't matter, AJ wouldn't let go of his arm.

"Don't they have their own speakers in the club?" the shorter cop quipped.

"Ah, yes, yes they do. But Danno here is something of a perfectionist, he likes to use his own equipment. Makes him think it sounds better." AJ squeezed Danno's arm, who nodded enthusiastically.

"I see," remarked the cop, but he clearly didn't.

They trooped upstairs, where after a curiously strange knock at his little brother's bedroom door, AJ led them in, to a scene of nine kids playing around on different gaming consoles. AJ was almost visibly relieved to find that there wasn't a bottle in sight.

"It was my little brother's birthday recently," he explained. "And he wanted to have a few friends over to play on his new toys."

"Do their parents know that they're here?" The shorter one asked sceptically.

"Of course." AJ replied instantly before one of the kids could accidentally give the game away. "I have a list of their parents' phone numbers and addresses downstairs in case of an emergency, if you'd like to see? And obviously all their parents have my house and mobile numbers in case they need to get ahold of them."

"No, thank you, that shouldn't be necessary," the shorter one replied a little downheartedly before sniffing the air. "There's a strong smell of smoke in this room."

This time AJ was stumped, inwardly seething at Wayne for smoking at all, let alone indoors when he knew what was happening. Jack decided to intervene.

"Ah, yes, that's my fault actually. I was playing young Wayne here at Fifa earlier and I had a smoke then. Mr Johnson here has already made it clear to me that he doesn't want anyone smoking around his younger brother and I have been told not to do it again." He feigned guilt by looking at his shoes and the policemen seemed both astonished and helpless as they couldn't think of anything else to say.

AJ smiled as he shook the policemen's hands on their way out. "Not at all, not at all. I appreciate that you have to do your job and I'm only too happy to help." He smiled sympathetically as apologies were offered for wasting his time. He closed the door behind them and breathed a huge sigh of relief.

Jack watched them return to their car through the window, and smiled as they mumbled something into the radio before driving off, flashing lights off and siren silent, as though the patrol car were a dog creeping away with its tail between its legs.

"They gone?" AJ asked between puffs of a cigarette. Jack nodded. "Sweet. Wayne!" He yelled up the stairs. The scamp poked his head over the landing in response. "Get your mates outside! Time for a street footy tourny!" AJ looked for Danno again. "Turn those beats back up!" he said when the cockney had finished his long-awaited toilet visit.

"Aren't you worried that they'll come back?" Jack asked.

"Who, the pigs?"

"Yeah."

"Nah. You remember that guy who called just before they arrived?" Jack shook his head. "You know, the one with the scanner?" Jack shook again. "Well, anyway, he's my lawyer. Right about now he'll be onto their boss about harassment or something. They won't be back tonight."

Jack smiled. He now knew that he'd seriously under-estimated AJ, and decided to just forget what had happened and join in the street football. The combination of alcohol and sugar in the Bacardi Breezers had a stimulative effect on the kids, whose high pitched screams and energetic scurrying around after the football was sure to wake the dead.

CHAPTER THIRTY-SIX

Josh sat back on his bed in a good mood. He'd spent the last three hours wriggling out of doing his homework and now it finally seemed as though his father had given up nagging for the night. Usually it took until around bedtime for the excuses to have the desired effect, but tonight had seemed a little easier than usual. *Maybe I'm getting better,* he thought. *Or maybe dad's finally seeing the light.* He didn't see the point in homework in any case. What's the point in going to school if they just give you more work to do at home? And holiday work!? That's just stupid.

As he sat there mulling over which excuses had worked the best, for future use, the sounds of kids chirped through his window. He looked out into the street to see a football match. One that looked like it lacked rules, or proper teams, or goalposts. At his private school, Josh was always forced to play rugby or hockey or other such rubbish sports, and he had actually been sent to the headmaster once for playing football in his lunch break. 'A sport for hooligans and degenerates.' the headmaster had called it, while incidentally sporting a cricket jersey. 'I'll not have a pupil of mine waste his future with pipe dreams of a decadent pastime.'

Josh's eyes lit up. He never got to play anymore. His parents hadn't seemed that bothered by the letter home about said incident, and they hadn't mentioned anything to him. Maybe they didn't mind. Quick as a flash, Josh opened his homework book and wrote down a jumble of random and completely wrong answers to the set questions, for insurance purposes, and ran out of the bedroom looking for his trainers. He tore down the stairs so fast he barely kept his balance, and hared out of the door as quickly as possible, in the hope that he wouldn't be noticed, or rather that if he was noticed he'd already be gone. It was a vain hope.

"Where do you think you're going?" his mother asked as he tried to escape.

"Uh, just out for a bit. I've done my homework, don't worry." he replied, slamming the door behind him to prevent being called back before time.

He sprinted up to the first person he saw and asked if he could join in. The person in question happened to be Jack, who was standing in defence of his six-man team with a can of beer in one hand and a half-smoked cigarette in the other.

"Er...your parents know you're out here?" Jack mumbled out of ceremony. Josh nodded enthusiastically. "Oh. Well, sure. You can be on my team I s'pose. Fuck knows...I mean Goodness knows I don't have the energy to keep up with this lot."

Josh immediately hovered around waiting for the ball, and when Jack finally fouled one of the opposition (not that any free kick was coming) he slid it over to Josh disinterestedly and wandered off. Straight away Josh tore off up the road, quite skilfully dodging attempted tackles and fouls on his way, before tumbling under a hefty challenge from another kid he'd managed to nutmeg. He collapsed in a heap, scraping his knee and bursting into tears on the spot.

It had, unsurprisingly, been Graham who had reported a 'domestic disturbance' to the police a little over half an hour earlier, and as he watched the squad car slip away quietly, he congratulated himself on a job well done. That is, until barely two minutes later, when the noise erupted again and prevented him hearing himself think. Having dialled the police once more, he had been further incensed when the desk sergeant had informed him that they had already investigated the matter, and furthermore were aware of the possible question of harassment.

The football match was just kicking off while he was half cursing the over-tolerant society and half wondering if he should go over himself. The sound of his eldest hurtling down the stairs distracted him momentarily, and he heard the words 'I've done my homework', which aroused his suspicions instantly. Just as he was about to call Joshua in to explain where he was going, the front door slammed, and Graham strode out to find out what was going on.

He had been about to yell at his son for all manner of reasons as he stood in the front doorway when he saw something incredible. While his mouth tried in vain to call out Joshua's name, the rest of him was struck dumb with amazement and parental pride, as he watched his boy sleekly dance past both kids his own age and much older, mesmerising all with the ball as he did.

For a moment, Graham just stood there with a look of admiration. Then he saw the scruffy hair disappear towards the ground and he heard a yelp of pain. Instantly riled, he marched off towards the group of players, who had gathered around the fallen star to see what could possibly hurt so much.

"Ah get up you pussy. It's just a scratch," one of them remarked after seeing his knee.

"Out of the way, please," Graham commanded as he approached. "Let me through." He knelt down by his son. Upon seeing the blood-soaked shorts, he feared a serious injury, but when he saw that it was indeed just a scratch, he found it hard to contain his relief. Parental duties do not involve realism apparently, when it comes to injuries to their children, and even though the so-called injury barely qualified as damage, Graham immediately scooped Josh up in his arms and carried him back to the house, comforting him as he went.

After they'd disappeared inside, the footballers milled around for a few seconds, trying to decide what to do, before Wayne flicked the ball up and began playing tricks on his nearest opponent. Sure enough, the act was a catalyst to the game restarting again as though nothing had happened.

Graham laid his son out on the sofa and called for Alice to bring tissues. Josh had finished crying now, and instead was just annoyed that the sum of his involvement in the match had been five seconds of dribbling and two minutes of blubbering.

"Do you feel better now?" his father asked compassionately.

"A bit." Josh replied, nodding weakly.

"I've had it up to here with them." Graham announced as he turned to face his wife, who had started padding the cut with tissues. "It's disgusting the way the police have responded, and now this."

"It was just a game of football." Alice tried to pacify her ever-reddening husband.

"And what about the noise? And the swearing? And the drugs and alcohol?"

Alice didn't reply. "Well then," he concluded, "something must be done. If the police won't help us, we shall deal with them ourselves."

"Now, Graham, do be careful." Alice ran through her mind the many possible disastrous situations that could arise. She was unable to air them, however, as Graham had already made his mind up.

"Hello?" He barked down the telephone after dialling hastily. "Is that you, Reverend? Yes, it's me. I need a favour."

"Oh, Lord," Alice mumbled.

CHAPTER THIRTY-SEVEN

Jack yawned impatiently as he waited for his kettle to boil. He wasn't drunk, but he certainly wasn't sober, and the smell of coffee that had greeted him upon entering his kitchen had whetted his appetite for a cup. He didn't know where the smell had come from, he certainly hadn't made any recently, but he didn't really care either. As he got older, Jack had gradually realised that the more alcohol he drank, the less he seemed to care these days. Not about his health, or how much he'd had, more about the menial things going on around him. Such as tonight, he hadn't really noticed when Kathi had left, if she'd left, due to the amount of beer he'd taken. Now he didn't care whether she'd gone or not.

He poured the hot water into a mug already half full with sugar and instant coffee granules. The taste was over-sweet, but of course he didn't much care. He wandered through to the living room with his mug in one hand and a fag in the other. The sight that greeted him was not the most enthralling. Marky was lying on the sofa in a brandy-induced coma, evidently having been so for quite some time, yet his left arm was hanging down the side of the chair, with his hand suspended in what appeared to be a bowl of warm water. Jack looked at the ensuing result and felt thankful just for the fact that his hammered friend was lying on his back, or else he'd have to get the leather covers changed.

After a few seconds silent mirth at the situation, he decided it was best to leave him there as he was, not wanting to disturb the beast until it had recovered. So he half-heartedly threw a rug over Marky, and plodded up the stairs to his bedroom, spilling his coffee everywhere as he went. He opened the door and found another unexpected sight. There was someone in his bed. In his mildly intoxicated state, Jack's mind ran to the implausible first. *A burglar who'd got overly tired at working his night shift? A friend Marky brought round? Perhaps one of the partygoers from across the road who took more than they could handle?* In any case, Jack was in no mood for hospitality, particularly when firstly, it was his bed and he was tired, and secondly, the pain from having scalding hot coffee spilt all over his hand had belatedly made its report to his brain, and caused him to curse under his breath.

The body under the covers stirred slightly, but made no other signs of having heard him. Torn between reclaiming his bunk, and dealing with potential third-degree burns on his arm, Jack hurried out towards the bathroom to deal with the physically painful problem first. While enjoying the soothing sensation of cold water, his sense of perspective finally caught up with him. Marky's missus had kicked him out. Jack knew that they fought, and on occasion there were serious disputes, but they had always kissed and made up by the next day. This time it was different.

Jack had always held the suspicion that one day their union would end messily. Rachel, two years older than her man, was at the age where women become unhealthily interested in long-term plans. Future goals include a ring on the finger and a bun in the oven. Marky, on the other hand, was still only twenty-five, hardly out of the 'live for the weekend' lifestyle, spending his pay cheque as soon as it arrived, and whose long-term goals were mainly different versions of seeing Manchester City play at Wembley. At the start it had all seemed well enough; he made her feel younger than she was, while she gave him regular sex that he didn't have to pay for. Mostly.

Whatever was to happen, Jack concluded, could happen tomorrow. He was too drunk, too tired, and too disinterested in anything other than the gradually-subsiding ache on his hand. He patted his arm dry on a nearby towel, and stumbled back to his bedroom. Temporarily forgetting his unwelcome guest, he almost crashed through the door, and looked in amazement at the graceful figure of Kathi, his former date, lying on his bed, staring at him provocatively.

"Er...I thought you were asleep..." he stuttered, wondering what she was doing here, but not daring to ask.

"It's a bit early for that, isn't it?" She cooed. "It's barely nine."

"Well...what were you...I mean...are you..." Jack failed to find the right way of speaking his mind.

"Oh I was just resting while I waited."

"Waited for what?" He asked gullibly.

"You, of course." Her smile had gone, he found himself defenceless in her gaze.

"Wha...what do...er..."

"Yes?" Not a single blink.

"Was that your handiwork, downstairs? Marky, I mean." He acquiesced.

"Oh, yes. I couldn't resist."

There would be times in the coming weeks where Jack would have killed to recall this moment more clearly. It wasn't the alcohol which robbed him of his memory, though he would happily blame it, it was his utter powerlessness to do anything but obey the gaze. He was at the time wondering what the fuck was going on, but his body didn't care what his mind was doing, and that *was* to be blamed on the alcohol.

CHAPTER THIRTY-EIGHT

"Alright, take care man." AJ closed the door as the last stragglers left the house. It was gone four am and the place was a mess. Still, mission accomplished though. He'd wanted to make his home feel more like a home he was used to, and he'd done that now. Short of throwing some decaying washing-machines into the front garden, and boarding up several of the windows, he now felt like he was at ease here. It wasn't the dozens of empty cans lying around the floor, nor the lingering odour of beer and stale smoke, the place just seemed more natural to him now. Before it had almost felt too clean, too nice.

Wayne was busy scrabbling through discarded cigarette packets to see if anyone had left any in them. He was surprisingly lucky on quite a few occasions.

"Hey, Bruv, there's something wrong with the dog," he called when he saw AJ. "Mum called to say he's running around in circles chasing his tail."

"What's wrong with that? All dogs do that." AJ reasoned.

"Yeah, but then he attacked a radiator or something. Mum's fretting, man. She says she's had to lock him in the spare room cos she's afraid he'll go for the kids."

At the mention of his children, AJ took the information seriously. He didn't get to see his kids as often as he liked, in fact he barely got to see them at all. Charlene, their mother, had insisted that she should look after them and that he would only get access at weekends. AJ had been powerless to argue at the time, as apparently her older sister was banging a judge or something. Ever since he'd won his money, he'd told his lawyer to sort it out so he could see his kids as often as he liked.

Now at the mention that there was even the slightest minimal chance that they were in danger, AJ wasn't interested in what 'all dogs do' and he grabbed his jacket and hurled himself into his car.

"Am I coming too?" Wayne asked through the window as AJ struggled to get the thing to start.

"No, stay here. I won't be long." And then he tore off in third gear, forgetting to release the handbrake in his urgency. The resulting smell flooded the area, and Wayne hurried back inside in a fit of coughing, only to fumble around in his pocket for his fags.

"Mum, it's me. Lemme in!" AJ yelled while almost taking the door to the flat off its hinges. He only stopped bashing on it when it opened. His mother's face was white as a sheet. "Where are they?" he demanded. "Are they alright?"

"Yes they're fine, love." Flo replied reassuringly. "That dog's gone fucking mental though."

AJ wasn't listening, he'd seen his kids in the kitchen and had rushed over to them, hugging them tightly as though they were recently freed hostages.

"You're gonna have to take it away somewhere." Flo told him as she came into the kitchen after him. "It needs looking at and it can't stay here."

"Well I can't leave them here." AJ retorted, hugging his children tighter.

"They'll be fine. You need to sort that animal out."

AJ grudgingly agreed, and after reluctantly letting go of the two most important people of his weekends, went scrabbling round the kitchen looking for something.

"What're you after?" his mother asked, bemused.

"Some rope. I didn't bring a lead, and I don't think he'll thank me if I grab him by the ear."

"Well there isn't any rope here."

AJ stood up and thought quickly. He noticed an old garden hose coiled up behind the sink like a starved snake. Quite why it was there was a mystery, the flat had no garden, and as far as he could remember, AJ had never, until now, lived in a residence where a hose would be needed. *Doesn't matter,* he thought, *it'll do.*

Ten minutes later, AJ was driving back towards Appletree Close at something of a crawl. Vieira had indeed not taken kindly to being tethered, much less to a strange rubbery leash that was tied to the back of his master's car. Half galloping behind the car, half gnawing at his leash, Vieira's mood was rapidly deteriorating. He'd pestered his master regularly to take him for more walks, but this was taking the piss.

As AJ came onto the main road through town, he sped up slightly, conscious that this was just the sort of thing that random people would want to stop him and chastise him for. Inwardly he was quite proud of his ingenuity, but he knew that he had to get home quickly, preferably avoiding any cops on the way.

As he turned down a side-street to avoid the main night spots of town, a cyclist passing the other way became so caught up in rubbernecking the bizarre scene that he ran straight out in front of a red light and into the front of an oncoming lorry. The ensuing scene did enough to distract attention away from AJ's mini-parade as passers-by rushed to the aid of the shaken cyclist, who was by now regretting his decision to have 'one for the road'.

Finally, he arrived back at the Close. The streetlights were buzzing contentedly, their dull yellow haze masking all natural light save for a bright full moon. AJ looked at the celestial body for a while, wondering if Vieira was displaying symptoms of being some sort of werewolf. Then, wondering further whether he should let the unruly creature into the house, he got out of the car and looked at his dog. There was carnage in those eyes.

"Well, there's sod all I can do for you tonight," he addressed the beast, cautiously untying the end of the hose from the bumper of his car. Vieira seemed to take a moment to assess the situation, then he slumped to the ground with a groan. "What the fuck is the matter with you?" AJ muttered impatiently, but the dog didn't hear him, he'd passed out. AJ poked the twitching body hesitantly, then decided that maybe it was best to leave him where he was, he was obviously happy. AJ tied the hose back to the end of his car, and wandered into his house, all the while racking his limited knowledge on dog behaviour as to what exactly had happened.

Vieira's sleep was deep and dreamless, no chasing rabbits here, no hunting prey or fighting rivals. The cause of his irrational manner, the bottle of suspicious pills he'd wolfed down while guarding his master's house, were beginning to pass out of his system finally, but their side-effects and consequences would linger on for a while yet.

CHAPTER THIRTY-NINE

The first thing Jack noticed as he stirred from his slumber was that he was cold. A slight shiver both reinforced the feeling and woke him further. He opened his eyes slowly, only for a powerful blast of sunlight to blind him from the window. The shock seemed to awaken more of his senses, and as a headache kicked in, so did the need to purge a large amount of liquid his bladder was currently storing.

He squirmed up slightly into a slouched sitting position, and realised that he was alone. Not an unusual situation to find himself in, he woke up every other morning alone, but something seemed wrong with it today. The need to piss hadn't gone away, and he hurriedly stumbled out of bed to answer the call. As he stood up he realised that he hadn't any clothes on, and the memory struck him. Immediately his male pride smirked at the realisation that he'd got laid last night, but then he wondered where she'd gone.

He shuffled off to the toilet to relieve his bladder of its unfairly large burden, and while there he went through the now mundane process of trying to piece together his movements from last night. *Let's see, I remember meeting some cops. I remember playing street footy. I remember the kid Josh crying for a half hour. I remember coming home…And that's it. Bollocks, I wasn't that drunk.*

After deciding that the rest of the night would come back to him in its own time, he put on his dressing gown and wandered downstairs for a cup of tea. As he passed the door to the living room, he noticed a bulk on the sofa. Once he saw the slightly damp patch on Marky's jeans, he remembered a lot more, and his short fit of laughter at the sight woke the Manc from his slumber.

"Eh, what are you doing here?" Marky slurred.

"I could ask you the same question, to be honest."

"What? Are we at yours?" Marky raised his head slightly and looked around the room. "Oh yeah, we are."

"What the hell happened to you?" Jack asked ambiguously, half hoping for an explanation, but half hoping to draw Marky's attention to his trousers.

"Oh, fuck." He noticed. "Jesus man, I dunno what happened." Jack smirked and offered tea to his guest. "You got a spare pair of trousers I can nick?" Marky called after him.

"Not if they're gonna end up like that." Jack replied, enjoying himself.

"Nah, look man…"

"Don't worry about it. There's some upstairs." Jack decided not to prolong his mate's embarrassment for too long. At least for the moment.

Thank fuck some Victorian Lord decided to annex India and nick all their tea, Jack thought as he let the traditional British 'comfort drink' work its magic. *And thanks for conquering America, too,* he thought as he took a drag off a cigarette. Marky appeared by the kitchen doorway, and Jack handed him a cup.

"Cheers mate," he mumbled in-between sips. "Listen, you're not gonna tell anyone, are you? You know, about…" He pointed to his crotch.

"Nah, don't worry," said Jack, crossing his fingers behind his back. "So, how are you gonna go about getting Rachel back?" He'd remembered why Marky was here while making the teas, and figured that the sooner he could get his mind onto a subject that didn't directly involve him, the less his head would hurt.

"Oh Christ, Rachel. I'd completely forgotten."

"I'm not surprised. Judging by the smell of you, you must've drank half the brandy in town last night." Marky looked sheepishly at his feet. "So how bad is it?"

"I dunno mate, we've had fights before and all, it's just this one she actually sounded like she meant what she was saying."

Jack snorted. He was having second thoughts about this. Marky and Rachel's stormy relationship was based on a foundation of mutual disagreement, amended by aggressive passion. The fact that they had a fight every now and then just seemed to be part of the normal run of things to him, an outsider. Anna, his former affair partner, was unusually interested in celebrity gossip magazines, and occasionally when he was at her house, he'd flick through some of them while passing time. According to the somewhat unreliable stories he read in them, most couples nowadays had a 'thing' that they did to keep the spark in their relationship. Some did weird things in bed, some did weirder things that should have been done in bed in public, others tried hobbies together and generally it seemed a load of bollocks to him. To be fair, he'd accepted it all with a pinch of salt, reading about how Actress X and Pop-star Y liked auto-asphyxiation, and he'd generally just put his lack of understanding down to the fact that he had nothing in his life to compare it to.

To him, Marky and Rachel's constant bickering and yelling and spending as much time pissed off with each other as making up for it was just their 'thing'.

"Look, man, call me indifferent if you like, but I'm sure the whole thing will blow over within a couple of days," he finally said, trying to comfort his mate without having any actual ability or knowledge of what he was doing. "You'll call her, she'll come back, you'll both shag each other's brains out and that'll be the end of it for another month."

Marky didn't seem as optimistic, which was worrying. Jack had always had the suspicion that one of the key reasons for Marky and Rachel's 'thing' working, was that neither of them actually knew about it. But the fact that he still couldn't see it happening now was more of a problem. As the case clearly seemed genuine, and in his anxiety to get Marky out of the house before he puked everywhere, Jack broke two of his lifelong oaths; firstly to interfere with a mate's relationship, and secondly, and perhaps more alarmingly, to do something about it on a Sunday.

"Look, mate. If you want, I'll go over there and try and sort it." He put his hand up to silence the inevitable reminder of a glaring flaw in his plan. "I know she doesn't like me, but I think that might help. Look, I'll go over there, tell her what a state you're in without her, and she'll realise that if it's bad enough for me to come and tell her, then it must be serious."

"I don't think she'll buy it, man. If you're gonna try that you should call her or something. But even then, she'll not believe you." Marky stole one of Jack's fags from his packet, a sure sign that this wasn't a drill or a hoax. Marky hadn't smoked since he was fourteen.

"No, I'll go and see her. I think it'll help. Plus, you know man, I've gotta start doing stuff on a Sunday. It's getting fucking annoying when I see the calendar and realise that my inexplicable childhood fears will prevent me from moving for a day." Jack dropped his half-smoked fag into his half-drunk tea, placed the cup casually on the floor, and began climbing the stairs back to his room to get dressed. Each step suddenly felt heavier, as though something inside him knew that he was about to go against pretty much all of his few moral principles. He never did anything on a Sunday, he never interfered with mates' relationships, Anna aside, why the hell was he changing now?

CHAPTER FORTY

Ralph rang the small bell by his bed furiously. The Major had given it to him to call for assistance when he needed it. He'd forgotten to mention, however, that his episode with the speaker system had left him partially, and probably selectively, deaf. His response times were measured in hours. Ralph had been ringing the damn thing constantly for about forty-five minutes now, and his hand had lost all will to effectively grip anything.

Eventually he gave up. He hadn't felt this bad since he'd invited a pair of visiting Thai businessmen over to view his work. At least that night had ended happily for all parties, even if both Orientals were now apparently HIV positive.

He looked down at his leg under the covers. The bandaging had been changed about six hours ago, but the smell had returned. The Major had said that it was nothing to worry about, that it was 'the smell of healing'. Ralph doubted it very much. He'd become interned in the spare bedroom of the Major's house for several days now, unable to leave, and he was getting quite distraught. He'd badly wanted to see a doctor and be treated properly, but the Major wouldn't hear any of it. Said that it was 'just a flesh wound' and that he'd be 'up and about in no time'. There had also been a comment about how he might have a limp, but that he should be fine with that by now, followed by the sort of dark chuckle you usually hear the villain in a Bond movie give as he tells 007 his plans to conquer/destroy/rule the world.

Finally Ralph heard the slow tramping and denounced muttering coming up the stairs, the sign that his call had finally been answered. It was accompanied, as always these days, by the energetic skipping of Betsy, who had returned to full health. And voice. She'd obviously discovered something in the garden that she disapproved of, and was not slow to make herself heard about it. Every night the incessant yapping began as it became dark outside, and would not stop until either she grew tired or morning came. The Major's new found lack of hearing seemed to be beneficial in this case too, as the few times that Ralph quizzed him about it, he'd had no idea what he was talking about.

The door opened and Betsy raced in first, scurrying over towards the bed, and hopping up enthusiastically. She hopped straight onto the bandaging on Ralph's bad leg, and following a cry that would have awoken the dead from the invalid tenant of the bed, hopped straight back off again and cowered behind her master's legs.

"There there, girl. Pay no attention to the decrepit layabout." The Major rubbed behind her ears while speaking, completely ignoring the look of murder in Ralph's eyes. "What is it now, Blakeney?" he demanded impatiently after tending to his pet.

Knowing full well that complaining about the dog would lessen his chances of getting any help, Ralph ignored the throbbing pain that had just surged up his leg, causing him to very nearly bite his lower lip clean off. "The smell's returned, I really want to see a doctor."

The Major looked to the heavens for any sign of salvation from the witless griper in the bed. "How many times, Blakeney, are we going to have this discussion?"

"As many as it fucking well takes for you to listen!" Ralph lost his temper. He'd had enough. He wanted out. Not just from the pain in his leg, but from the house, from the Major, from the hooligan next door and from the Close in general. "Can you not fucking see what's fucking happened?! My leg's green! It's fucking green! Please! I'm begging you, Get me the fuck out of here!"

The Major stared at him, completely nonplussed. "Would you mind not swearing in front of Betsy? She has a slightly nervous disposition."

Ralph goggled, how could this be happening? How on earth could the old twat be so pompous in the face of such obvious human suffering?

"Look," he pleaded, "Just take me to a hospital. I'll give them a fake name. I won't mention you, or anything that has happened here. I'll just say I was attacked by a bear or something? Oh for God's sake please!" he whimpered.

The Major studied him carefully. Having this whining fairy out of his way would be a blessing. Whether he could trust him or not was the question.

"All right, calm down. All right, Blakeney. I'll take you to a hospital. I won't take you to one around here, but I'll take you to a hospital." He stood there for a second, running over the pros and cons of his plan. It was now his intention to drop the nancy off at a hospital at least a hundred miles away from here. Blakeney could give all the false details he liked in any hospital near or far, it wouldn't matter to the hospital workers, they'd just patch him up and tell him to piss off, of this the Major was sure. What he was really worried about was if Blakeney gave anything away that could lead to suspicion towards him. That had to be avoided, so therefore the further away, the safer. Also, the next stage of his plan was due to start off tomorrow, and having an alibi that he was over a hundred miles away at the time might come in handy, as long as Blakeney could be contained. At a busy A&E unit in Manchester, Leeds or Liverpool, the staff wouldn't have time to listen to his ramblings about any 'incidents' happening in a quiet Close near the M40.

"Take this." The Major handed Ralph a small vial of clear liquid he'd had in his pocket.

"What is it?" Ralph asked suspiciously – the first time he'd ever cared about what drug he was taking in his life.

"It's a painkiller. Let's just say that the ride to the hospital might be a touch bumpy, this will ease that."

Ralph needed no further invitation, wolfing the little vial of salvation down in one gulp. The Major watched him as he sunk back down under the covers of the bed, losing consciousness by the second. He knelt down by his head just as the last grip on the world of the waking was being loosened.

"Badgers, Blakeney. Not bears. Badgers were what caused this. They had huge razor teeth and blood-red eyes. It was badgers."

"Badgers…" Ralph mumbled without moving his lips.

The Major left the room, satisfied that the drug would have the desired effect. He'd seen its potency first hand, when in the Army, while watching a biological weapons trial on some unsuspecting recruits. During the tests, the 'volunteers' were given half the dose he'd given Ralph, and then verbally given an image as they drifted off to sleep. In every case the volunteer would wake a couple of hours later screaming in terror and gibbering about whatever image he'd been given. Most had never recovered. The Major had recovered a small stash of the substance from the labs before it had all been destroyed, mindful that it might come in handy at some point.

He fumbled around in a box under his bed. "Ah, there they are, the old service issue." He smiled, looking at the pair of earphones left over from his time as an Artillery commander. The journey to Leeds would be noisy, that was for certain, and he wanted to make extra sure.

CHAPTER FORTY-ONE

Jack stared at the door in front of him in trepidation. He had no idea what he was about to do, or say. It appeared that this certainly was a task easier said than done. He'd been waiting there for about five minutes before he realised that if he didn't do something soon, one of the neighbours of this very plush area would be onto the Bill sharpish. He knocked quietly. Obviously no answer - a mouse would have made more noise. He knocked louder, and seized up when he heard the sound of movement from inside.

The door was opened by a small woman in her fifties, though she obviously wanted to conceal the fact. Jack tried hard not to smirk at the ridiculous amount of make-up on her face, and had even more trouble trying to not gag at the pungent reek of half a can of hairspray. His eyes gave him away though, and the cautious hospitality afforded by most people to strangers to their door disappeared from the woman's face immediately.

"Can I help you, young man?" she asked firmly, one hand secure behind the door, the other impatiently planted on her hip.

"Er, yes. Is Rachel in at the moment? Please? Thank you." Jack tried his hardest to sound polite, but years of avoiding conversations that required a degree of decorum had taken their toll, and his tone was fractured and insecure.

"Oh, so you must be the selfish pig who's abandoned my daughter?" The arm behind the door was now crossed over with the other in a defiant protective stance.

"Excuse me?" Jack replied, bewildered. *Marky hasn't even met her parents?! Jesus fucking hell, what am I doing here?!*

"You're not Mark?" She sounded slightly apologetic, but the defiance remained.

"Er...no, I'm a friend of his, and Rachel's," he lied, though he tried to make it sound as though he was just trying to be compassionate. "I heard about what...happened, and I wanted to make sure that she was alright." He stared at his shoes, afraid of the response he was about to receive.

"Well, obviously she's very distraught," the small woman began, as if she were about to launch into a lecture on how men could be inconsiderate of women's feelings and so on. Luckily, she saw that Jack was obviously insecure about being there, and relented. "I'll just get her for you." No invitation inside though.

Jack nodded slowly while still staring at the laces of his shoes. He definitely did not want to be here. This was why he didn't interfere with friends' relationships. Plus, moments like this one were hardly the greatest adverts for Sundays either.

He only looked up when he was sure that she had gone. In a way, he was glad that she'd forgotten to ask him his name. That could have been messy if Rachel had dismissed him via her mother without even seeing what he wanted. He heard the small woman call Rachel's name out, and listened fearfully as the sound of confrontation came hurtling down the staircase of the house.

He saw that she had the faintest trace of a smile on her lips as she turned into the hallway to the door, and the smile vanished as soon as she set eyes on him.

"What do you want?" she asked icily. As she reached the door, she crossed her arms and struck an identical pose of defiance as her mother had done not ten seconds earlier.

"I've...er...come because of Marky," Jack began. However, he wasn't allowed to get very far.

"How bloody typical. Not man enough to come and see me himself, he sends you of all people to plead on his behalf! Well you can tell that selfish wanker that he knows what I want, and I'm certainly not going to have that discussion through you!"

"Rachel, please." Jack tried again, as the door started to close in his face. "Marky doesn't know I'm here." That seemed to get her attention.

"What?" She asked suspiciously. "Why are you here then?"

"Because I'm worried about him." Jack continued, grateful that at least it seemed he would get a chance to plead his case, even if the trial would still be biased. "He turned up at my house last night. He was in a real state. Worst I've ever seen him." He wondered if he was playing the sympathy card a little too heavy-handedly, but then again, he had no idea what the fuck he was doing anyway, so it was worth a shot.

"What...what do you mean? Is he alright?" The coldness in Rachel's eyes was gradually replaced by concern.

"Not really. He drank heavily last night. Came over to my house and moaned about how things were all fucked up between you two. He was a mess, I've really been worried about him." Jack realised even as he said the last part that somewhere he'd made a mistake, as Rachel had now gone through the full spectrum, and was seething with rage.

"He got pissed?! We break up and he gets fucking bladdered?! I should have known it! And you come over here because you're worried about him? You shouldn't be coming to me, you should be calling AA or someone like that!" She was purple, and Jack was hastily planning his escape in case any nearby objects found themselves thrown at him.

"Rachel, seriously, he's ill. He needs you back..." Even now he knew it was futile. This woman had made up her mind, and now it was more a case of damage limitation.

165

"You know what's wrong with you two?" Rachel pointed at him lividly. Jack had a fairly shrewd idea that he was about to find out. "You two still think it's the fucking nineties. Getting fucked on lager and weed, going to Britpop gigs and generally caring about nothing but the next night out! Well it's no longer the nineties, and you're no longer nineteen. The both of you need to wake up and realise that it's time to grow up! Tell Marky if he can't handle that, then he can go and find some dumb tart to date instead, because frankly I've had enough of your childish attitudes. As for you...well...oh fuck it! You'll never learn until you get a job."

Jack was actually relieved when the door finally slammed in front of him. His ears felt like they were inside furnaces, and his mouth was as dry as a desert. What was he going to do now? Marky would kill him when he found out how this had gone, and Rachel would kill him if he tried to fix it after that verbal bombardment.

Bollocks to this, he thought. *I'm never getting out of bed on a Sunday again.*

CHAPTER FORTY-TWO

"So you understand the situation, Peter?" Graham took a contented sip of his coffee while he let the clergyman digest his story. He felt it fitting that Peter's sermon this morning had been on the subject of safer streets, and had taken the opportunity to discuss the situation with the vicar after the service.

"Well, yes, I suppose. And now you want this wayward soul shown the correct path of light?" Peter mused happily over the possibilities. He loved a challenge, and trying to turn young offenders in the Juvenile Institute towards the path of Christ was a large part of his working week. He had over two hundred successful conversions at that institute, 'more than Jonny Wilkinson' he used to joke at religious conventions. The idea of being able to get his hands on some real raw material from the rough end of town was more than a little appealing to him. Despite pleading every month with the bishop, he was never given the finances to set up any outreach centre in the Greenmeadow Estate. Now he had the chance to break into the social circles there with this young man and his problems.

"Absolutely, it is my belief..." Graham checked himself, reached out, and took Alice's hand in his. "It is *our* belief that this lost sheep has his heart in the right place, but merely needs the right guidance. Guidance that only someone like you, Peter, are in a position to give. We have tried, but to no avail, it needs a more experienced hand."

Alice was slowly seething more and more. Her husband could be a devious bastard when the mood took him, and this was his career high in the field. She hadn't forgiven AJ for what he'd done to her cat, but what he was about to receive from these two conspirators was cruel and unusual punishment indeed. If Graham had just asked the vicar, then all well and good, a visit from a man who firmly believed that his name was already on the canonisation forms waiting for his death was probably fair justice, but Graham had already made similar requests to half a dozen other religious groups around town before church this morning. Jehovah's Witnesses, Mormons, Methodists, Catholics and even an old friend who'd become fascinated by Scientology had been asked to visit AJ, and all of them at the same time tomorrow morning. Graham had already left a message on the answer machine at his work that he was ill and wouldn't be going in tomorrow, just so that he could watch.

"Is there anything else you think is important to add, darling?" Graham finally asked, a smile as wide as the Thames and concealing motives just as dark.

"Could I have a word with you, husband?" she replied frostily.

"Of course." Still the smile remained, even though Graham knew that Alice never addressed him as 'husband' unless she was really fuming about something. "Excuse us, won't you, Peter?"

"Of course, I'll just be over at the altar clearing up." The Reverend left the vestry and almost skipped up the aisle towards the head of the church, obviously excited at the prospect of tomorrow's calling.

"What the hell do you think you're doing?" Alice hissed at Graham once the vicar was out of earshot. "You'll cause a war sending all those people to his house! He doesn't deserve it."

Graham decided attack was the best way to defend his neatly laid plans. "Don't you care what he did to Joshua?"

"Oh don't give me that! Josh fell over playing football on tarmac, *he's* hardly to blame for that!"

"Oh, and what about Jadis? Did she deserve to be kicked in the ribs? Or did the glass deserve to be smashed against the wall?"

"Turn the other cheek, Graham," she replied straight-faced.

"Rubbish. This isn't some young scally trying to rip us off, he's a menace to society and a danger to our children!"

"Don't!" she snarled, surprising herself with the amount of chagrin she found in her voice. "Don't use our children as an excuse."

"What excuse? You've seen what they're like, do you really want young Joshua running around smoking and addicted to drugs?"

"You're being ridiculous, what do drugs have to do with this?"

"Everything, I don't want our children exposed to that sort of behaviour."

"When have you ever seen him taking drugs?!" Alice became more and more exasperated. "And anyway, you and I know perfectly well that Jack next door smokes cannabis regularly, yet you've never had much of a problem with it until now. Now that it's convenient to bring it up."

Graham had grown tired of the conversation. After nearly twelve years of a marriage where Alice had agreed with everything he said, the sudden exposure to contradiction was totally alien to him, and what was more he was having none of it.

"Alice, I am doing this with the best of interests at heart. I am thinking only of the safety of my children. If you can't accept that, then tough, you'll just have to sulk."

On any normal day, Alice would have buckled and submitted to her husband's will, as had been the case for the past dozen years. However, now that she had found a release for years of pent-up frustration at playing the obedient housewife, she wasn't about to let it go.

"I'll be at my mother's," she said quietly but with firmness. "I'm taking the children with me. You can call me when you grow up."

She trotted off before her astonished spouse could find the right words. As she sat down in the car outside, doubt crept in. *What have I done? I'm risking my marriage over some kid I don't even care about.* By the time she realised that she could have gone back and apologised, the car was already halfway down the road at twice the speed limit, racing towards home.

No, she thought. *I'll pick up the children, go to my mother's, and let him think about what he's done for a while.* The doubt still nagged at her as she pulled up next to her house, but it was now largely being ignored, as a new and almost exhilarating feeling of a little slice of freedom was tentatively taking root.

CHAPTER FORTY-THREE

"Have you even been to sleep yet?" AJ stood in the doorway to his brother's bedroom watching him hack some orc-like creature to death on his computer. It was well into the afternoon, and AJ had spent most of the night cleaning up the house before he had gone to bed.

"Nah, man. Gotta kill these fuckers. Gotta reach level twenty." He quickly gulped down a mouthful of cold coffee from a mug by the side of the computer, without breaking his stare at the screen.

"Christ, Wazza, you'll screw your eyes up or something." AJ shook his head as he wandered out into the hallway, ignoring a muttered reply from Wayne. He half-stumbled down the stairs and went into the front room to check that it was as tidy as he had left it the night before. It was not. Wayne had obviously been down to watch a film while he'd been in bed, and the smell of stale smoke and beer hung in the air. He looked down at the TV, there was an empty DVD case lying on the top with the word 'Hostel' on the front.

"Fucking hell, Bro, you'll have nightmares after watching this," he muttered to himself. He sniffed the air again, the smell was accented with that of smoked joints. "You'll have more than just nightmares," he muttered.

As he opened the curtains to let some light into the clammy room, he noticed that there was something hanging off the back of his car. It looked like a green rope of some form. *Shit, the dog!* He remembered.

"Wazza?!" He yelled up the stairs.

"What?" came the irritated reply from Wayne, expecting a row for his late night film-fest.

"Did you bring the dog back in?"

"No. Why, where is he?"

"Oh, bollocks." AJ began to worry. Having seen the evil state Vieira had been in the night before, there was a big chance that right now he'd gone off hunting for shoes, preferably ones that were being used.

"Bugger, bugger, bugger." He lit a cigarette and paced the hallway. This was a real problem. It wasn't just the fact that there was a mad dog on the loose, for that he could just call up the RSPCA or a vet. The problem was that Vieira was a Japanese Tosa, a rare descendant from a line of fighting-dogs, and a huge one at that. Legally banned by the Dangerous Dogs Act, possession of one without a court order meant problems. AJ had won him in a bet at a pub two years ago, when he was just a puppy. He'd never met the guy he won him off before, and had never seen him again. Back then, a friend of his had told him that he'd be better off getting caught with a gun, but he'd been smitten with the pup, and named him after Arsenal's then midfield hard-man in appreciation of the dog's infatuation with nipping people's ankles.

"Wazza, get the fuck down here now!" AJ was in no mood for pleasantries. Wayne sauntered down the stairs, taking as much time as possible.

"What now?"

"Vieira's gone missing. We gotta get him back." AJ put on his coat and picked up his keys.

"Why? Just let the pigs pick him up, I'm tired." Wayne began to slink back up the stairs, he'd reached level twenty now, and wanted his overdue sleep. AJ grabbed him by the collar and frog-marched him out of the front door.

"The state he was in last night, he's gonna do some serious damage to someone," AJ told him as they approached the car.

"Is he chipped?" Wayne asked.

"Is he what?"

"Chipped? You know, those little computer things they stick in their necks so when they go missing people know who they belong to."

"Of course he's not fucking chipped. He's a fucking illegal dog!"

"Right, so has he got a collar tag thingy?" Wayne stopped walking.

"No." AJ began to get annoyed.

"Well then no-one's gonna know where he's from, so we ain't gonna get into shit for it." He turned and went back to the house. He returned five seconds later to an unimpressed brother. "Give us the keys, then."

AJ handed them over in resignation. He'd always known that the day might come where he would have to give up Vieira, and while he never looked forward to it, due to the state the dog had been in the last time he'd seen him, leaving him was decidedly easier than he thought it would be. Wayne was right though, there was no easy way to trace Vieira's home or owner, and save for people who knew that he belonged to AJ, there wasn't much the authorities could do. Even the thought that they might put him down didn't really bother him anymore; the dog had threatened his kids, and therefore had crossed a line. As for any collateral damage to human limbs caused in the time period between now and his capture, AJ didn't care now either. The people in this area were all wankers and deserved it in his opinion.

"Alright, I'll be back in a minute, I gotta go warn Jack." AJ decided that he owed him at least that much for being the only guy in the postcode not to have wished him dead as soon as look at him.

CHAPTER FORTY-FOUR

Later that night an old beige Volvo was chuntering up the M1 with dogged determination. The sound of the wheezing engine, however, was drowned out by the blood-curdling screams from inside the boot. Ralph, strapped down to protect both him and the upholstery, had awoken from his drug-induced nightmare.

"For goodness sake be quiet will you!" The Major was decidedly annoyed. First, the weak-willed fop had woken up a full two hours earlier than he had hoped, then he had discovered to his horror that the leather lining on his old Army-issue earphones had been attacked by a horde of moths, rendering them useless. In fact he was beginning to believe that they were actually making the horrible noise louder.

Ralph continued his ranting regardless. It had started out with cries of fear at the sight of imaginary three-metre long badgers, but after a fluorescent yellow lorry overtook the car the screams had become all but nonsensical.

"Let me out! Argh! Leave me alone!" Ralph tried to kick out but for the thirteenth time in five minutes he realised that his legs were tied down.

The Major decided that he had had enough. It was still another hour and a half at least to Leeds, and a further hour on top of that to avoid the heavily populated areas where he would be almost certain to be caught with that racket going on in the background. He looked around at the motorway and surrounding area. It was largely rural farmland at the moment. There wouldn't be a better opportunity than this. He slowed the car down to as low a speed as possible without arousing suspicion, and waited while the trickle of other motorists dried up. When he was confident that there were no other cars around, he pulled up on the hard shoulder and flicked his hazard lights on.

"Be a good girl and stay." He patted Betsy on the head as he got out of the vehicle. She had been more that a little disturbed by the howls coming from the back of the car, and twice already she'd tried to drown them out with a chorus of her own, to no avail.

The Major stared at the sight before him through the back window of the boot. Ralph's leg stank to high heaven, and his body was contorted in a distinctly unnatural position. He'd eaten most of his hair, and there was blood trickling out of his mouth from where he'd broken a tooth trying to bite through one of the straps around his arm. For the first time since he'd first met him, the Major actually felt a twang of sympathy for the wretch. Actually it was less sympathy, more just pity.

"If I had a gun with me I'd do the humane thing," he mumbled apologetically as he opened the boot lid. "As it is, this should do the trick, though it'll be a darn sight messier." He untied the straps around Ralph's legs, being careful to avoid the inevitable kicking out that followed as soon as the limbs' owner realised that they were free. The Major warily untied Ralph's hands, and jumped backwards in anticipation. Ralph did not disappoint, after a few seconds of feeling his wrists, he hurtled out of the car and disappeared through the line of trees by the side of the road.

The Major was about to call out to him, but realised the futility of trying to tell a drugged-up lunatic to come back and run the other way, and he decided to make his exit as soon as possible. He'd been decidedly lucky that no cars had passed throughout the whole episode, and concluded that that sort of luck should not be wasted.

As he sat back down in the driver's seat, Betsy climbed up onto his lap, placed her front paws on his chest, and began licking him enthusiastically. He had thrown out the scary creature from the back. To her, he was a hero. He rubbed his pet behind the ears and rested his head back in appreciation of the new-found silence.

"Well, best be off then, eh girl?" He carefully placed Betsy back in her spot in the front passenger seat, and started the engine. After a few complaining grunts, the car pulled away smoothly. The Major decided that he would continue on as far as the next junction, turn around, then take a less high-profile route home. It wasn't that he was worried about the repercussions of what he'd done; as far as he could tell he'd done nothing wrong, it was more that he still needed to be away from the Close for most of the coming morning, and taking the back-route south would add another couple of hours on his journey time.

Ralph's foray through the trees and bushes would have been decidedly more painful than it actually was, had his dementia not meant he felt virtually nothing as he was scratched from head to toe while staggering through the plant-life. He stumbled down the bank on the other side, tripped, and landed face down in a freshly-laid country pancake. Half passing out for roughly the fiftieth time that day, the sound of the Major's car leaving startled him, and he looked up to see a giant bull staring back at him. At least ten feet high, and with horns that seemed to glisten in the moonlight, Ralph was now quite certain that he was in the presence of the Devil himself, and fled as fast as he could in no particular direction, shrieking in a disturbingly high-pitched voice for any number of Gods from various different religions to save him. The bull, having only that afternoon been introduced to four different in-season cows, was mercifully in no mood for chasing down the strange animal in his patch, and it sauntered off to try out the grass on the other side of the field.

Not sure and not really caring whether the Beast was following him or not, Ralph hurdled a barbed wire fence which happened to be giving off a buzzing sound, and kept sprinting once he'd picked himself up on the other side. His consciousness had returned to take over partial control of his actions, and he felt as though he were watching himself from afar. The physical Ralph was testing the world cross-country record, while the cerebral Ralph was wondering what the hell sort of a trip this was anyway. Out of breath, parched dry, and severely disorientated, the physical Ralph collapsed near a fence and lay panting while staring glassy-eyed at the stars. Cerebral Ralph had lost interest in what his body was now doing, and was currently joining the dots of the stars to make silly pictures.

Two hundred yards away, woken by a shrill squealing that sounded like a dying pig, the farmer who owned the land went downstairs to fetch his gun, convinced that he was being rustled.

CHAPTER FORTY-FIVE

"Ah yes, could I speak with Miss West, please?" The American twang in the accent grabbed Kathi's attention as she sat up in bed. At least it explained why she was being phoned at four in the morning.

"Yes, I'm speaking."

"Ah, Miss West, my name is Max Campbell. I'm the director of financial planning here at Tekkron, maybe you've heard of us?"

"Yes, I have. You've got an office in London, near Westminster," she replied. Of course she'd heard of them. They were one of the largest corporations in the City.

"Ah, good. Well, I'm sorry to call you so early in the morning. It's eight in the evening here and we only just finished a board meeting."

"That's alright," she lied. Since she lost her job she'd discovered that the extra couple of hours' sleep every night was a welcome silver lining, though she was impressed by the fact that this company held board meetings on a Sunday evening, which to her spoke of dedication.

"Yes, well. Like I say we've just been having a board meeting to discuss the proposed expansion of our business, and we've decided to take on a new team of personal financial advisors. There sure is a darn shortage of them here in Seattle."

"I see." She did not.

"Well, anyway, we've been liasing with our branch in London, and they recommended you for the position. We heard about the circumstances surrounding your...ah...dismissal, there's no problems there. We understand that you were made the scapegoat for liquidating a company that happened to be owned by a...er...hang on let me just check my papers. Ah yes, a Lord Tilburn. Frankly, Miss West, we're impressed that you had the hardiness to make that call, and we're looking for people like you to join us over here. People who can make difficult decisions and stand by them."

"Er...thank you." Kathi stuttered. It was the first opinion that she had heard about the incident that had been the same as hers. Just because a private company was owned by one of the Law Lords, it didn't mean that it didn't have to pay its bills. The whole situation had been a sham, and as she'd been the one to pull the plug, she'd been the sacrifice offered at the proverbial altar in appeasement to Lord Tilburn, after threats were issued that the rate of corporate taxation on financiers might suddenly leap up unexpectedly.

"Anyway, I'm flying over to the U.K. later this week, and I'll be in London for most of the trip, so what say we organise a meeting, just go over the general details of the post, and discuss any queries you may have?"

"Yes, that would be appropriate. Would you like me to prepare anything in advance of the meeting?" She began to slip back into the office-speak that she'd lost practice in these last few weeks.

"No, no. Just bring yourself and any details of what you'll need to move. We understand that leaving your country can be difficult, so perhaps it's best that we approach the problems head on straight away."

"Hang on, you want me to move out there? To Seattle?"

"Er...yes ma'am. Our new team will be based out here, but due to the nature of your knowledge of the British system there will be a lot of travelling to London and back involved. I hope this won't be a problem with you."

Kathi sat there silently for a couple of seconds. Was she really ready to up sticks and leave behind everything that she had known? The prospects of a job like this were astounding, and she knew that offers like this didn't come around often.

"I'll take it. I'll be at home for the first half of this week, so if you just call and let me know when you'll be in the City, that would be perfect."

"Alright then. May I just say that having seen your file myself I think you're really gonna enjoy it out here, and I think you've made the right decision. Goodbye now."

She hung the phone up without another word, and then sat in bed staring silently at the wall. America. Seattle. It sounded too good to be true. After being fired for being too professional, now she was being hired again in an even better job. On the one hand she could barely contain her excitement, on the other she could barely conceal her trepidation.

Tekkron were a big company alright. Everyone in financial circles knew about them. They were known as the sharks of the economic world, ruthless and efficient. That suited her perfectly. No more of the English 'jobs for the boys' mentality. Now she had a chance to work in a truly professional environment. There really was no decision to make. Having turned its back on her, now she'd decided that she was more than happy to turn her back on the English market.

She went through a brief list of people she'd have to tell about her moving. Her parents, obviously, though she wasn't really sure how it would change anything with them. She only saw them once a year, and even then hardly spoke to them. Also a few friends in the City, but that was more for gloating purposes. Aside from a couple of supportive former colleagues, there wasn't really anyone else. She realised that the thought should have made her sad, but in truth the more she contemplated her big move, the less she cared about everyone else.

Unable to sleep, she went downstairs to make a coffee. *Might as well get used to getting up at proper times again*, she thought. A million images ran across her mind as she waited for the coffee machine to pour her cup. She'd been to the States twice before. Once as a student, to see Wall Street – her version of sightseeing – and once on a business trip, which had lasted all of three hours before she'd been back at the airport boarding the return flight. Now she thought of virtually every movie she'd ever seen that was based in America, and the waves of different images make her almost giddy in anticipation.

CHAPTER FORTY-SIX

The Major watched as Betsy lapped up her bowl of cola energetically. The night shift staff at the service station looked on disapprovingly. The Major didn't care, he was peering over his road map, trying to plot his route home. Suddenly a thought hit him, and he picked up a leftover newspaper off one of the empty seats near him. Flicking through to the back pages, he found what he was looking for. 'Hapless England pray for washout' read the headline over the cricket news. According to the paper, which had been written on Saturday night, England were floundering in their test match against the West Indies at Trent Bridge, and could only hope for the poor weather forecast to help them scrape a draw from the game. It had bucketed it down throughout the Midlands most of yesterday, though the South had had one of the warmest days of the year. Therefore, provided the weather now improved, there was almost certainly going to be play today.

"Trent Bridge is only another hour's drive away, shall we go, girl?" he addressed Betsy, who was already feeling the effects of vast amounts of sugar in her drink. She wagged her tail enthusiastically in agreement.

The Major breathed a sigh of relief. He'd been pondering what to tell anyone who questioned him what he was doing halfway up the M1 at four am in the morning, and now he had his excuse. The test match in Nottingham was hardly likely to be sold out, but he felt he could play his 'old and absent-minded' card by pretending not to understand that and therefore wanting to get there early. Moreover, he was getting very tired, having not slept since Saturday night, and he could think of no better place to catch up with a comfortable nap than at a cricket match, not least one where one side would be trying desperately not to do anything.

"Well it's settled then, Betsy dear. We shall go and cheer on dear old England in the Test." The Major put the paper back where he found it and poked at his sandwich suspiciously. He never usually ate service station food, preferring to pack his own for long-distance journeys. However, this particular excursion hadn't exactly been thoroughly prepared beforehand and it had veered so wildly away from the initial plan that he had thought that just this one occasion wouldn't matter. Now he was feeling decidedly queasy, having only just had one mouthful of the sandwich, so he offered it to Betsy to see what she thought.

Betsy took one look and a quick sniff of the food and growled menacingly. There was no way she was touching that, it was growing new life. She finished her cola and hopped down from her seat, her little tail wagging furiously. She didn't quite understand why, but she felt like she could run all the way home without panting. The Major watched as she scurried off to investigate the few other people in the seating area. He then gathered the sandwich up in a napkin and went off to complain.

"Look here, I don't know what you call this, but it certainly isn't food," he began, staring up at the waiter behind the till, undaunted by the fact that he was dwarfed by the employee by a full foot. The waiter, who happened to be a new arrival in the country from Malaysia and who spoke very little English, stared back at him blankly, hoping that if he said nothing then this strange little man would go away.

"I say, answer me will you?! Even my dog won't touch it, I demand a refund immediately!" Still the waiter stared back impassively. The Major was turning red, after holding an officer's rank for his entire Army career, if there was one thing he hated, and one thing he was most definitely not used to, it was being ignored.

Just as he was about to explode into a rant about Johnny Foreigners, respect for elders and general common politeness, the Major's attention was drawn away by the sound of irate yells coming from a pair of truckers in the seating area of the diner. Betsy, her eyesight still somewhat inaccurate following her run-in with the double-glazing of the french windows back in the Close, had assumed that one of the trucker's shoes was a decent substitute for a lamppost, and had just finished watering it in her own way. While one of the drivers had found this hilarious, his colleague had naturally not been able to see the funny side, and was currently scrabbling around trying to catch the mobile watering-can to give her a piece of his mind. A job made considerably more difficult by the fact that Betsy weighed about eight pounds and could sprint twenty yards in a little under two seconds, while the trucker weighed nearer two hundred pounds and would have trouble completing a twenty yard waddle in less than two heart attacks.

"Betsy! Betsy, come! Good girl!" The Major rescued his dog from being squashed.

"Is that your fucking dog?!" The trucker wheezed, scrabbling around for a cigarette to calm him after having done more exercise in a minute than he usually managed in a year.

"Yes, she is, and I'd appreciate it if you didn't use such coarse language." The Major eyed him darkly. In his opinion people in this state of health, or lack of it, should be institutionalised.

"It fucking pissed all over my shoe! Look at it!" He screamed, unaware that the very few other people in the service station had started gathering around to watch. He stuck his leg out in front of the Major to show the effects of

Betsy's relief, and nearly fell over backwards as he lost his shaky grip on balance.

"Well I am sorry, but if you will let your legs get to be so thick then you can't blame a dog for mistaking them for lampposts. Now if you don't mind we have a long drive ahead of us and I need to get going." He took one more look of contempt at the speechless driver, "and by the smell of you, you need a wash anyway." he added, before marching out without a second thought.

By now, the trucker's co-worker had literally fallen off of his chair laughing, while the assorted spectators were either quietly nodding to themselves in agreement with the Major, or staring intently, hoping for a second act. Unfortunately for them, the exhibition was over, as the offended driver simply sat back down in complete disbelief, finished his smoke, immediately replaced it with another, and for the first time in twenty years he pushed his dinner away.

CHAPTER FORTY-SEVEN

Jack groggily reached out of bed and picked up his incessantly vibrating mobile from off his bedside table. He looked at the screen. *Marky. What the fuck do you want at this ridiculous hour?* He pressed the answer key.

"This had better be fucking good, it's nine in the morning for fuck's sake." he slurred down the phone, still half asleep.

"Oh I'm sorry Mr 'I don't have to go to work'. I've got news."

"Look, mate, if this is to do with you and Rachel, I can't be bothered to deal with it right now. Come round after work if you like, but I only got like ten hours sleep last night so I'm too tired at the moment." He went to hang up, but an unnatural squeal from the other end stayed his hand.

"No, wait, it's nothing to do with that. You know City got Liverpool in the cup draw last week?"

"Yeah...Again, I'm happy to take the piss out of your shite team, just not at this time of day."

"Nah, listen to this...Guess who just won two tickets to Anfield to see it?!" Marky couldn't contain his excitement. Jack, suddenly a lot more awake at the sound of his church's name, shot up out of bed as though he'd been electrocuted.

"Don't fuck with me, you got tickets to it?"

"Damn right I did. Won them on a phone-in last night. Was gonna tell you about it then, but what with you and your weird thing about Sundays I thought I'd leave it 'til today. Gonna get to watch the mighty City teach your show-ponies a lesson!"

Jack smirked. While he'd never hear the end of it if that were the case, he was confident that he wouldn't be the one leaving Anfield depressed.

"Anyway, so sorry for disturbing your mid-morning nap, you lazy knob. I'll come round this evening so we can celebrate, you know, start preparing you for the shock you're gonna get when we win!"

"Whatever mate. Anyway, see you later." Jack hung up, but now he couldn't go back to sleep. Why would he want to? He was going to Anfield! For a Cup game! Living as far away from Liverpool as he did, he didn't get to watch his beloved team nearly as much as he'd have liked, especially not at Home. He was on the waiting-list for a season ticket, but as the time-scale between applying and finally getting one was measured in decades, the only times he got to see them were either through friends who had spare tickets, or competitions.

After a few minutes further contemplation as to possible scores, line-ups, and most importantly, potential banter for Marky when City lost, Jack decided that there was nothing for it, he might as well get up.

"First time I've been up this early since school," he grumbled away to himself as he tapped a key on his keyboard to bring his computer back from its slumber. Seventy-four new e-mails. *Fuck's sake. Who keeps sending me all this junk?* He looked through the list, there were some pretty alarming headings by some of the messages. He had once made the mistake of giving his e-mail address in reply to what he thought at the time was a slightly dubious but tongue-in-cheek message from a hot-looking girl on a personal profiles website. As a result, nowadays he received anywhere between fifty and a hundred junk messages offering anything and everything from second-hand Lotuses to Viagra for less than four dollars. Inwardly he didn't really mind the junk mail, it had become part of his daily routine. Clearing out his inbox for him felt therapeutic, almost like a fresh start to each morning, before he happily went off doing bugger all for the rest of the day.

After a quick trip to shed his morning glory, Jack trotted downstairs to see what state he'd left his house in from the night before. After his dressing-down by Rachel yesterday, he'd avoided talking about the subject with Marky by the only way he knew how; beer, joints and console gaming. Seeing as they both knew about the football cup draw by then, they'd played some early tasters of the match, with Jack letting Marky win a few to keep his mind off his estranged girlfriend.

The sight of empty beer cans and dog-ends lying around didn't exactly delight him as he looked into his sitting room, but seeing as he was up and had the time, he decided to clean it up there and then. A very rare occurrence normally, but today seemed to be the day for breaking habits.

He fetched his vacuum from its hibernation in the cupboard under the stairs, and was just in the process of looking it over in bemusement when he remembered what AJ had said yesterday evening. That vicious dog had escaped, and that it was acting aggressively. Or in AJ's words, 'He's gone fucking mental man, and we can't find him. So look out when you go outside'.

"Fucking animal was always mental anyway," he muttered to himself as he finally found the 'on' switch to the vacuum. Just as he was about to turn it on and get started, the beeping sound of a large van backing up attracted his attention away. He looked out into the street to see what was happening, and saw a huge Royal Mail delivery van parked right outside AJ's house.

Subconsciously grateful for the interruption to his chores, Jack watched intently as a squat little man in a postman's uniform hopped out of the front of the van and trundled round to the back. After opening both doors, he hauled out two huge sacks that were virtually the same size as him, shut the doors, and began dragging one of the sacks towards the front of Number 1.

What's he gone and bought now? Jack had a fair few ideas. They were much the same as the ideas of things he wanted to buy when he first moved into his own house, and he chuckled at the silliness of some of them. Remote control Helicopters. Twenty-four man paintball kits. 2,000 CC quad bikes. They had been fun times, though his bank manager had disagreed.

This looked different though, there were seemingly no large crates or parcels, just these two sacks that looked as if they more likely contained people than paragliding equipment. He dismissed it with a shrug, reluctantly returning to his vacuum, when the sound of a car drew his gaze back out of the window. In fact it wasn't a car, it was a fleet of cars. A procession. All of them pulling up around the delivery van, blocking it and each other in.

CHAPTER FORTY-EIGHT

AJ opened the door to find a clipboard thrust into his chest. He looked down at it dubiously, then at the small round man who had handed it to him, then at the two large brown sacks that were sitting by his doorway.

"What the fuck is this?" He wasn't in the best of moods. After another fruitless search for Vieira, he'd gone off to his mum's flat to pick up his kids, only to have to drop them off at their mother's barely an hour later. He always found it difficult handing them back, but having spent so little time with them this weekend made the occasion particularly upsetting.

"If you'll just sign here, please. It's for these two sacks of post. There's so much of it that the office wanted the delivery recorded." The postman looked up at him disapprovingly.

"Yeah, OK, whatever." AJ didn't really care. He scribbled a doodle on the clipboard and began hauling one of the sacks through the doorway, while the postman turned around just in time to see a horde of various cars swarm around his van, preventing him from leaving.

"Can you get those people to move their cars so that I can get out please?" The postman looked aghast. He'd been up since four am sorting out this kid's mail, and was anxious to get home.

"Er...no. Sorry mate I don't know any of them," AJ said dismissively after briefly looking up at the scene for barely a second. He grasped at the end of a piece of string that was hanging off the top of the larger sack. Before the postman could tell him not to, he gave it a sharp tug and the bulging bag blew open ferociously, spilling its contents everywhere.

Letters of all shapes, sizes and colours formed a mini paper fountain for a second as they all made bids for freedom in different directions.

Meanwhile the drivers of the fleet of cars were all approaching AJ's house at various speeds. Some carried large books which appeared to be bibles, others handfuls of pamphlets, while one had a briefcase. Seemingly recognising each other, to a man they quickened their pace towards the door in a bid to arrive first, until it became a virtual race as they jostled to be first in line.

AJ was now watching the approaching squad with a look of bewilderment. He didn't know any of these people, yet they all seemed extremely anxious to meet him. The frontrunner was a tall imposing man with thick-rimmed glasses, a white collar, and a very determined look. He thrust his hand out in front of AJ as a greeting, almost barging past the frustrated postman as though he hadn't seen him.

"Mr Johnson?" he demanded.

"Er, yeah. Who are you?" He took the man's hand weakly, watching him tread obliviously all over the pile of letters on the porch, much to the postman's chagrin. Not that AJ cared.

"I'm here to save you. Tell me something, young man, do you know Jesus?" He glared straight at AJ poker-faced, his eyes magnified to disturbing proportions by the thick glasses.

"Ah, yeah. He used to live across the road from me in the Greenmeadow. Nice guy, dodgy beard though." AJ grinned, not exactly happy that this ominous figure seemed to be trying to get into his house, but smug at his joke.

"My boy, I'm serious. Do you believe in the one Christ?" Again the stare.

"No. But there's a family across the road who'd love to meet you…" AJ was cut short.

"Then I'm afraid that you are going to Hell. He who does not accept the Christ as his saviour is doomed to eternity..." Now it was the large bespectacled man's turn to be interrupted, as a smaller man, with equal fire in his eyes, barged in front of him to have his turn.

"Mr Johnson, I believe you have not been baptised?" The small man asked with mock pity.

"Not been what now?" AJ didn't know where to look, new arrivals were now flanking the current owner of the temporary soapbox that was AJ's porch, all of them trampling over the letters. The postman was by now having a nervous breakdown, and AJ was quietly lighting a cigarette while he watched the whole scene unfold as though it wasn't him they were talking to.

"Mr Johnson, did you know that your Theton Levels are dangerously high?"

"Mr Johnson, are you aware that when Christ returns to Earth to rule in Zion on the American continent that your soul cannot be saved unless you turn to the true path?"

"Mr Johnson, have you found spiritual enlightenment?"

"Mr Johnson, we are still waiting on your tax return forms."

In the garden next door, hidden in the shrubbery, two blood red eyes watched the scene unfold with considerable interest. Having destroyed an entire warren of rabbits over the last day and a half, Vieira thought he'd had his fair share of hunting for the time being, but seeing his master seemingly under attack from this strange collection of humans had ignited a protective spark in the dog's hitherto scrambled senses.

Certain that the human who he seemed to remember used to feed him was under attack from a rival pack, Vieira tore through the shrubbery, dragging most of it behind him, and launched himself into the throng of people with his trademark terrifying cacophonous barking. The associated members of various religious orders didn't have a moment to react. One second they were just about to turn on each other for their differing beliefs, the next they were crashed into by a beast of considerable size at high speed. They collapsed like a row of skittles, some screaming in shock, some screaming in pain, and some just screaming for help.

Despite their different creeds, to a man they all believed that the Devil/Xenu/Spirit of bad Karma had come to strike them down, and they all scrabbled around trying to escape to their cars. Here the deeper-lying distrust for each other's beliefs came to its full fore, as Catholic pushed Buddhist to the ground, Methodist tripped Scientologist in an effort to gain vital yards, Mormon was rugby tackled by Jehovah's Witness who wasn't about to be left behind on his own.

Three people escaped the fracas relatively unscathed. AJ quietly closed his front door and went off to watch TV, not really caring what happened. The postman hid beneath the pile of letters as soon as the attack started, then made his escape while the animal was chasing down the herd of theologians. Finally, the man with the briefcase, who was a tax-inspector, shinnied up a drainpipe and dug in.

The whole incident was watched by a pair of spectators who couldn't take their eyes off what was happening, for very different reasons. Jack spent most of the time in hysterics at the scene, while next door Graham Hamilton was spitting venom. This had definitely not gone as he'd intended.

CHAPTER FORTY-NINE

"I'm telling you I wasn't trying to steal your fucking cows! How the hell could I anyway?" Ralph sobbed. His wretched night had gone from bad to worse in the last few hours after he'd been dragged at gun-point through two hundred yards of mud and shit by a fanatical farmer, convinced that his herd was in danger. Now he found himself tied up, again, to a heavy wooden chair in the dingiest of sheds he'd ever laid eyes on. The irate country bumpkin was now sitting opposite him, still pointing the gun menacingly, trying his hand at imitating a Gestapo officer.

"You'll not be having owt away tonight, laddie." The bushy white eyebrows slanted angrily. Ralph wouldn't have been quite so exasperated had he been able to understand even half of what the Northerner was on about. He didn't quite know what was more worrying, the fact that some deranged old farmer was pointing a gun at him with apparently no interest in excuses, or that his accent seemed to indicate that Ralph was nowhere near his home, the Close or civilisation in general.

A door in the darkness away to his side creaked open, and a plump middle-aged woman bustled in. She was carrying a mug of tea and a look of scorn.

"Has he confessed yet?" She spoke purposefully, while handing the tea to the man whom was seemingly her husband. "Hanging's too good for the likes of him. Stealing our livelihood an' all." Him was Ralph, and Ralph was beginning to wonder if everyone north of the Wash was as thick as the cowpat that was still clinging to his face.

"Please believe me! I don't want to steal your cows. I just want to go home!" He began to wail. The briefest of glances between his captors suggested that maybe they were starting to get the message.

"Then tell me how you got out here then." The farmer crossed his arms, gun and all, sitting back awaiting a story.

"I've told you, I don't know. I don't even know where I am. Where the fuck am I?!" He looked around the large dark shed deliberately as if to emphasise his point.

"You're about five miles away from Dodford. I take it you're not from around here, then?" the wife chirped up while her husband looked curiously at his tea, evidently unhappy at the lack of sugar in it.

"Do I fucking sound like I'm from around here?! Where the hell is Dodford?" He regretted his outburst as he finished it. The gun was back pointing at him.

"Mind your language, laddie. There's no call for it."

"Oh, forgive me." Ralph replied sardonically. "I didn't realise that it was common courtesy to be polite towards kidnappers." He tried what he thought was a dark look. It seemed to merely amuse his captor.

"You're a weird one. Mind you I s'pose coming from down South it's no surprise, you're all idiots down there." He thrust his mug of tea out to his wife. "Sugar, woman!" His wife scurried out irritably with the mug.

"Quite," Ralph muttered. "So could you at least tell me where Dodford is then?"

"Just told you, about five miles away, as the crow flies, and there's plenty of them…"

"No!" Ralph yelled then instantly looked sheepish apologetically. He spoke softly "I mean where's the nearest large town or city?"

"Ah right, that'll be Barnsley. About twenty miles from here. I've got to go in later today for the market. Good thing I caught you when I did else I'd have nothing to market, eh?" He grinned at his joke. Ralph hid a variety of dark thoughts behind a fake smile in response.

"Barnsley?! Where the fuck is that?" Aside from his haunting recent trip to Liverpool, Ralph had never travelled north, avoiding crossing the midlands like the plague, and as such his geography of the area was more than a touch poor.

"You must be a right cretin. Yorkshire!" The farmer seemed genuinely insulted by his captive's ignorance.

"Oh my God." Ralph wondered how the hell he'd got up here. His memory was a blur. He could remember being attacked by a giant badger, and then subsequently nearly crushed by some weird giant yellow metal monster. While he was still scared shitless by both images, the sight of those two gun barrels pointed straight at him had a galvanising effect on his focus. He couldn't take his eyes off them, nor his mind, and in a way he was slightly thankful for that, as the images in his head were terrifying.

"Well, I doubt you're a rustler then. Everyone knows Barnsley if they know cattle." The farmer looked studiously at Ralph. "The question, then, is what *are* you doing up here?"

"I don't know. I really don't," he pleaded. "I don't remember how I got here, and I really want to go home. Do you think you could take me? I'd pay you obviously..."

"Do I look like some sort of fucking taxi service?!" The farmer exploded, leaping to his feet in anger. As he did, he inadvertently pulled one of the triggers on his gun. The shots flew straight into the floor, but a couple of the pellets bounced back up and found themselves embedded in the nearest object in their flightpath. That object happened to be Ralph's wounded leg, and after having a mild heart attack at the shock from the sudden sound of the gun blast, fresh pain surged up his body.

The farmer was unaware that he'd hit anything, or anyone, and was staring at the gun bemusedly, when he noticed that Ralph had begun foaming at the mouth. He prodded him carefully, before untying his hands. As the rope fell to the floor, so did Ralph's unconscious body.

"What did you have to shoot him for?!" the farmer's wife grumbled as she handed his tea back, two spoonfuls of sugar heavier.

"I didn't hit him I don't think. He just started dribbling everywhere. Don't know what that bandage on his leg is all about either." He took a swig of his tea, contented that it tasted adequate.

"These Southerners," his wife tutted. "Did you find out if he was a rustler or not then?"

"Don't think he is. God knows what he's doing up here."

"Well you might as well take him to the hospital then. That bandaging reeks to high heaven. You can drop him in later when you go to market."

"Aye. Meantime I've got to get on; cows don't milk themselves."

CHAPTER FIFTY

The splintering chime of breaking glass rung through the room, breaking the silence for a split second. Graham wasn't usually a violent man, in fact not since puberty had he let any real raw emotion break out of his control, but today he was truly pissed off, and he had banged his fist down on the dining room table so hard that a glass on the edge had jumped off in an ill-advised bid for freedom. His plan had failed. On paper, sending a half a dozen overbearing religious zealots into the domain of ungodliness that was Number 1 Appletree Close looked like a winning solution. In his mind when concocting the idea, Graham had imagined their constant bickering with both each other and AJ would drive him mad, infuriating him to the point of mental breakdown. In reality, after watching the debacle unfold before his eyes in ever-increasing disbelief, he'd looked at AJ's face as the front door was closed, and even from across the road, he could tell that the youth hadn't been in the slightest bit bothered.

It was only now, after most of the cars had driven away, crunching each other as they barged through the bottleneck that was the entrance to the Close, that Graham had been able to look back out at the aftermath. There was one car left, its owner had one foot perched precariously on the small ledge jutting out over the front door of AJ's house, and one hand gripping the drainpipe. He was furiously engaged in an animated phone call on his mobile while the beast sat patiently below him. Twice the poor tax inspector had nearly fallen off the ledge due to excessive gesticulation, and both times the dog had jumped up enthusiastically in an effort to help him down.

Graham sat wondering what to do next. The arrival of that animal had certainly been fortuitous, but it hadn't seemed as though its absence would have made a difference, such was the apparent disinterest from AJ. He'd obviously gone about this the wrong way. He'd tried the indirect approach, and while admittedly it had been a touch underhand for his tastes, its spectacular failure prompted thoughts of a shift in tactics.

"I'll get that little bugger, and I'll do it myself if necessary," he muttered to himself. It was time for a more aggressive attitude. But how? He couldn't confront him directly, that would probably just provoke a belligerent reaction from the youth. What he needed was a way to antagonise AJ and force him out without him knowing it was happening. Graham now knew that he needed AJ to think of the option to leave, rather than have it offered to him only for him to reject. He needed to come to the decision himself. *It's hopeless,* he thought. *Whatever I do will be too strong and implicate me, or too subtle for that thick yob to understand.*

A wail of sirens and the eye-catching urgency of flashing blue lights interrupted his pondering. He looked out of the window to see an assortment of emergency services vehicles pulling up outside. A pair of police panda cars escorted a fire engine, with an ambulance and pet control van following close behind, in a brisk procession up the street, before unnecessarily skidding to a halt outside AJ's house.

Vieira was at first startled by the arrival of this procession of noises and lights, but after a brief growl at the tax inspector to make sure that he didn't try to escape, he wandered over to sniff out this curious new development. He trotted up to the nearest vehicle, which happened to be the lead panda car, ironically occupied by the same two officers who'd left their smell in the Close not two days ago when they'd come over to see his master. Neither of them seemed very keen on getting out, which Vieira thought was a bit rude. He'd come over to greet them and sniff their arses, surely the least they could do was get out and let him. He tried his own brand of encouragement by barking heavily, jumping up and putting his front paws on the side of the car.

"Fuck, Jesus, bollocks!" A startled Constable Miggs squawked at the sight of a gargantuan canine that was obviously trying to break its way into the car. "I knew there was something dodgy about this place!" He fumbled around his belt for his mace, but then decided that opening the window to use it would be a pretty silly idea.

"Better tell the vet. That thing looks like it'll need enough tranquillisers to floor an elephant." His partner looked worried. When the station had received a call out from an apparently 'hysterical' tax inspector and this address had been mentioned, they had both not been too bothered, suspecting another hoax. What had greeted them was in fact the largest hound ever to set foot west of the Ural Mountains of Siberia, and the gaze in its evil eyes looked as though it belonged in that inhospitable wasteland too.

Afraid to leave the car for fear of being shredded, all the emergency services personnel in the Close held a short conference over their radios to work out the best option. The fire and ambulance servicemen were adamant that they weren't leaving their respective vehicles until the beast was subdued, or preferably dead, and their view was shared by Constable Miggs and his partner. The vet was in favour of sedating the animal, as she didn't believe in needlessly killing animals, but she insisted that she wasn't doing it on her own. The suggestion was to call out the armed response unit 'to be on the safe side' according to Miggs, but he was told by the station to 'grow up' and that 'highly trained armed response squads are not here to shoot pooches'.

While the discussion about who should try to deal with the canine conundrum continued, Graham Hamilton made a snap decision. He had realised now that he would have to suffer for his cause, and that there wouldn't be a better opportunity than this. He had to do this, to win back his home, his wife, and his life. Without stopping to consider how ridiculous his plan was, he opened the front door and strode out towards the first police car. The officers in the car didn't see him at first, but thankfully for his sake, the vet did. After a couple of seconds of fierce protestations through her near-soundproof van windows, the vet realised immediately what was about to happen, so she scrabbled around on the passenger seat for her tranquilliser gun and hurriedly loaded a dart into the chamber.

Too late though. Graham had managed to get to within three metres of the squad car by the time Vieira noticed him. Bounding towards him with a fresh vigour, he launched himself at this new stranger. Graham just stood still, closing his eyes and bracing himself for the impact. He never felt it. The vet had wound down her window, aimed, and missed. Well, she missed Vieira, but succeeded in hitting Graham, right in the neck. The tranquilliser was a particularly potent one too, designed to be ultra-fast acting. Graham was out for the count before his head hit the front lawn.

Vieira was puzzled by this development, but lost interest immediately in Graham. He wasn't about to interact with a body lying on the ground. After deciding that there was nothing much else to do, he wandered off through the bushes near the Hamilton household and away onto the golf course. He'd completely forgotten about the tax inspector, but the scent of rabbit had caught his nostrils, and it *had* been well over an hour since his last vermin-hunting foray.

CHAPTER FIFTY-ONE

"Boom, headshot!" Jack fell about the floor laughing after he saw Graham drop to the ground like a bag of wet cement. This morning had been better entertainment than watching Australia lose a match of any sport whatsoever. Marky looked out of the window where the emergency services were tentatively getting out of their cars to deal with the casualty.

"What was that fucking animal anyway? Looked like some giant Labrador on speed or something," he muttered while glancing around to see if he could see it.

"Oh AJ's dog. Vieira I think he's called. Mostly harmless." Jack got up, noticed that the fun had stopped for the moment, and went off to put the kettle on.

"Mostly harmless?!" Marky followed him out looking bemused. "What'd you call harmful?"

"Dunno, if he'd started eating the body maybe that'd qualify. You want a brew?" Jack fished around for a mug in the cupboards. He owned nearly fifty mugs, just a habit he'd picked up through amassing them from various holidays, and yet finding a clean one was rather less easy than finding syphilis on the moon.

"Christ, man. Don't you ever do any washing up? Or do you just buy new stuff when everything gets too dirty to use?" Marky looked around the kitchen disapprovingly. Jack's sheepish look confirmed his disbelief. He knew that his standards were poor, increasingly so now that Rachel had left him, but this kitchen looked as though it was two evolutionary stages away from intelligent life.

"Tell you what, I wouldn't half like to get to know that vet though, she was fit." Jack tried to change the subject as he reluctantly scrubbed the scum from off two of the less filthy mugs he could find.

"Well if her choice of men's as poor as her aim, you'd be well in with a chance. Gotta agree though, I'd give her one, easy." Marky was having second thoughts about his cup of tea.

"Yeah well you're not giving anyone one for a while. You need to get your missus back and you need to do it soon."

"I know, I know. Can we just please change the subject, we went over this last night already. Anyway you never told me what she said to you yesterday." Marky stole one of Jack's cigarettes, two new habits he had formed, both of which were starting to get on Jack's nerves.

"How come you're here anyway? You said you had work all day." He tried to deflect the conversation away.

"Oh, slow day. Nowt coming in 'til the afternoon so I thought I'd drop over. Kind of handy too, the boss is ill and won't be in 'til tomorrow, so it means I get to get paid for spending such quality time with you." He pinched Jack's cheek. Jack swatted his hand away. He wasn't in the mood for sarcasm.

"Anyway, while we're on about women, how's things going with you and that bit of fluff from across the road? You got anywhere with her yet, or are you doing your usual incompetent fucking dithering about?" Marky looked at the tea that Jack had handed him, it looked a bit too dark brown for his taste. While Jack turned away he threw the contents of the cup down the sink.

"I'm not telling you that, you'll only broadcast it in some local fucking newspaper the first chance you get." Jack tried to look sincere but his silly grin gave him away.

"Wahey, nice one, lad. She any good?"

"Wish I could remember. It was the other night, you know the one where you had your little 'accident'."

Marky's smile disappeared completely. "Ah don't worry, I've not told anyone. Anyway it was that night."

"You seen her since?"

Jack looked at Marky's mug, then at the dirty brown water trickling away down the plug in his sink, and figured out what had happened. He threw his tea away too. "We should probably go to the café round the corner," he agreed as he waved away Marky's apologies before he could offer them. "And no, I haven't seen her since, but come on mate, it's only been a day."

"Two." Marky corrected him.

"Well one and a half, whatever. Still, it's hardly that long." He put on his leather jacket in the hallway. It wasn't particularly cold out, but he did sense that if that bloody dog were still around he'd need a bit of protection.

Marky followed him out of the front door with a thought. "Hey, what are we gonna tell the fuzz if they pull us?"

"Pull us?" Jack asked with a sceptical look. "We're not in a frigging nightclub."

"No, you know what I mean, If they wanna question us about that dog."

"Oh, I dunno. Just say you've never seen it before."

"Fine. If that's the case, how come we're standing out here, pissing about waiting to be viciously attacked by the fucker?"

Jack and Marky looked at each other quickly. Then they ran towards Marky's van, spurred on by what they thought was a deep growl coming from the nearby garden of Number 6.

"Open the fucking door!" Jack yelled as he discovered that the passenger side was locked.

"I'm fucking trying!" Marky retorted as he fumbled about inside his pocket for his keys. After finally finding them, they were just getting in when Constable Miggs noticed them.

"Hey, you two!" The policeman called to them. They ignored him. "Stop! Police! Stop!"

"You were right, they wanna talk to us." Jack said as he put on his seatbelt.

"Yeah, well I've got to get back to work later, and spending half the afternoon at the local nick is gonna screw that up." He started the van and screeched away across the front lawn of Number 6 in order to avoid the gridlocked little road full of emergency services vehicles.

CHAPTER FIFTY-TWO

"That was close," Jack mused over his cup of tea, which in his opinion wasn't much cleaner than the one he'd just thrown away back at his house.

"Close?!" Marky asked incredulously. "Close is when you get away! They'll be round here in a minute with a search warrant and fuck-off big truncheons."

"Ah well. Gives me something to do this afternoon. Seriously though, they're not gonna arrest us you don't think?"

"Nah. They'll just want our opinion on your lad across the road and his evil pet." Marky sipped his cup of tea, and stole another of Jack's cigarettes.

"Fucking buy your own will you?! Anyway if that's all they want, what did we run off for? We could have just said we'd be back later."

"I don't fancy talking to a copper. They're annoying little wankers, always trying to pin something on you."

"This isn't fucking Manchester, where everyone has a gun in their car." Jack laughed. He had doubts about the so-called gun crime reputation of Manchester himself, having never been there, and Marky's suspicious reaction supported his belief that most of it could be put down to police heavy-handedness, and trying to look hard.

"Ah well. You can tell them what you like later. Personally I also didn't like the idea of talking about that knobber over the road to them."

"It's weird, I've never been in a police car before. I've never even been in a station before either," Jack mused distractedly. "What? Oh." He realised what Marky had said. "Still don't like him, then?"

"Well no, it's not that. He's probably got a good heart on him, but you know, the way he dresses, for fuck's sake. And the way he talks. The way he acts, the music he listens to, the car he drives. Shit like that." He stubbed his smoke out irritably.

"Come off it man, you can't judge someone for the car they drive!" Jack tried to reason.

"That's not true. I'd not trust anyone who drives one of those weird VW hippie vans."

"No, okay, fair point. But realistically, it's all superficial. He's just...different, you know, to us." Jack tried to think of the right words, but found himself tongue-tied. "I mean, he probably thinks the same about us."

"Eh?" Marky looked confused.

"Well don't you see? He likes underground, we listen to indie. He drives a shit car with a cool stereo. You drive a nice van with a shit stereo. Seriously man, that thing spews out more white noise than a grunge concert, you gotta get it fixed."

Marky nodded distractedly. A police car had passed by slowly outside, though it hadn't seemed to notice his van, which he'd parked around the back to buy them some time.

"And anyway, it's not as if he's French or anything. He's not all that different from us. Just a twenty-something-year-old lad living in suburbia."

"Why do you have to keep defending him?" Marky demanded. Jack's constant sticking-up for AJ had initially just been a minor irritation, now it was getting annoying.

"I suppose I feel sorry for him, to be honest. I mean it's not the 1940's anymore; where the rich were rich, the poor were poor, and the only time they ever crossed paths was when the rich sent the poor off to die in wars. He's not done anything wrong for fuck's sake!"

"No well, maybe you're right," Marky eventually submitted. He was getting tired of arguing about it, particularly as it wasn't a subject he was very interested in in the first place.

"Good. Now, on to more pressing matters. What are you doing about Rachel?"

"Oh not this again." Marky put his head in his hands wearily.

"Yes, this again. Come on, man. She's the best thing that ever happened to you, and apart from sending me off to get my head bitten off, you've done nothing about it."

"She had a go at you?" Marky hadn't heard about this, and Jack regretted saying too much.

"Er...yeah. Sorry mate, it all went tits up." Jack looked timidly at his feet under the table.

"Fuck it, my hopes weren't high anyway." Marky gave a sigh, before trying to pinch another cigarette. Jack made no attempt to stop him this time, conscious that he'd probably just upset an already depressed man.

"So that's it? You're not gonna try?"

"She'll calm down in a while. She'll come back eventually, she always does," Marky mumbled to his cup of tea.

"I dunno, she sounded pretty adamant when I spoke to her."

"That's what I was afraid of."

Jack looked confused. "But didn't you just say she'd be back?"

"I was trying to convince myself, not you." He drained the remnants of the cup and gestured to the waitress for another. "I dunno what I'm gonna do without her, mate. The house seems so empty, you know? I come home from work, she's not there. I go to bed, she's not there, I get up..."

"Yeah, I get the picture."

"It's killing me, man. It's fucking killing me. I've not been single since I was nineteen, it's weird man, it's kill..."

"Killing you, yes I got that too. So we need a scheme then."

"A scheme? What sort of scheme?" Marky asked suspiciously. Jack's schemes were not marked with the highest success rate, and his contingency plans when everything invariably went wrong usually involved nothing other than retreating to the Rosebush with a fresh pair of twenties in his wallet.

"Some big gesture springs to mind. She said you needed to grow up, well actually what she said was that we both needed to grow up and stop living in the nineties, but anyway, I think you need to prove to her that you're ready to commit to her."

"Alright, how?"

"Fancy buying a ring?" Jack asked. He wasn't hopeful.

"Not really."

"Okay...we'll have to think of something else then."

CHAPTER FIFTY-THREE

"It's alright, sir. It's safe for you to come down now." Miggs beckoned to the distraught tax inspector who was still clinging rigidly to a drainpipe that was rapidly losing its structural integrity.

"Have you caught that beast?!" The inspector screamed back in anxiety. "I'm not coming down until you've killed the fucking thing!"

"It's all under control, sir. If you'd just like to come back down so that the paramedics can attend to any injuries you may have." Miggs stood to the side to let a pair of nervy firemen prop a ladder up against the wall next to the drainpipe. All the emergency services personnel in the Close were keeping one eye on any sudden movement in gardens and bushes, but for the time being the animal seemed to have disappeared. As such, they had tentatively gone about their jobs, mindful that the sooner their task here was complete, the sooner they could leave.

Miggs had tried again to call in armed backup and had initially only succeeded in receiving a further ear-bashing from his superiors for being a 'drama queen'. Finally Control had agreed to send a pair of police marksmen who had nothing better to do round to investigate, on the understanding that unless the dog actually attacked anyone, Miggs would stop pestering them. The car had arrived a few moments earlier, and the sharpshooters were obviously keen on making a big day out of the whole scenario. One of them had positioned himself on top of the fire engine with a clear view of the whole Close, while the other was busy wandering around the various gardens behind the houses searching for the beast. Every now and then he would yell: "Contact!", and everyone in the road would run for cover, only to see a smirk on the other sniper's face and get increasingly annoyed at the sick game they were obviously playing.

"We're not the bleeding SAS, mate." The sniper on top of the fire truck grinned as he said to Miggs finally. "We don't yell out 'contact' when we see something."

"So what do you do then? Just shoot on sight I suppose?" Miggs had asked snidely. He had once tried out for the Armed Response Squad but had been turned down on the grounds that he couldn't shoot straight.

"If we've got the order to, then, yeah. Other than that we wait for the order, then we shoot on sight. We're snipers for fuck's sake, not commandos."

Miggs walked away with dark thoughts about people who thought they were high and mighty simply because they carried guns. "What is it now?" he asked one of the fireman through the din of the tax inspector who had started wailing for his mother again.

"He says he won't come down until he's sure that the dog is dead. To be honest, mate, I feel pretty much the same. That thing looked well wrong." The fireman pulled the zipper up on his jacket and crossed his arms as if underlining his point.

Miggs ground his teeth in irritation. He had to get the civilian to safety before he could proceed with any proper investigation. A thought struck him, but he dismissed it instantly as being ridiculous. However, the longer he stood there impatiently listening to the bawling from the tax inspector, the more it struck him as being worth a shot. Literally. He walked back over to the fire engine and called up to the sniper who was fiddling around with the scope on his rifle for no apparent reason.

"Hey, mate?"

"What?" The sniper continued fiddling, disregarding Migg's presence.

"Do me a favour would you?" Miggs whispered so no-one else could hear. "Radio your parter and tell him to fire off a shot into the air for me could you?"

"You what?!" The marksman looked at him goggle-eyed.

"Tell him to fire off a shot in the air. This guy over here on the drainpipe has lost it. He won't come down until he's sure the dog's dead, and if your mate lets one off and then calls out that he's killed it, we can get the guy out of here and continue with the investigation." Miggs looked pleadingly at him, inwardly cursing himself for having to speak to the arrogant knob.

"Alright, I don't see the harm in that." The sniper laid down his rifle and put his radio to his ear. "Charlie, come in Charlie?"

The radio crackled back at him.

"Charlie, let one off in the air. No I'm not having a laugh, let one off in the air. Don't hit anything though for crying out loud. Then radio in when you have. Yes I know I'll be able to hear it from here, just let one off and radio it in, I'll explain when you get back."

A single crack sounded from behind the back of Ralph's house. Everyone was silent, then the radio crackled again. The sniper on top of the fire engine listened in, then looked at Miggs and nodded.

"Alright now, sir. We've just been told by Armed Response that the dog has been neutralised." Miggs craned his head back as he addressed the tax inspector, who only seemed more nervous by the sound of the gunshot. "You can come down now, sir. Let these nice gentlemen from the Fire Department help you down the ladder and we can take you away from here."

The idea of leaving seemed to galvanise the tax inspector, and he gingerly climbed down with more assistance that was really necessary. As Miggs watched the paramedics lead him away to the ambulance, he nodded a grudging thank you to the sniper, then turned to face AJ's door. He rang the bell, took a deep breath and drew himself up to his full height.

"What do you want?" AJ asked disinterestedly after answering.

"Could I have a word with you about everything that's happened here just now, *sir*?" Miggs eyed him darkly. He'd got him now for sure.

CHAPTER FIFTY-FOUR

The Major looked around in despair at the crowd around him. It hadn't been like this when he used to watch his local County Cricket Club as a boy. The spectators in the time of his youth had been quiet, reserved and dignified. This motley collection of football hooligans was anything but. Some insensitive idiot was relentlessly banging a huge drum around twenty rows away to his right, and he was sporadically accompanied by a trumpeter, who played some incessantly catchy and annoying movie theme tune as though they were the only notes he knew.

He was even more aghast at the dressing of his fellow fans. While he would be the first to admit that his attire wasn't entirely appropriate – an old cardigan and only his third smartest trousers – he was shocked at the apparent popularity of wearing very little. Three rows in front of him, there was a party of women wearing Union Jack brassieres, and nothing else above the waist. In his day they'd have very swiftly been asked to leave and not return.

Conversely, some of the spectators had gone to the other extreme. One man, at least he thought it was a man, sitting near him was wearing a costume made up to look like Big Ben. The Major was seemingly the only one sitting in the enclosure who failed to find this amusing in any way, and he became ever more annoyed every time someone passed by and remarked at how they apparently saw the wearer of the costume in the London Marathon.

Betsy meanwhile was having a whale of a time. The Major hadn't bothered to tether her properly, and she'd slipped her collar and gone about happily sniffing anyone and everyone she could. To her, these were interesting people, the sort her master had never introduced to her before. The attraction was reciprocated too, as the gathered throng of spectators took time out from their cheering, noisemaking and beer swigging to take turns picking her up, ruffling behind her ears, and feeding her whatever scraps were left over from their pasties/chips/chocolate bars. Soon after a pair of irresponsible lads with too much money had bought her her own pint of lager, then exchanged wagers on whether she'd streak onto the pitch and piss on the umpire.

By now, she was feeling decidedly queasy. The combination of chip salt, pasty grease, chocolate and alcohol had given her a more than slight sickly feeling. Natural instinct then made an ill-timed call, and she waddled over to the grassy area she could smell. After wriggling through a gap in the advertising boards, she found a quiet secluded spot to perform her business. Unfortunately for her, the TV cameramen were bored of watching the West Indian fielders beaming at how close they were to winning the match, and had started panning around the ground in a quest to find something unusual to show.

After excessive use of the zoom functions on Betsy and her produce, the different cameramen decided to play a game by tracking the three nearest officials to the errant dog, and seeing which one would be the first to notice. In pubs, bars and living rooms up and down the country, bets were placed on how long it would take the officials to notice as they watched the poor excuse for entertainment unfold on TV.

The odds were significantly shortened over the next few seconds, as the English batsmen had actually decided to try and make a fight of the match for once, with Pietersen hammering an erratic delivery across the field for four. Betsy was staring curiously at a boom mike at the time, so when the red ball skipped up over the boundary rope and clattered into an advertising board her yelp of surprise was heard by four hundred thousand viewers. Almost to a man they began cheering along with the crowd as the little dog picked up the ball and scampered off with it, three flustered Nottinghamshire County Cricket officials in pursuit.

The Major had managed to doze off at the time, and was partially awakened by the cheering from the crowd. "Good shot!" he mumbled blearily, before he opened his eyes and realised what was happening. The big screen, normally used as an electronic scoreboard, was now showing the chase and even the English batsmen had begun cheering Betsy on. The West Indian players were less amused, mindful that they needed to get the Englanders out or risk the victory getting away from them. Some of the deeper lying fielders made half-hearted attempts to catch Betsy when she came near them, but she avoided them with relative ease.

Finally Betsy gave in. She dropped the ball on the ground and sat by it wagging her tail. As her pursuers cautiously closed in, the already volatile mixture of foodstuffs in her stomach was given its final push over the edge of stability by the exercise catching up with her. She coughed slightly, then emptied fourteen chips, half a pasty, two Mars bars and a pint of lager over the cricket ball, much to the chagrin of the officials and West Indians, but to the raucous laughter of nearly everyone else.

After seeing his Poochie ruin a Test Match ball on the big screen-cum-scoreboard, the Major realised that it was time for a hasty exit. He shuffled out from his row and began hurrying up the steps towards the exit, before an attack of anxiety struck him. He couldn't leave poor Betsy here, they'd put her in a shelter, or some such horrid place. With the weary resignation of a man who has just realised that there was no avoiding it, he trudged off towards the pavilion, where he was sure they would take her.

Two hours later, the Major's car chuntered slowly down the motorway southwards. Betsy was curled up in the boot, still somewhat ill as a result of her first ever exposure to chocolate. The Major was in a peculiar mix of dejected moods. Furious that someone had fed his dog chocolate, even more furious that someone had fed her beer, upset that she was ill, embarrassed at the dressing down he had received from the cricket officials and depressed at the lifetime ban he had received from Trent Bridge. His only silver lining was the smug content that at least the vagrant AJ was getting his comeuppance, though not as it happened, in the way that he had planned, as he would find out later.

CHAPTER FIFTY-FIVE

"I thought you said you had to be back at work later?" Jack leaned on the bar while the barmaid went off to fetch his order.

"Nah well, I called in saying I had a family emergency. Jimmy said he'd cover for me and not tell the boss." Marky flicked through the text inbox in his phone, hoping to find a message from Rachel that he might have missed, but to no avail.

"Who's Jimmy?"

"Ah, some Polish kid who started working with us a few days ago."

"Doesn't sound like a Polish name to me." Jack fumbled about for his wallet as the first of two pints was delivered to him.

"It's not. It's not his name. His real name's...er...Slobodan or some such bollocks. We call him Jimmy just cause it's easier. He doesn't seem to mind. He thinks it's a term of praise or something."

"Doesn't speak much English, then?" Marky shook his head in reply. "How do you know he'll cover for you, then?" Jack paid for the pints and walked over to the nearest table. All the tables were empty, it being barely eleven in the morning.

"Cos he's a gullible sort. Pigeon English and the like. 'My mother sick. Me go see her.'" They sat down and realised that the pub was empty. "Hey! Harry!" Marky shouted towards the bar. The landlord popped his head around the corner with a look of general contempt. "Stick the cricket on would you?" Harry wandered off muttering to turn the TV on.

"Why do you wanna watch the cricket?" Jack asked distractedly.

"Weren't you listening to the radio in the van?" Jack looked blankly back at him. "On the way here?"

"Oh, no. Sorry, mate I was miles away."

"Apparently there was this dog ran onto the pitch and ran off again with the ball. I wanna see what else's gonna happen." Marky looked at the TV as if to underline his statement, but unfortunately for him the match looked normal. "Bollocks. We missed it. Maybe they'll show it on the highlights reel. Christ, we're getting hammered," he added upon seeing the score.

Jack was still looking distant, staring at his pint as though he was trying to get the glass to move with telekinesis. A short deliberate sigh indicated that he had a problem.

"What?" came the inevitable irritable acknowledgement.

"Well, I don't know what to do about Kathi. I still haven't spoken to her since the other night. It's weird, I think I...I think I miss her."

"You poof."

"Come on, mate, be serious. We've spent most of the morning trying to fix *your* shitty relationship issues."

"Yeah but there's a difference there."

"What's that then?"

"I've been with Rachel for years, you're hung up on a one night stand."

"I know, that's what I can't get my head around. I've got all these weird...feelings. It's fucking annoying I can tell you. Every five minutes she pops into my head, it's like she's got control of my mind or something." Jack finally attacked his pint, hoping the sudden burst of lager would do its usual job of removing his self-consciousness. Or, failing that, just his consciousness would do right now.

"Well go round there then. Stop pestering me with all your *issues* and go and fix it." Marky's pronunciation of the word 'issues' was accompanied by a scornful sneer of distaste.

"Well I guess I'd better then." Jack looked at his half-empty pint glass. "Need some courage from the Dutch first I think." He offered Marky another drink and went up to the bar to order. After he returned, he looked up at the TV to notice that Pietersen had made his century, but England were still losing badly. "We should go down the bookies and put money on the West Indies. Make a few quid."

"Doubt it, they showed the odds just after the ad break, West Indies are one to seven to win. We'd make about twenty pence."

"Pity." Jack mused. "So are we decided on what you need to do?"

"No, we are fucking not!" Marky growled. The idea that Jack had come up with was beyond the pale. "I know you said I needed a big gesture, but that's fucking ridiculous, and damn well ungrateful on your part too!"

"Look, I'm not saying it'll be easy, but you've spent the whole morning bleating about how you want her back, and this is probably the best way. Besides, I don't see how it's ungrateful on my part, I still get to go…"

"*Probably?!*" The scornful sneer returned. "It's not the best way, not in an aeon! You'll have to think of something else."

"Well, I'm out of ideas. This could work. In fact, sod it, it *will* work."

Marky sat and thought deeply about the possibilities for a moment. Missing the Cup game, a live Cup game between City and Liverpool. His club's biggest match in a good few years, and the chance to rip on Jack for months if City won. All for his missus? It was drastic in the extreme for the sake of making up for an argument, even if this particular argument had been somewhat more serious than normal.

"Couldn't I just go round and apologise the next day?" He looked pleadingly at Jack for an answer he knew wouldn't be coming. "Alright. Fine. I hope you're fucking happy." He crossed his arms and dropped into a foul mood. "By the way, if City win you should probably know that I will personally hunt you down and make you pay. And then piss on your grave."

"Oh, understood." Jack managed a wry smile from behind his pint glass.

CHAPTER FIFTY-SIX

"Look, Ashley, we know the dog's yours. Just admit it and maybe you'll get off with just a fine." Miggs banged his fist on the desk irritably. Two hours of questioning had brought nothing from his detainee.

"Constable Miggs..." AJ's lawyer interrupted for the umpteenth time. "My client has been nothing but helpful in your inquiries. May I firstly remind you that he is not under arrest, secondly he cannot help the fact that he did not witness the incident, and thirdly you have no proof that the dog that attacked those people belongs to my client."

Miggs looked bitterly at the lawyer. He may be wearing a £1,000 suit and speak as though he'd gone to school at Eton, but this guy was about as clean as a whore's drawers. Quite how he'd managed to get to the station before AJ had even called for him was, in itself, decidedly murky.

"I see. Well could you at least tell me what all those people were doing at your house in the first place?"

"I dunno." AJ mumbled.

"You said that the postman delivered two large sacks of mail for you, what was all that post for?"

"Dunno."

"Well who was it from?"

"Dunno."

"Yes, well, nothing but helpful." Miggs muttered under his breath.

"I'm sorry, Constable?" the lawyer inquired belligerently.

"Nothing, forgive me. Well then, Mr Johnson, it seems that we've achieved all we can from this interview..."

"Inquiry." The Lawyer corrected him.

"This inquiry, yes, so thank you for your help. If you could just let us know if you're planning to leave the area any time soon."

"Why is that necessary?" AJ's brief was certainly earning his bread today.

"Well, we may need to go over this information again at some point, or of course if anything new comes to light that needs looking at. I'm sure Mr Johnson would be eager to be as helpful as he has been today." Miggs shuffled his papers together and stood to leave.

"Very well." The lawyer agreed after a short pause to think. "If I could just have a moment with my client?"

"In here? You're free to go you know."

"Yes, well, no time like the present." The lawyer shook Miggs' hand firmly with a look of warning that he was not to be messed with over this or any point.

"Fine." Miggs relented. "Constable Witherspoon will be outside, just let him know when you're done." He stormed out with an ever-darkening cloud brewing over his head.

AJ watched the door close. "Why are we still here? I wanna go home for fuck's sake!"

His brief put his finger to his lips and AJ fell silent and watched as the lawyer went over to a corner of the room where there was an apparently dormant tape recorder. He looked at it closely, before smiling, popping the deck open and removing the tape from inside.

"I had an idea they might try something like this," he grinned as he placed a similar looking tape from his pocket into the player and closed the lid. "Recording an interview without the consent of the interviewee or his representative." He placed the police tape in his jacket. "Just a little insurance."

"Is that really that bad?" AJ asked incredulously. He personally didn't care that he'd been recorded with or without his consent or knowledge.

223

"On it's own, no. But coupled with the Officer's aggressive interviewing technique and the fact that we have already filed a complaint for harassment with the Police Complaints after your...social event at the weekend, it just adds a little more weight to our side."

"So," he turned and sat back down opposite his client. "Is the dog yours?" AJ nodded, unsure how many other people might be recording him now. "I see. Did you witness the incident?" AJ stared at him blankly. "Er...did you see the dog attack all those people?".

AJ nodded again. "Why do you need to know? Surely it doesn't matter to you whether I did or not?"

"I'm trying to make sure all our options are covered. I don't want something 'coming to light in future' as that stupid pig put it that I'm not aware of. Now, who sent that mail?"

"I dunno."

"AJ don't fuck about. I need to know. What were all those letters about?"

"I seriously don't know. I never got a chance to open them before the filth dragged me down here. Whatever it is I'm not gonna need to buy any Rizla any time soon." AJ began rolling a cigarette as if to highlight his point.

"Very funny. And you can't smoke that in here. Now, find out what they are, then tell me. People don't just receive hundreds of letters by accident." He placed his notes into his briefcase and straightened his tie. "OK then, I guess that's everything covered."

"Thank fuck for that." AJ got up to leave.

"Oh there was one more thing..." AJ sat down again impatiently. "You wanted me to sniff around the owners of all the other houses in the Close for you, remember?" AJ nodded once more. "Well, I can tell you that of the five other houses in the road, only three are fully owned by their occupiers. Your mate Jack or whatever his name is owns his, the old guy next to you, and the woman at the end owns hers. The family opposite you are heavily mortgaged, beats me how they can afford it on their wages, but never mind. Also the artist apparently has three loans set against his property, all of which are in arrears."

"All what now?" AJ fiddled around with his cigarette restlessly.

The lawyer sighed. "He's in debt. Big time. I'd say that if you made him a decent offer, and his creditors heard about it, he'd be forced to accept. As for the family, same deal. You make them an offer of the full value plus say...five percent, then they'd have to accept or their bank would have words. The other three I can't help you with, you'll just have to try and persuade them."

"That's alright, two should be enough."

CHAPTER FIFTY-SEVEN

Jack stood nervously waiting outside the door and had a sense of deja-vu from his attempted pacifying expedition to Rachel's mother's house. This time it was for real though. Well, last time was 'for real' too, but this time he felt more pressurised as it was on his behalf that he was here, no-one else's.

"Oh, hey honey." Bright and breezy answer from Kathi who seemed to have regained her air of always looking as though she was too busy.

"Hi, er...how are you?" Jack had also regained his own air of incompetence and self-consciousness around women.

"I'm great, cheers. You? What went on out here, did someone die?" She pointed at the eerily silent street which only a short while before had played host to Vieira's little adventure.

"Oh, something about a dog I heard. They had Armed Response in and everything."

"For a dog? Seems a bit extreme. Oh well, you want to come in? I'm a bit busy at the moment but it's about time for a break anyway."

Jack nodded and followed her in. The house, or the lower level at least, was crammed with large cardboard boxes. "Break from what? Building forts?" Jack asked before cursing under his breath, not the best line ever.

"Oh I'm packing." Her overly upbeat manner called out from the kitchen where she'd begun making tea.

"Going somewhere then?" Another curse, this time for stating the bloody obvious. "Nice. I mean going somewhere nice?" He didn't know what to feel, though he now at least knew where their supposed relationship stood in Kathi's list of priorities.

"The States. I've been offered a post over there. I figured it was the right time for a fresh start. Time to move on, you know?" She almost danced back into the sitting room with two mugs of tea. Jack had never seen her so happy before, though having said that, he hadn't seen her in a great many different moods before.

"Well, congratulations." His face gave away his lack of enthusiasm.

"What's up?" she asked without really paying attention.

"Ah, nothing. I'm made up for you. I've never really seen the fascination with the U.S. myself, but good for you." He slurped his tea sheepishly.

"Well, it's a big opportunity for me. Plus getting away from the decrepit geriatrics running the British market will be a pleasant change." She glanced over at him, noticing that he didn't seem convinced. "Something's bothering you. I know when something's bothering you because you avoid making eye contact."

"How can you tell that? You don't know me that well." Jack realised the trap she'd led him into, and true to form lowered his gaze away from her.

"If I don't know you that well, why are you getting so worked up over this? I'm sorry, honey, what we had was fun while it lasted, but it was never serious, surely you knew that?"

Jack nodded silently. *Bugger, walked into that, and now I've got no way of convincing her to stay.* "But…"

"But what?" She'd begun packing more things into boxes.

"I want to get to know you…I don't want you to leave."

She stopped what she was doing and walked over to him, placing one hand on his cheek. "That's sweet, honey, but let's be honest, this was never anything more than a fling. I'm sorry that you seem to feel differently, but there's not a lot I can do about that." She patted his cheek and went off back to her packing.

Jack felt as though his stomach had suddenly disappeared. Part of him was wishing the ground would eat him up, so as to end this torture, part of him was angry at her for dropping him so coldly, and the rest of him was wondering why the hell he was getting so emotional over this. He'd lived next to her for years, and never felt anything, then one evening, Bang! All those sickly soppy poems inside Valentine's cards suddenly made sense to him.

"I...gotta go," he mumbled by way of excuse. "Good luck with everything...bye." He trudged out of the house. He thought he heard her say something in reply, but wasn't interested anymore.

Jack stared at the blank TV screen back in his living room. As far as he could tell, he'd been staring at it for a good half-hour now. His stomach still felt AWOL, and the two remaining joints of weed he'd just polished off hadn't helped. In fact they'd just made things ten times worse. Every time he thought about Kathi, he felt hollow and sad, but as is the way when stoned, his attention was quickly snatched away onto another train of thought at regular intervals. Then after following whatever winding road his mind would take him on for a few minutes, he inevitably thought about Kathi again and became more depressed.

He half wondered if this is how Anna had felt when he'd ended things with her. It wasn't that he was flattering himself at the prospect, but back then he hadn't been able to understand why she was so upset over him, now he seemed to appreciate her feelings more.

He finally summed up the courage to flick the TV on. The first channel that came up was showing some Australian soap, where, ironically some poor lad was pleading with a pretty woman not to leave him. Jack tried to turn it off, but the remote wasn't working properly, and his chemically induced lethargy meant he was stuck with it. He wasn't sure which soap this was, but it didn't matter. They were all the same really, some set on the beach, some set in suburbia, all of them poorly acting out life's pleasures and pains. He wasn't listening to the dialogue anymore, it was all pretty much the standard scripting for an early-afternoon soap episode anyway.

"Unless I'm very much mistaken, that's the potent aroma of Thai weed." A voice came from his hallway.

"Alright, mate." Jack mumbled without moving.

AJ wandered in and surveyed the scene before him. "Right, this is strange. No yelling at me for not knocking, no sarky comments about privacy in your house, and two spent spliffs on top of an empty beer can. What's the matter?"

"I'm not in the mood, mate. What do you want?"

"Ah just to say, if the cops ask you about Vieira, don't tell them he's mine, yeah?" AJ sat down on the sofa next to Jack, who was still staring blankly at the TV screen.

"OK."

"So what's up with you, then?" he said after a short pause.

"Ah, nothing. Girl trouble."

"What, has that that fit bird across the road given you your marching orders?"

"Sort of, yeah. She's moving to America."

"Really? That's unlucky mate." Another short pause. "So do you think she'll be selling her house then?"

CHAPTER FIFTY-EIGHT

"Shh, we don't want to wake Daddy yet." Alice hushed her excitable children as they sat by the side of the hospital bed. *Enjoy your rest, husband dearest, because when you wake up you'll wish you hadn't.*

Inwardly Alice was fuming, though she wouldn't let it show in front of the children. When she'd heard about what Graham had done, she'd stormed over here with the intention of giving him a piece of her mind. The police had told her that it had been an accident, and he had been shot by the vet by mistake, but she knew full well that he had only been out looking for that dog to prove a point. In a way she was a tiny bit disappointed that the tranquilliser had hit him and not the dog, that would have at least taught him a lesson.

Graham stirred at the sound of Joshua's PSP bleeping repetitively. He opened his eyes slightly but kept them closed enough so that it appeared as though he was still asleep. His wife's expression was not one he wanted to encounter at the moment. He closed his eyes again and tried to remember what had happened.

"I know you're awake." Alice interrupted his contemplation. "Your eyes moved."

"Daddy!" Mary leapt up onto the bed when she realised that he was conscious. "Daddy, we missed you!"

Graham flinched as the lump of child landed on his legs, but found himself confused that there was no pain. He'd expected jolts of agony to be racing their way up his nervous system right about now due to the wounds he had inevitable suffered at the hands of the Beast. Yet nothing, not even a minor sting.

"Hello, sweetheart. Have you been good for Mummy?" He distractedly interacted with his daughter. The look on Alice's face had grown darker. "Hello Jacob, Joshua." He nodded at each of his sons in turn. Jacob grinned cheerily and went on playing with his toys. Josh barely looked up from his PSP, acknowledging his dad with a short grunt.

"The doctor says that there won't be any side effects but they'll be keeping you in for the night for observation." Alice spoke coldly while avoiding eye contact.

"What happened to me?" Graham asked with genuine innocence.

"You were shot by a tranquilliser. According to the doctor, there was enough sedative in the dart to put a rhinoceros to sleep. What I want to know is, what on earth were you thinking?!" She stared at him with deep hostility. For a second Graham felt nervous that she was about to take the children away, such was the severity of her look.

"I...I don't know what you mean. I can't remember what happened. How did I get here?" This time his voice lost its guiltlessness and Alice saw straight through it.

"You know perfectly well how you got here. You deliberately went looking for that dog. I can't believe you could be so stupid! What the Hell were you thinking?!"

"Mummy said the name of the Bad Place!" Mary whispered in shock.

"Mary darling, right now Mummy's allowed to say the name of the Bad Place so that she can find out what Daddy was doing." Alice patronised her daughter affectionately.

"If you already know what I was doing," Graham interrupted before Mary had her morals skewed for life, "what are you getting so upset about? Surely you realise what I was trying to achieve?"

"You were actually going to let that dog attack you? To prove a point? To get rid of the young man across the road? In God's name, why?"

"It was the only thing left to do. Everything else that I'd tried had failed, surely you must understand?"

"Understand? That you would willingly allow that animal to mutilate you, perhaps even kill you just to harm someone you don't like?! I don't even know you anymore!" She was standing now, shrieking at her husband with a complete disregard for the effect her voice was having on other sleeping patients.

"Alice, the children..."

"Don't you dare! Don't you dare hide behind them now!" Her face had turned a deep purple.

"I'm sorry. Really I am. I don't know what came over me." He began to whimper; there was no acting here.

Alice sat back down and made no attempt to hide a small tear running down the side of her face. She couldn't believe that this was the man she had married. In fact, no, this wasn't the man she had married, he had left somewhere, perhaps never to return. Whoever this Graham Hamilton was, it wasn't the one she thought she knew.

By now even Josh had stopped playing his PSP. Evidently concerned by the situation, both he and Jacob had sat up on the bed alongside Mary and tried to get a word in edgeways. Now that the argument seemed to have cooled off, he and the other two children hugged their father, trying to prove a point of their own.

"Look at them." Alice mumbled. "That's the first time they've done that in years." She sniffed away the tear and sat up straight, looking her husband directly in the eyes. "I will not split this family up lightly, I will not deny my children one of their parents and I will not break our marriage vows without good cause, so listen to me very carefully, as I will say this once and once only. Stop this ridiculous crusade of yours, or find yourself a divorce lawyer, because I've had enough."

Graham sat open mouthed. Never in all their years of marriage had any argument or confrontation even come close to this moment, but never in all those years had he seen his wife with so determined a look on her face. That she was serious he had no doubt. That she would act on her threat if pushed he doubted even less.

He sat in his bed stunned, unable to speak. The children were still hugging him tightly, he wasn't entirely sure whether they were aware how compelling their act was, but he certainly felt the effect himself. He didn't want to lose them, or his wife, that much went without saying, yet this was the first time since he'd met Alice that she'd forced him into a corner in order to get her own way and it was strange and uncomfortable to him.

"What do you think we should do?" he asked meekly.

"Move."

"Move? Move where?" he asked wide-eyed.

"I don't know and I don't care. I don't particularly want our children exposed to that man across the road any more than you do, but he has as much right to live there as us. Therefore if we don't want to live near him, we must be the ones to leave."

Graham sat silently for what seemed like an age, thinking about what this all meant. Finally he sighed. "Then we shall move."

CHAPTER FIFTY-NINE

In another hospital, in another part of the country, another victim of Vieira's enthusiastic exploits was also coming round from his period of slumber. Ralph woke up feeling distinctly groggy, bursting for a piss, and with a certain sense of distress upon realising that he had no idea where he was. A flickering neon tube light above his head had begun to irritate him with its ceaseless buzzing, while from somewhere else an equally annoying repetitive bleeping seemed to be playing an automated melody to the light's percussion. He groaned loudly, hoping to attract attention from somewhere, and the pale blue curtains surrounding the bed he was lying in ruffled quietly as a large nurse came over to see what the problem was.

"Ah, you're awake. That's good." She wandered over to the IV machine which was responsible for the bleeping, looking over the readout nonchalantly.

"Who are you?" Ralph mumbled.

"My name is Nurse Susan. More to the point though, who are you?" She picked up his chart from the end of his bed and began writing in it.

"What do you mean, who am I?"

"Well, you arrived in A & E last night, dropped off by person or persons unknown. You had no wallet, phone or means of ID. So, sir, if I can put it another way, what is your name?"

"Ralph. Ralph Blakeney. Could you tell me where I am?"

"You're in Barnsley General Hospital."

At the mention of 'Barnsley', a tide of memories came flooding back. The field, the farmer, his obnoxious wife, and *that* gun.

"What's wrong with me?" he sobbed quietly, hoping to be told nothing, but knowing full well that he wouldn't still be here if that were true.

"Well, according to Prof, gangrene. At least that's what it says here on your chart. I'm not allowed to go into the exact details myself, mainly because I don't know them, but I can say that you're lucky to have got here when you did, a couple more days without treatment and you'd have lost your leg."

What little colour remaining in Ralph's cheeks vanished rapidly. He had a perverse urge to lift up the sheets and take a look just to make sure his leg was still there, but the thought of what it might look like made him feel too sick to go through with it.

"So anyway, Prof will be doing his rounds in an hour or so, you can talk to him then about it all. Until then, I need to know a few more things about you."

"Such as?"

"Age, address, spouse or significant other. I'm afraid you've got a fair few forms to fill out." She grinned wryly at him. Ralph mumbled several curses under his breath. She drew the curtains away and he stared out for the first time at his surroundings. Every single bed in the ward was occupied by old men with all forms of tubes and machines plugged into them.

"Am I in the geriatric ward or something?!"

"Yes. No room anywhere else. Anyway, you just stay here and I'll go and get the forms." She trotted off.

"I need a piss!" Ralph yelled after her, drawing disapproving frowns from the other beds. "Fucking accountant, making me fill out forms in my state," he muttered while she was out of earshot. There was no denying it, he was in Hell. He'd been shunted from pillar to post, drugged, attacked by a rabid dog, drugged again, dumped in a field, shot at, and finally left to rot in some godforsaken shithole of a hospital where the nurses were more concerned with filling out forms than treating injuries.

The strange thing, though, was that he didn't wish he was back home. He felt that he should, given all that he'd been through, but the thought of returning to the Close filled him with just as much dread as the idea that he might have lost his leg. He imagined that it was because of that hoodlum and his dog who were the main culprits for his being here now, yet even that didn't appear to be the real reason. Something inside him didn't want to go back home, and it was disturbing that he couldn't put his finger on it. Ralph shut his eyes and did something he had never even considered doing in his life before. He prayed. He prayed for anyone or anything out there to help him out, to get him away from this horrid mess he had found himself in. He was not a religious man, but having decided that this was indeed his version of Hell, it felt fitting that he appealed to the greater forces in life that he was now sure existed, given the way they had treated him recently.

"Well well, Ralph Blakeney. This is indeed an honour." The man in the bed next to him spoke. His face was open but tinged with pain, no doubt as a result of the many tubes and needles sticking out of his body at all angles.

"Do I know you?" Ralph squinted at the old man, trying to find some recognition of who he was. None came.

"No, you don't. I wish that were not the case though. I've been meaning to meet you for some time now, but alas in my infirm state I rarely travel south anymore. Allow me to introduce myself. I am Gerry Newman, owner and proprietor of the Leeds Central Art Exhibition Hall."

"I've never heard of it."

"No I doubt you have, we set up earlier this year as a rival to Leeds City Art Gallery. Anyway I have to say I am a massive fan of your work. The exhibition you created in homage to the Tamal Tigers was particularly moving; it brought a tear to my eye. I also hear you're entering into the Turner this year. I must say it's so refreshing to see vibrant young artists such as yourself not constricting themselves with the narrow-mindedness of the general populous in refusing to support an exhibition outside of London."

Ralph gave a small hollow laugh.

"So anyway, I'll come straight to the point, Leeds Central is losing money. We need a big name to hold an incumbency to draw the crowds away from City, and I think you are just the man. What do you say?"

Ralph was speechless.

CHAPTER SIXTY

"What the fuck is all this?" AJ looked aghast at the mountain of letters stacked up in the hallway. While he'd been gone, Wayne had taken it upon himself to search through the two suspicious sacks from the postman in the hope of finding money, the end result being that the hallway had a new paper envelope carpet laid out.

AJ examined the first letter he picked up. It was hand-written, addressed to him personally. He tore it open and read through the first few lines. Whoever wrote the letter, Stan Dillon being the name signed underneath, was apparently in dire need of £25,000 to pay off several missed payments on his mortgage and credit cards. AJ had never heard of a Stan Dillon, certainly not one who lived in Darlington. He dropped the letter back onto the floor and opened the next one. Same result. This time a Harry Walker was asking for £12,000 to pay legal bills following a messy divorce. Once again hand-written, once again addressed to AJ personally.

The next five letters he read were all the same, and in the end AJ gave up and tried to wade through the mess to make himself a cup of tea. About halfway through the hallway he noticed that some of the letters had been addressed by computer, not hand. This was where the ever-scrounging Wayne had opened the second sack. He tore open the letter and saw that it was typed, and very official.

According to the blurb, it was from a company called Gigimax Telecom, who were seemingly delighted that AJ had decided to choose their services for his telephone and internet supply. An account number had been set up, with direct debits arranged to be paid on the fifteenth of each month. A simple mistake perhaps, but the worrying sign was that they had the correct bank account details.

AJ stuffed the letter into his pocket for future reference and picked up the next typed envelope he saw. This one was from County and Western Gas, who were also delighted to be chosen to provide him with services, namely gas and electricity. Again a direct debit had been set up, and again they had the correct bank account details.

AJ looked in horror at the rest of the pile. There must have been over a hundred letters there, each one looked very similar to the two he'd already opened. This wasn't funny anymore, if he didn't fix this quickly, he was set to lose around twenty five grand a month on these hoaxes.

At first AJ thought he'd been the victim of identity theft. He'd known a guy who used to live on the estate who occasionally subsidised his income by pinching people's bank account details. After spending as much as he thought he could get away with, out of some warped sense of decency the lad would subsequently pull a stunt similar to this in order that the owner of the compromised bank account would be able to claim on insurance. This couldn't be that though, AJ had looked at his bank details on the internet the previous day and everything had been fine. Besides, the details on the letters weren't for the account where his winnings had gone.

He had two bank accounts, one where the money from the lottery was stored, a high interest account set up for him by his lawyer, the other being an everyday current account where each week a certain amount was transferred into for him to live off. Very quickly AJ realised that if he didn't push large funds into the current account, the charges that missed direct debits would cost him would be astronomical. Maybe that was what the ID thieves were hoping for.

He had no time to speculate about it now. He scrolled through the phonebook in his mobile and found his lawyer's name quickly. He'd been calling him a lot lately.

Later that afternoon Jack, AJ, Wayne and the lawyer were sitting round the table in AJ's living room. Jack had been initially reluctant to get involved but needed something to take his mind off Kathi, while Wayne had been promised a Playstation 3 if he got off his arse and helped. The mound of letters had now been transferred mostly onto the table, with the rest piled neatly on the floor. All had been opened, all had been found to contain either requests for money from indebted people or official notices of services soon to be provided.

"Final count, there's 273 beggars, and 100 commercial notifications exactly," the lawyer stated bleakly. "The company letters are equally split. Twenty-five for phone and internet, twenty-five for gas and electric, twenty-five for water and twenty-five for various insurance policies, mainly car." He half threw one of the pieces of paper he'd been holding onto a pile on the floor.

Jack glumly watched it drift down and settle. "Shouldn't companies check things like this? I mean if two companies are trying to provide phone and net to the same address wouldn't it show up on the computer or something?"

"They should, but they rarely do. These letters are all to state that services have commenced, so as each company starts pumping gas in, or setting up a phone line, they'll all cancel each other out. Therefore you get into an even deeper mess as each provider will think that you've cancelled the service without telling them, and they'll try and get you for the whole year's contract. The insurance quotes won't even provide for that, this time next week you'll have twenty different car insurance policies and five house insurance." The lawyer picked up one of the hand-written letters. "As for these," he waved it in the air, "they won't affect your bank balance so long as you don't reply to them. However, to get over 250 responses in less than a week, from all corners of the country, shows that whoever set this up made sure that a lot of people saw it, and therefore you'll be getting a hell of a lot more coming.

AJ said nothing. Wayne folded one of the letters into a paper aeroplane and threw it across the room into the fireplace. Jack picked up one of the typed letters again and glanced through it.

"Is there any way of finding out who did this?" Jack asked without much hope.

The lawyer thought silently for a moment. "Depends how far you take it. Whoever did this surely wasn't enough of an idiot to do it from his own house, or on his own mobile, so tracing the number won't help. Neither will pestering the companies for the tapes of the phone-calls. Not unless you get the police involved. The question, in a nutshell, is who had both the motive and the ability to set this all up? They had to have your account details, they had to know that you had a fair bit of money, and they had to really hold a grudge against you. I've seen the police fraud squad in action and I can tell you the ones round here will have never had anything on this scale to deal with."

AJ tore off a small piece of one of the letters and defiantly rolled it into a cigarette. "So what do we do?"

"Well that part's obvious. Call up each and every one of these companies and cancel the orders. However, there is another problem. If they've got your bank details, the sky's the limit with the Internet. You'll have to cancel the account."

AJ nodded slowly, taking it all in. He fished his mobile out of his pocket and gave it to the lawyer. Then he snapped his fingers expectantly at Wayne, who handed over his mobile too, which AJ promptly gave to Jack. "Alright, then. You take the car insurance. Jack, you handle the gas and leccy. I'll deal with the water and we'll split the phone and 'net when we're done." He picked up a handful of the hand-written notes and thrust them into Wayne. "Wazza, you can start us a fire."

CHAPTER SIXTY-ONE

Jack prodded his cup of tea apathetically with a dirty spoon. The 'hold' tune coming from the phone had changed to Karma Chameleon by Culture Club, a song Jack particularly disliked due to the fact that it represented a dark time in the British Music Industry to him. A time where UB40 and Spandau Ballet were disturbingly allowed to roam the country freely.

This had been his seventeenth call to gas and electricity companies, and despite the call timer on the mobile screen clocking in at nine minutes, it was by no means the longest. That honour had gone to none other than British Gas themselves, who had redirected his call through eleven different switchboards, at least six of which were in Asia, only to find that he had managed to get through to the correct department the first time.

The worrying thing for him though, was that he seemed to be streaking ahead of his two competitors in the phone rally. The lawyer insisted on quizzing everyone he spoke to on the phone as to how and when the bogus accounts had been set up, while AJ invariably lost his temper after being put on hold for more than ten seconds. The reason it was worrying was that were he to finish first, AJ would undoubtedly assign him the bulk of the phone and Internet bills. That would be taking the piss.

Jack slurped his tea deliberately noisily, hoping whatever twat keeping him on hold from the other end would get annoyed by the sound. He looked out into the hallway where he could see the Close through a window by the stairs. It was mainly quiet and tranquil, though there was a uniform bobby patrolling the other end of the road, obviously on the lookout for the loose animal that had caused so much carnage earlier that morning.

He watched as a large van crawled through the Close and pulled up gently next to Kathi's house across the way. It was a removal truck. Jack was initially astonished that she had organised this all so quickly, before he remembered who she was exactly. The woman had become a machine again. No longer the supposedly fragile troubled soul that Jack had inadvertently become involved with, now she was back to 'Career Bitch' mode.

The tune on the phone faded out and Jack completed the monotonous procedure of cancelling the account for the seventeenth time. The woman on the other end sounded as though she'd rather not be there, which Jack felt was unnecessarily ironic, given that he'd yet to meet anyone who enjoyed making these calls.

After around another hour of calling up companies, Jack had finally finished his lot and felt that he was buggered if he was going to do the Internet ones too. He mumbled an excuse about needing to check something in his house and left the room as AJ began yelling at the phone again. After peeking out of the front door and carefully checking for the bloody dog, he trudged out across the road towards his house.

The sun was shining, the birds were cheerfully chirping from the trees, even the copper was whistling, yet Jack could not have been less enthused. Lately he'd been concerned that he'd been thinking about what his plans for the next week would be, rather than just for tomorrow. About whether he'd go food shopping on Friday, for better deals, or on Thursday, for quicker queues at the checkouts. He'd begun turning his back on his previously comfortable day-to-day existence and opening his eyes to a wider world of long-term plans, and it scared him. He didn't know where he would be this time next year, or in five years and frankly he didn't want to, but he'd been pondering it.

True, he had more than enough money to keep him in a moderately profligate lifestyle for the next fifty years, assuming he didn't blow it all on a trip to Las Vegas or an ill-advised investment. He felt he justified his wealth by throwing it around on occasion. Not in an ostentatious or pretentious manner, more out of a sense of compassion. At least he hoped so. He gave money to the Cancer Fund, he topped up Graham Hamilton's salary (admittedly without his knowledge), he gave change to beggars and buskers every time he passed them, and these were his 'good deeds'. He liked the feeling it gave him to hand over to the needy, though now he just realised that he wasn't doing any of this because he actually cared, he was doing it simply because it made him feel better.

Jack entered his front door with morbid visions of his life being compared to that of the post-haunting Ebeneezer Scrooge, with the Victorian's coming out marginally better off. At least Scrooge had inwardly accepted the fact that his charity was for self-preservation. Jack, on the other hand, had only just begun to understand the motives for his seemingly selfless actions.

He poured himself a shot of bourbon and looked out of a window into the Close with new eyes. He watched quietly as the removal men scurried to and fro with Kathi's effects. He glanced across to his left where the Hamilton household was strangely silent. Back across the Close the Major's house also looked empty, as did Ralph's. He thought briefly about calling Marky and going down the pub in an effort to wash away his dejection, but knew that Marky had more pressing things to attend to at present; mainly the attempt to reconcile with Rachel. The even more drastic thought of calling Anna occurred to him, making him realise just how seriously he was taking this sudden loneliness he was feeling. *No. I've burnt that bridge,* he thought glumly.

Later that day, for no particular reason that he could explain, Jack found himself sitting in the Rosebush watching horseracing on the big screen. He didn't like horseracing, he didn't like sitting drinking on his own in a pub, or anywhere for that matter. He just found himself there after having decided to go for a walk. He watched as various groups of people came in for post-work drinks, early dates, and just general socialising. Couples sharing a joke that no one else would understand, gangs of spotty teenagers shuffling towards the bar hoping not to get ID'd, blue-collar workers shooting pool while still in their overalls having just got off-shift.

"This is stupid," he grumbled out loud to himself, causing several nearby patrons to glance at him apprehensively. He ignored them, finished his drink, stubbed out the remnants of a cigarette that had expired some time ago and stormed out.

CHAPTER SIXTY-TWO

"It was that fucking wanker, I knew it!" AJ yelled out at his unwillingly captive audience. "He did this. Fuck knows how, but he did it, and I'm gonna get him!"

"Look, calm down." The lawyer tried to down-play the situation. He wasn't really sure why he was bothering, in the first place he was also more than a bit peeved at having spent the afternoon speaking to gormless cretins cancelling services that should never have been ordered, while secondly the idea that his client might go off and assault the Major in reprisal would at least mean a big payday for him when the warrants were issued. Nevertheless, professional duty required him to at least make a vague effort to restrict his client's actions, not least given that if AJ were to really fuck up and do something stupid right now, he wouldn't be able to represent him as he'd be implicated for sure. "Please just don't do anything rash, you don't even know for certain that it was him."

"Oh I know it was him. Makes perfect sense. That fucker has wanted me out of this place from day one. He's not getting me out that easy though."

The lawyer looked puzzled. Setting up this elaborate charade had obviously taken a lot of time and effort, therefore it could hardly be labelled as 'easy'. "Well, we can get on to the police about harassment, possibly, but without concrete evidence we'd only be wasting their time and ours looking for anything else."

"Fuck the police. He's gone too far for that."

More puzzlement spread across the lawyer's face. Either the set up had been 'easy', or it had been 'too far'. His client's repeated ability to mix the severity of his allegations

246

was giving him a headache. "So what do you plan to do?" he finally asked with weary apprehension, more through knowledge of the breed rather than experience of his client's actions.

"Oh, don't worry. I know something about him. Something he wouldn't want anyone to know. Something that will ruin his fucking life."

The lawyer shot up from his seat faster than a firework. "As your representative I must formally warn you about the possible consequences of blackmail or attempting to blackmail anyone."

"I ain't blackmailing him. What the fuck would be the point in that?"

"Well...er..." The lawyer sat back down again, wondering with dread where this was going. "To get him to stop harassing you I thought?"

"Bollocks. Too late for that." AJ fished around in his pocket looking for his car keys. Not present. He went out into the hallway where Wayne had just managed to spill a can of Stella Artois which he'd been trying to sneak up to his room. AJ ignored him, at least the little scally had had the good sense to mop it up. Added to how helpful he'd been this afternoon AJ figured he was due a bit of leniency. He fished around the pockets in the jackets hanging on a rail by the front door and still couldn't find the keys.

The lawyer came out into the hallway and saw AJ hare up the stairs like a man possessed. "What is this big secret about Major Forsythe then?" he asked Wayne, who, having given up trying to find a mop, had proceeded to flick the errant beer into a dustpan with a yardbrush with limited success.

"Dunno. Didn't know there was one. Do you know?"

"No. That's why I just asked." The lawyer was half a step away from adding 'you fucking idiot' when he heard AJ thundering back down the stairs, keys in hand.

AJ raced out of the front door without so much as a wave and sprinted towards his car, clicking the electronic lock repeatedly in his enthusiasm.

"Wait!" The lawyer called after him. "What is this secret? For your own sake tell me!" He figured that at the very least he could start preparing a case for the defendant prior to the crime.

"Haven't got time to explain it." AJ called back, now sitting in the car revving the engine impatiently. After a few second coughing the rumble smoothed out and AJ tore off with his handbrake still on. "Google him!" he shouted out of the window as he disappeared around the corner.

The lawyer went briskly back into the house, finding Wayne now chattering away on his mobile while trying to push the remaining liquid into the dustpan with a disinterested foot. "Excuse me." he coughed to the boy.

"Hang on a sec." Wayne muttered at the phone. "What?"

"Could I use your computer quickly?"

"Give us a hand and you can." Wayne smiled crookedly.

The lawyer sighed. He should have known better. "What do you need a hand with?"

Wayne looked down at the laminate floor to where the beer was now closing in to the skirting board by the wall where the phone line connected.

The lawyer looked at him pleadingly. "This is a £1,000 suit," he reasoned.

"And these are fifty quid kicks. Yet it's not like I ain't complaining." Wayne gave a short sneer and wandered off, leaving the lawyer half irate and half confused by the kid's poor grammar.

Twenty minutes and a pair of lager-soaked trousers later, the lawyer found himself tapping AJ's laptop impatiently as he waited for it to load up. The unpleasant child had tested his patience to the extreme by refusing to give up the password for logging into the computer, which the lawyer felt was unduly unfair seeing as he needed access for Wayne's brother's sake. After more irritated tapping the laptop finally chimed its nauseating welcome riff at him and he clicked what he thought was an internet browser. It was, in fact, a file-sharing program which after welcoming him proceeded to resume thirty-two different porn downloads.

After hastily closing the program, worried more what the evil child would try and do to him were he to discover the situation than the actual legality of file-sharing, the lawyer found good old trustworthy Internet Explorer and brought up Google.

"Major William Forsythe." He spoke aloud while typing. After a second's hesitation as he wondered what exactly he might be presented with, he hit the 'Enter' button and found the colour drain from his cheeks when he saw the results. "Oh dear God no." He yelled. "No. No. No!"

He slammed the laptop screen shut and raced out of the door with no real idea of what he was going to do, just the fierce notion that he had to do something. *Anything.*

CHAPTER SIXTY-THREE

"What do you want?" Rachel looked at him scornfully. Jack hadn't expected a warm welcome from her, but it still caught him off guard.

"I need to see Marky," he mumbled by way of excuse.

"*Mark* is busy at the moment, I'll tell him you stopped by." The door began to close.

"Please, Rachel. Just let me speak to him. I won't be a moment."

After a second's pause for thought, she relented and went in to fetch her reinstated boyfriend. Or fiancée, Jack noted, after seeing a large diamond stuck to her ring finger. He wasn't allowed to follow her in.

Eventually after what Jack thought was a hissed argument, Marky came to the door sheepishly. Jack took one look at him and would have laughed out loud had he found the sight as funny as he should have.

"Mate, you're wearing an apron."

"Yeah, I know. So?"

"So?! So take it off for fuck's sake, you look like a faggot."

"I can't, I'm cleaning." Marky was deliberately avoiding eye contact throughout the conversation.

"You're what now?"

"Cleaning. You know, general tidying of house contents and the like."

Speechless, Jack looked at him long and hard for a good few seconds. After recovering his frayed composure he searched for a delicate way to express his views on the matter.

"Mate, what the fuck are you doing to yourself? No, no. Scratch that. What the fuck are you letting that woman do to you?"

"Jack, that's my missus, show a bit of respect lad."

"Your missus or your mistress? It's difficult to tell the difference right now."

"And it's exactly that sort of chauvinistic attitude which is keeping people like you single and sad." Marky recited from memory.

"OK, ignoring the fact that I know that those are Rachel's words that she's force-fed you and made you repeat, this has nothing to do with sexism. It's about who you are, and this," he pointed at the apron, "is not who you are. Why are you just letting this happen?"

"Because I'm scared, alright?" Marky snapped, ripping off the apron more out of genuine anger rather than an attempt to make a point. "I'm scared that I'll still be down that bloody pub with you in thirty years time, watching City lose every week, getting pissed and chatting up birds half my own age. I'm scared that I'll still be fixing engines for eight quid an hour with a bunch of immigrants who don't speak English. I'm scared that all those blind ambitions I have will remain just that, with no hope of them ever happening for real."

As the dust settled the two looked at each other unflinchingly. Jack's face was incredulous, disbelieving the words he had just heard. Marky's, on the other hand, hid nothing. It was bare of all pretence and showed only genuine fear.

"Here, you'd better have these." He handed Jack the pair of tickets to the Liverpool Manchester City cup tie. "You can tout mine at the game."

He began to shut the door, not only on Jack but most probably on their friendship too, when Jack called after him. "Is it really all worth it? Does it really mean that much?"

251

The door stopped and Marky half turned back to answer.

"Yes." The door closed.

"How can he change so quickly? Why would he let himself fall into all the shit he's in?" Jack groaned while half admiring a picture of Sigmund Freud on the wall of Frank's office. After refusing to accept that Marky had maintained mental stability during his transition, he had sought out his psychiatrist friend, who had initially been sceptical about Jack's request, but having noticed that there had been no sarcastic comments or derogatory comments made he'd decided to go along with it.

"Maybe we should stop focusing on Marky and pay more attention to you," Frank said from behind his desk while doodling on a notepad in an effort to look professional. "From what you tell me about this Kathi, she sounds a very interesting woman."

Jack scoffed. "You're welcome to her if that's the way you feel."

"No, what I meant was, as far as I can see she is seemingly somebody who is very reliant on being in control. Be it of her work, her social or personal life or anything else for that matter. Probably all of the above. She most likely viewed you as a comfort blanket; someone to control, having had her powerful position at work undermined."

Jack sat up straight on the cliché of a couch. "So how exactly is that paying more attention to me?" he asked, for want of a better question.

"Well, people who like to feel in control of situations...no we don't call them control freaks, that's derogatory," he stopped Jack's interruption before it was born. "Anyway, as I was saying, people who like to be in control are often using it as a form of defence against some deeper insecurity. The same could be said of you, except unlike Kathi, you haven't figured out a way of dealing with it yet."

"What sort of insecurity?"

"Oh I don't know. Maybe she was bullied at school, maybe her parents abused her, the possibilities are limitless, we could speculate all day on the subject."

"No, I mean me. I don't have any insecurity. Not that I'm aware of anyway. My life was just fine until everyone else started changing."

"Really?" Frank asked half as a question and half as a statement of doubt.

"Well, I have been pretty bored recently."

"Bored? Come on, you've got to do better than that."

"How do you mean?"

"Dogs get bored. Goldfish get bored. Infants get bored. Twenty-five year old males who have enough money to live permanently on an aeroplane do not get bored."

"So you're saying I'm depressed?"

"I didn't say that."

"But you're implying it?"

"Yes."

"Oh." Jack sat thinking for a moment. Frank didn't press him. Apart from the fact that the session was on the clock, he personally got more satisfaction out of his job when the patients discovered their issues themselves.

"So what do you suggest I do?" Jack still didn't believe he was actually depressed, but was interested nonetheless in what Frank would tell him.

"Well, you don't have a job, have you considered getting one?"

"Er..." Jack implied with the syllable that he was waiting for a better idea.

"Have you considered travelling? You've got the money, go out and see the world. Go discover things and the like."

"I do go travelling. I went on holiday less than six months ago."

"Weekend binges in Prague and Amsterdam are not holidays. They are just the same as what you do here every weekend, only more expensive and with better-looking prostitutes. Have you even been out of Europe?"

"Yes. I went to Cyprus a few years ago."

"That's in Europe. Plus I'm betting you went to Ayia Napa?" Jack nodded. "Again, just another form of weekend bingeing."

"Well, where do you think I should go?"

"I don't know. For fuck's sake, Jack. Go see the pyramids, go climb Everest, go to the U.S. It doesn't matter. All I'm saying is that maybe a trip abroad might help you discover yourself."

When Jack left the building a few minutes later it was in deep thought. He'd decided to see a shrink to get his head cleared up, but now he was even more confused than before. As he meandered down the street he passed by a travel agent, and thought he'd have a look in just for the hell of it.

CHAPTER SIXTY-FOUR

The beige Volvo limped reluctantly around the corner and sighed with relief as the Major pulled the handbrake on and switched off the engine. The streetlights had buzzed on in unison to welcome them home; it had been a hell of a trip. After having returned to the South, he had decided to take Betsy for a refreshing walk up in the woodland outside town, where the newly famous mutt had found something interesting down a small hole in the ground. She'd squeezed down into what appeared to be an abandoned rabbit warren, (come to think of it, she hadn't seen hide nor hair of a rabbit for some time now in the area) and had had a fair amount of fun scurrying around the tunnels.

The Major had mistakenly believed that she'd been trapped and had spent an hour digging up the warren with a spade he kept in the car in an anxious search for his beloved pooch, only for her to appear next to him, wagging her tail happily. The fresh air had done her the world of good, though she did become somewhat cagey when she spied two young lads with a cricket bat across the field, her recent experience still fresh in her memory.

As he left the car, his composure deserted him briefly and he couldn't resist a quick glance across to AJ's house in the hope of seeing some fallout from his latest plot. To his bemusement the house appeared empty, no car in the drive, no lights on. He allowed a small wry smile to take control of his face for only a second, while his imagination wrongly pictured various consequences he hoped had taken place.

As he was about to enter the front door to his house, he caught a glimpse of the slightest movement in the corner of one of the windows. He ignored it, assuming that his eyes were playing tricks on him in the dusk light. The door creaked open as the makeshift panelling moaned in protest.

Must get that fixed, he thought to himself. *It'll never hold out if an intruder wanted to get in.* Having said that, the original door itself hadn't been able withstand Jack kicking it in, but standards had to be kept up and he couldn't very well take his stance against the anti-social behaviour of his neighbour with a shoddy front door.

Wayne watched the door shut and the lights go on in the hallway, then the kitchen. For a second he'd been worried that the old fool had seen him in the window, but nothing had come of it and it wouldn't matter soon in any case. He pulled his mobile out of his pocket and tapped off a message to his brother. 'Target Akwired.'

The Major placed a bowl of fresh water on the floor for Betsy, who eagerly drained the lot. He wandered through to the living room. After flicking through an out of date TV guide he turned on the set and passively skipped through the channels. Nothing but bad News and Reality TV, definitely not his cup of tea. *Ah, tea. There's a thought.* He pottered back into the kitchen to brew himself a cup.

Outside, cars began to appear in the Close. All various makes and models, though all had a distinct second-hand look mixed with an oppressive selection of spoilers, neon lighting and stickers. They all pulled up in a motley fashion across the small road. Some pulled up on the grass, some drove happily and uncaringly into the seemingly empty parking slots of various other houses around the Close. Once each had found a spot that they were happy with, the occupants of the cars clambered out and began assembling in a similarly dishevelled congregation as their vehicles. There were at least six people to each car, and not one of them looked happy to be here. Eventually a wheezing Nova slid up behind them and AJ hopped out to join in.

In all, the crowd numbered around fifty strong, and as AJ stood in front of them the rumble of discontent grew ever louder, until the Major poked his head out of the front door to see what the hell was going on. Upon seeing him, the mob erupted in seething rage. Chants of Paedophile Out! and other assorted variations on that theme rose up into the previously tranquil evening air.

At first the Major was speechless, shocked to the very core at the sound of *that* word being yelled at him. Then he opened his mouth to retort but still he could not find a word to say. Finally he panicked and slammed the door shut, racing with all the speed his ageing legs could carry him at towards the phone.

The crowd outside took this act to be one of guilt and, assuming that he was trying to flee without facing their vigilante justice, poured forward as one wave towards the door, still screaming white fury at the man they believed a monster. The front door of the Major's house crumpled like wet tissue under the will of the crowd and they scrambled into the house. The frontrunners spotted their target cowering by the telephone in the hallway and they lunged towards him, dragging him away while he grasped in vain at the receiver, having only had time to dial nine, nine before the cord snapped.

AJ watched on from outside as his former neighbours from the Greenmeadow Estate acted with all the unmeditated bigotry that you'd find in a tabloid editor's wet dream. They dragged the helpless pensioner out of his house by his legs and dropped him on the grass in-between two of the cars. From there they circled him as a pack of wolves would a large wounded elk; not quite ready for the kill, but not about to let him away. The insults grew louder and more vicious as he lay helpless on the ground, threats of various tortures were spat at him while he searched in vain for any form of salvation. They didn't touch him though. Despite all their thoughts of pain and death for the creature they believed to be less than human, throughout each and every one of their subconscious was the knowledge that to kick him, to punch, to physically lay a finger on him in anger any more than they had already done would be to cross a boundary from which there would be no return. Yes, they had dragged him out of his house, yes they had thrown him to the ground, but no, they could not harm him.

The Major was not to know this though. Lying on the ground awaiting his fate all he could think of was the names of former comrades from his Army days who had met more dignified ends than this. A landmine in the Gulf War had blown his roommate from Sandhurst apart and now the Major thought him lucky. All he could do now was hope that it would be quick.

AJ looked at him worriedly. This was not going to plan. He had hoped to scare the old twat, not to kill him. In the mob now circling the accused, AJ had unleashed a monster he could not control. This wasn't just self-preservation that he was worried about, repercussions with the police and such like, he was genuinely concerned for the Major's safety now.

The first suggestions of what to do next were being passed around the crowd, who had run out of threats. Upon hearing this, AJ leapt into the middle and grabbed his enemy, hauling him out of the throng as quickly as he could. While the mob was left in a mixed state of disbelief and disappointment, AJ almost threw the Major into his car, jumped in himself and tore away with the door still open.

"Thank you." The Major stuttered quietly. AJ was about to reply, but now he didn't know what to say. The car sped off down the main road with no particular destination planned as yet, and the two men sat in silence while a full moon beamed behind a weak cloud ahead of them in the night sky.

EPILOGUE

The Major's public exposure of past crimes uncommitted finally broke his resolve. It says much about the training of Army Officers that it took a blow of that magnitude to make him surrender and submit, but after thinking long and hard about this strange new world and his place in it, he eventually decided to see out the rest of his years in a small cottage on Salisbury Plain. From this peaceful backwater he spent much of his time devoted to gardening. The peace was broken habitually by the comforting rumble of artillery fire from the horizon and the regular convoys of tanks and armoured vehicles running around the fields nearby, as is customary on the Plain. To the Major it was as though he had finally found his home. No longer part of the Army, but neither completely separate from it. His unwarranted reputation fortunately did not follow him south. AJ's lawyer had agreed to act on his behalf in preventing any news finding its way into the mucky folds of some irresponsible tabloid newspaper.

After all the posturing and plotting, the Major and AJ ultimately parted on fairly amicable terms, with the younger man even going so far as to make his younger brother help pack the elder man's possessions for him. That this was actually a punishment for Wayne after AJ found an ounce of skunk in his bedroom was not mentioned, AJ preferring to let the Major believe that this was an act of goodwill thereby smoothing the passage.

Betsy initially took to the new found freedom of an entire plain like a swallow to the sky. However, her optimistic opinion was soon dented by her nearly being blown apart by an unexploded tank shell, an attack by the local cat mafia, and repeated attempts of hostile courtship by an elderly but enthusiastic Alsatian from the nearest house over the hill. Eventually she decided that it wasn't all that bad staying in the house with her master for large portions of the day, and despite her advancing years she even managed to learn to roll over and howl in tune to the theme of Coronation Street.

Kathi's new job was a dream come true. Having been brought up during her working life in a 'job for the boys' environment in London, she was ecstatic to find that things were done much more professionally in the States. Her commanding and overbearing manner frightened her colleagues but impressed her bosses so much that she found herself promoted within three months. Unfortunately this led to her downfall, as her 'insecurity' as Frank had put it in fact turned out to be nothing more than a cry for attention in a society dominated by those who didn't approve of her, thereby acting both as its own life support and magnifying factor. In her new job she received all the attention she craved and more, causing her to lay off her aggressive streak. This, in turn, affected her work, which was obviously soon noticed by the powers that be, and finally she found herself back at the same level she had started at, only this time no one paid her any attention at all.

Ralph's new position as permanent incumbent at Leeds Central Art Gallery was initially a resounding failure. Unlike the owner, Mr Newman, who happened to be growing ever more senile by the day, no one in Leeds had heard of Ralph Blakeney. On the opening night of his first display at the gallery, only six people turned up; four of them happening to be a group of Danish students who thought they were in Leeds City Art Gallery and who left despite the best efforts of Ralph to coax them to stay. After the gallery had closed for the night, three hours early, Ralph had taken full advantage of a three for the price of two offer on wine at the local offy. He was found later the next afternoon lying unconscious on the floor in a puddle of his own vomit.

That he was found by the first visitor to the gallery of the day and that he happened to be lying in an empty exhibition cubicle contributed to the misunderstanding that he was in fact performing an act. The visitor, who was by chance the bored editor of a local newspaper, was both stunned and impressed at the dedication of this new artist, and with nothing much else to print that day wrote a feature-length article on what he had seen. The crowds came flooding in from then on. The gallery's profits surpassed the owner's wildest dreams, while Ralph was just happy to have an excuse to get royally pissed every night in order to keep the act up.

The Hamiltons spent a few weeks living apart following the sale of their house. Alice lived at her mother's house for a while with the children while Graham toyed with the idea of becoming a priest. After deciding that he wouldn't enjoy the job as much as he'd first imagined, Graham rejoined his family and his marriage was stronger than ever.

They moved to Canterbury and settled in a quiet residential suburb overlooking the cathedral, where Graham spent most of his free time irritating the Archbishop at every opportunity with recommendations on how to improve the running of the Anglican Church.

Their new house was much more suitable in Alice's opinion. She had always thought that living in Appletree Close was somewhat pretentious on their part, given that it had taken both of their incomes to keep the bloody place. Graham too approved of the new accommodation, though when he was transferred to his new post in the Kent County Council he was more than a little bit peeved to find that his wages had been reduced with no explanation from his new employers. After threatening his old ones with legal proceedings for not disclosing exactly why he had supposedly been paid too much, he finally found out about Jack's subsidy. Though initially outraged, he was soon able to view the whole matter in a much more appreciative fashion, choosing instead to believe that the Lord does indeed work in mysterious ways.

The children loved Canterbury even more than their parents. Uprooting to a new school seemed to bring the three closer together, though Josh had picked up on some of Wayne's slang, which regularly had his parents cursing, particularly when Mary started copying him.

Marky and Rachel tied the knot after an engagement of just two months, Rachel, evidently eager to tie her man down before he had second thoughts. In a quiet ceremony of family only, all had almost gone according to plan, until Marky's true colours made one last attempt to announce themselves. As the bride and groom stepped up for the first dance, the band broke out into 'Some Might Say' by Oasis while Marky, fairly well tanked up on cheap champagne, tore off his jacket and shirt to reveal a Manchester City strip underneath and began yelling along wildly out of tune.

After the understandable following period of coolness between the newlyweds, Rachel 'accidentally' managed to get pregnant, and the change that overcame Marky was nothing short of miraculous. He gave up lager as though he'd become allergic to it. He applied for a wide range of new higher-paying jobs, subsequently taking on the position of head mechanic for the local bus firm. It wasn't that he was a particularly good mechanic, it was just that no one else in the repair shop spoke English, while he had decided to learn Polish to be able to get through to Jimmy at his old job.

The marriage wasn't without its ups and downs. Marky's insistence on naming the baby Elano if it was a boy particularly tested Rachel's patience, but the two went on to grudgingly accept each other as being the love of their lives.

AJ started his own property company with the remnants of his winnings. Having bought up every house in the Close, some for knock-down prices, he arranged for his children and their mother to have one house, his own mother another, one for Wayne on the strict understanding that he didn't 'fuck about with the gas mains' and one for rent to three couples from the Greenmeadow Estate. The house that he rented had been the Hamiltons and was the smallest, but it took the combined incomes of all three couples to deal with the rent, council tax and bills. The only house to remain unoccupied was the Major's, AJ preferring to have the building converted into flats in a move that netted him three times the amount he paid for it. With the sudden change in the variety of people living in Appletree Close, by a strange quirk all the houses in the area had their council tax brackets reduced.

With a very nice new house, which happened to be free, and the threat of being screwed in court if she dared oppose him, AJ's children's mother allowed him free access to his kids whenever he wanted. Happy now that he'd achieved the only real goal he'd had over the last few months, AJ took it upon himself to provide his children with the father figure he'd never had.

Vieira eventually returned to the home of his master when he'd eliminated his food supply by killing every rodent in a three-mile radius. AJ knew that he couldn't keep the dog any longer, but stoutly refused to hand him over to be put down. On a dark rainy night one weekend AJ coaxed Vieira into the boot of his car and drove away. He got to the Devon/Cornwall border before deciding that he'd gone far enough, and left the deranged animal in a nearby field. AJ contented himself with the knowledge that out here Vieira would be able to look after himself. Vieira had hundreds of square miles to roam around in and no master to obey, so was delighted by this turn of events. By a strange coincidence, sightings of the fabled Beast of Bodmin Moor tripled over the following months.

Jack decided at the travel agents that a proper holiday might not help him discover whether he was depressed or not but should at least be fun. After deciding to try out

Australia, he packed his bags and flew out for what he thought would be a couple of weeks. He ended up enjoying it so much that he flew back to England at the end of the break and promptly sold his house to AJ for a bargain price just so he could move out there all the sooner.

He spent his time divided between working at a beach bar near Sydney and performing stand-up sets at a local comedy club, where he discovered that in order to get good laughs in this country with his accent all he had to do was insult the England Cricket team.

After some time in Oz he became restless and tried out travelling again. He toured south western Asia for several months, where his collection of Liverpool Football strips made him extremely popular with the locals.

When he finally started pining for the miserable weather and excessive taxation that was his home country, it was with a heavy heart that he returned home. When he got there he saw that the Rosebush had finally been closed and was due to be demolished. Obviously it had been missing his custom, so he bought it, appealed against the demolition order, renovated the pub exactly as he liked it and finally he found his happy medium between not having a job but having an occupation. There was always the lingering threat of Police raids on the premises, particularly given that two of Jack's most regular customers were AJ and Wayne, but it seemed that the now Sergeant Miggs was happy to turn a blind eye, obviously keen to avoid any contact with the residents current or otherwise, of that Close.